The Dark Takes Fools

Book 1
The Long Way Home
A Space Opera Adventure

by
Mark Henwick

Published by *Marque*

The Dark Takes Fools

ISBN : 978-1-912499-51-9

Published in 2024 by Marque

Mark Henwick asserts the right to be identified as the author of this work.

AMZ240609

AUTHOR'S NOTE

The Long Way Home was originally written as a serial book,
delivered in monthly episodes through my newsletter.
Books retain the episode structure.
Enjoy.

Episode 1
The End of the War

E1. Chapter 1

"I have a plan."

Bjorn Thorsson snorted. "Course you do."

We were both down to a quarter of a magazine for our weapons and we were crouching in a muddy ditch, halfway up a supposedly extinct volcano that had become active again under heavy bombardment from space. The mother of all pyrocumulus thunderstorms was unloading a year's worth of rain on us, and through the clouds of steam, my IR detectors were picking out the glow of lava creeping toward our ditch. The lava would reach the ditch in three minutes. It would fill it in ten.

Our armored combat suits laughed off small arms fire, and were designed to continue operating underwater or in a vacuum, but I suspected lava exceeded the specifications.

Our objective this morning had been to destroy a vital part of the planetary defenses of Rhea 4. It was a fortified fire-control installation buried in the lip of the volcano, which, despite the eruption, was still operating. It was only a half-klick away, but it might as well have been on the moon, because an automated plasma cannon had been deployed on an embankment right above us just as we'd reached the base. It was spitting a constant stream of vivid blue-white bolts at anything it considered a threat. The cannon fire meant the rest of our platoon was pinned down a quarter-klick behind us. Trouble was, give that tiny electronic brain enough time and data, and it'd work out where the platoon was hiding. That cannon was capable of blasting through whatever they were sheltering behind. It'd catch them if they came forward or retreated.

Same for us. The cannon couldn't depress enough to fire at us in the ditch, but we couldn't climb the embankment, and we couldn't get out of the ditch. I didn't even want to try standing up.

The lava was going to reach us in two minutes now.

"Skelling, Thorsson, sorry to disturb you on your rest break." Gunny's voice crackled through the lightning interference on the comm. "That cannon is starting to be inconvenient."

"Which cannon is that, Gunny?"

Probably wasn't my best acknowledgment. I was saved from Gunny's reply by the cannon zeroing in on her comms signal and vaporizing the ruined building she was hiding beneath. Not a problem for her and the rest of the team in their combat suits, but there was no other cover to hide them when they dug themselves out.

That job done, the cannon pointed down as far as it could and blew several huge craters just meters downslope from us.

We crouched lower, pressing ourselves hard against the soft, slippery mud.

All our supporting bombardment had stopped. Ground attack had been blown out of the sky by the same planetary defenses that we were here to take out. The cannon pinning us down didn't seem to be low on plasma charge. Our platoon was stuck. We were stuck.

It looked like, one way or another, this was our day to die.

Or not.

"Janice, that plan..." Bjorn said.

Using my full name, eh? He was obviously getting concerned. I hadn't really had a plan before, but I did now.

"Dig," I said, forcing one armored hand deeper into the mud.

"Into the side of a *volcano*? An *erupting* volcano? Crazy much?"

"In and then up. It's an embankment. It's compacted earthwork, not rock. It's probably already unstable with all the rain. And if it's not unstable enough, we set off one of the bombs."

"They're supposed to be for destroying the installation."

"Yeah, well, we have two of them, and anyway, better than being cooked."

Bjorn grimaced at the red and black wall of lava clearly visible now, even through the rain and steam, inching along the ditch. "Good point."

It turned out that armored suits dug well.

Lava filled the ditch behind us, but fortunately, the mud of the earthwork was so liquid it flowed around us, sealing us off. At which point, it became more like swimming blind than digging. We were inside the earthwork and we couldn't see anything.

"My inertial sensors say we're moving downward," Bjorn panted after a couple of minutes of lung-bursting work.

He was right. The mud was moving by itself. It was making a noise like a growl, which grew and grew. And the faster we dug, the faster we seemed to be sliding down the slope.

Really fast...

"Hang on!"

We linked arms and locked our servos just in time. It seemed we'd succeeded in undermining the cannon's platform, and once it started sliding, nothing was going to stop it.

My suit speakers maxed out with the noise so I couldn't even hear myself scream.

For the first time since training, I switched on my helmet lights, otherwise known as *I'm here, shoot me* lights. They didn't help.

We were rolled over and over, blind, helpless, battered by rocks and twisted every which way. Even with the armored suits, we were in trouble.

Maybe this was our day to die, after all.

Then, suddenly, the turbulence thrust us up onto the surface of the mudslide.

I couldn't clear my visor, but I felt Bjorn pull me up onto something. The world settled a bit; we were still moving, but we seemed to be *on* the mud instead of inside it.

I let rain sluice the visor until I could make things out.

We were clinging to the underneath of the overturned plasma cannon, surfing it down the side of a volcano on a roaring mudslide. The whole thing was heaving and bucking, and we'd either hit something and turn over or run out of liquid hill soon, but we'd enjoy it while we could.

"Was this in your plan?" Bjorn yelled, one gauntlet pounding the metal of the cannon as if to make it go faster.

"Sometimes you gotta improvise," I shouted back.

Relief after terror. We were laughing so hard, the tears ran down our cheeks.

The command channel in my helmet blared into life.

It was Gunny yelling on the comms. "Skelling! Thorsson! What the hell do you think you're doing? Stop messing around! All units! Stand down. Cease fire. All units, cease fire."

There was a long wash of static, then Gunny's voice came back, weary but exultant: "It's over, people."

∞ ∞ ∞ ∞ ∞

Now that they had decided that the war had finally ended, they started shipping whole brigades out as fast as they could board them. We lifted off Rhea 4 the next day.

It made sense; there were military units you use for peacetime duties, and then there were frontline units like the ones on Rhea 4: the 1st Frontier Assault Brigade and the Terran Volunteer Mobile Infantry.

But maybe the more important thing for them was that some units were permanent, while we weren't career military. The sooner Earth government got us off their payroll, the happier they'd be. There was no profit in this war.

War... Officially, the 'Dimitras Incursion' wasn't a war, whatever it felt like while we were fighting it.

Me? Janice Skelling. From Calloway, in the Ensylas Sector, far out on the Parvi Arc. Private (for the third time—'authority issues' and 'attitude'. Got a problem with that, *bud*?). Assigned to Alpha Company, 2nd Battalion, 3rd Mobile Regiment, 1st Frontier Assault Brigade.

Shit. You could spend all day chewing through names like that, which is probably one of the reasons why we were usually called the Acid Penguins, even by General Thoomis.

And make no mistake, we were all happy to stop fighting and just go somewhere that wasn't beat down or blown up, but while everyone else celebrated, it was at that point I started to worry. That's the way I'm wired.

We had to go back to Earth first; that was just the way the bulk of space transport worked—inward and outward from the center. But the ship they used for us? The TSS *Wingate*, the Terran Marine Corps' just-launched, state-of-the-art troop transport ship. So new it had never been shot at, and only had one layer of paint on the bulkheads down in marine country.

And it all worked. Even the freaking showers.

It was a vacation at the military's expense, with more time to think than I'd had in years.

Like: why a war, even one that wasn't called a war, had ended, and yet planets that could barely afford to feed themselves were still paying Earth to build ships like the *Wingate*.

E1. Chapter 2

"Hey, come on, Jan! We're *finally* going home," Bjorn said as we stood at the viewport, watching the blue-green jewel of Earth spinning beneath us.

"I know we're not all here," he went on, misunderstanding my silent mood. "You're thinking of Hal, aren't you?"

He held up his hand, fingers and thumb spread. I couldn't refuse the ritual. I put up my hand to touch his, finger to finger, thumb to thumb. The Five, we called it, because there had been five of us from Calloway originally. Feeling lost among the two thousand recruits of the Frontier Brigade, this had been our little group's greeting to remind us we weren't alone.

There were only two of us left. Solveig had died first. Then Enoch. Then such a long gap when we'd begun to think we were invulnerable. But Hal had died in the first nightmare drop onto Rhea 4, just one month ago. Happy-go-lucky Hal. So close. He'd almost made it.

I squeezed my eyes shut.

We'd all known the risks when we'd signed up.

Calloway was a system at the very limit of the Frontier, unless you counted complete dead-ends like Yorkham. We hadn't expected to be visited by Frontier Brigade recruiters from Earth and we told them truthfully, ignoring that we were actually pacifists, we couldn't *afford* for people to leave. But then they told us what the pay was, and that it was in Terran dollars. Not enough to make it worthwhile back on Earth, maybe, but out on the Frontier, Terran dollars were the only way to buy the Inner Worlds tech that hard-pressed colonies were so desperate for. And we *were* desperate; we'd discovered Calloway had a long-term atmospheric cycle which fed a chemical change in the soil, and we were heading for a huge die-back of crops unless we could buy the kind of terraforming tech that would reverse the changes in our fields.

Everyone had met up or connected by comms to debate, because that was the way we did it on Calloway. We'd worked out that five of us signing up for a standard three-year tour would make enough for eight of the bio-processors we needed. It would be enough to stop starvation, no more, but it was a compromise between hard choices.

The Church declared that anyone who volunteered would be deemed guiltless in their eyes.

Everyone who'd met the military requirements had put their names forward, and the five had been chosen by drawing lots. The recruiters had allowed a couple of contract amendments. In the event of death, payment would be made to the end of tour. The survivors and our cargo 'within reason' would be shuttled down to the surface of Calloway at the military's expense.

And so, the five of us became soldiers in the 1st Frontier Assault Brigade.

Our choice hadn't been wanting to take Earth's side in some dispute about whether they had the right to export their marginal citizens into the Dimitras Sector.

No.

It'd been a stone-cold assessment of the trade-off between the temporary or permanent loss of five people who couldn't be spared, and the purchasing power of hard Terran currency for the three years they'd originally said we'd be signed up for.

And we'd done six years. Double the original tour—yeah, always read the small print, folks.

But still...

"Something's going wrong," I said. It was the same gut feeling I'd learned to trust in combat.

"Paranoid much?" Bjorn laughed. "Hey, it's okay. We all have doubts and failures of confidence at the end of a long project. It's natural. But we did it, Jan! Look, just picture their faces when we arrive. The whole colony will be there."

I couldn't help but visualize the 'shuttle port' on Calloway. The bleak expanse of vitrified rock on the coast near the town. Would they really all take the time to come out to greet us?

A huge longing swept through me to see the family again. To return to them, alive, the risks of military service to body and soul vindicated, bringing the *literally* lifesaving bio-processors, which were in storage at Ensylas, waiting for payment.

All the emotions I'd kept locked down for so long started to seep out, and my eyes blurred up.

Bjorn bumped shoulders gently. "Betcha looking forward to the expression on your old Uncle Nikolai's face, aren't you?"

I had to laugh through the tears.

"Nah. That would be childish," I said. My least favorite family member had bid me farewell by saying he never expected to see me again. That I was just running away, and I wouldn't amount to anything, anywhere.

Maybe I was looking forward to him eating his words, a little bit.

Bjorn had cheered me up and I gave him a one-armed hug. Not too much. I had kind of a thing about him, but, well, he was probably bad news. Not a bad man, but not a good bet, if you get my meaning. And maybe almost as much as I was for him.

"Come on," he said. "Let's go watch the parades."

∞ ∞ ∞ ∞ ∞

Earth was humanity's home, but not home for the Frontier Brigade, which might be why we didn't get to touch the planet that we'd spent six years fighting for. Or maybe they thought that we'd all jump ship and disappear into the teeming billions of Earth's population.

Probably *that*, because it was the heart of the problem all over.

Earth and the closer Inner Worlds wanted to export their excess populations and import raw supplies in exchange for their advanced technologies.

The Margin wanted more people, but only the 'right' kind. And they didn't want to export their resources—*couldn't*, in some cases.

And lastly, there was the Frontier, the furthest reaches of human expansion, the most desperate colonies. No one wanted us, except to fight their wars.

It was a sore point out on the Frontier.

Anyway, the military decided to keep the Acid Penguins in orbit, aboard the Ganga, the huge military transshipment station.

In the Ganga's cavernous concourse, we watched while the Terran Volunteers paraded. There were speeches. Presentations. Medals. Buffets with champagne for the senior officers. Beer for the rest of us.

When the celebrations ended, the Terran Volunteers were paid off and shipped planet-side on the space elevator, leaving the Frontier Brigade to wait for our transport home.

The *Wingate* had already left, gone to get the next shipload from the Dimitras Sector, and the military didn't have enough transport ships to visit every part of the Frontier, so they contracted merchanters whose cargo pods could be temporarily converted to barracks.

While the transports fueled up and got a shakedown from our Brigade engineers, the Terran Marines put on a last-minute recruitment show for anyone interested.

They had a good turnout.

Yeah, they were offering free food and alcohol.

And the show was slick, I'll give them that.

New, higher-powered armor. Glossy visors with improved tactical information. Better comms. Working active camo. The latest Mark 5 Tactical Assault Weapon.

Very impressive.

It was like a line had been drawn down the hangar. One side the Terran Marines, all clean uniforms, fresh faces and unmarked armor. On the other side, us.

We'd been requested to assemble in our battle kit, bar the helmets, and we looked more like a ghetto gang than an infantry company.

We'd spent the war shedding bits of malfunctioning suits, experimental equipment and surplus gear, sloughing off decorative coatings while gathering scars, dents and mods, until we'd emerged like a new sort of metallic insect: hard-shelled, dark, with the sort of dull sheen that comes from unremitting use, but everything functional and deadly.

I'd worked on every inch of my equipment, right down to the power servos and the slick mechanisms of my Mark 3 Tactical Assault Weapon, as if my life had depended on it. Because it had.

All that pretty kit on the other side wasn't going to impress us, and the marine recruiting sergeant didn't get much interest until right at the end.

"So what you going to do?" he asked us, leaning against the table with all the food and alcohol. "You've spent six years getting good at being soldiers. Now you're back off to the farm and the factory, richer, but still scratching a living in the Frontier." Big pause to look around. "Or you could join the Terran Marines. Do what you know best, but with the latest, finest equipment, dedicated support, and supply divisions." He paused again. "And the way things are going, you probably won't even have to fight."

He smiled when he said it, and we smiled back, because by this time, we all knew that was bullshit. You didn't recruit like this for peacetime.

"Who the hell are they going to war with?" I whispered to Bjorn.

He just shrugged.

The recruiter saved his best argument for last. "Oh, and there's a new law been passed this week in the Terran Council," he said. "After a five-year stint in the Terran Marines... you get citizenship."

It was like a shockwave flashed through our ranks. Hellfire, that was some bribe.

And while my mouth was still open in shock, I got Gunny hissing quietly in my ear. "He doesn't mean you, Skelling. Or your partner in crime."

Bjorn and I turned around together.

"Crime? Gunny, that's libel," I said, with my innocent, shocked face on.

"Not unless I write it down," she replied. "And anyway, it would still be true."

Gunny was okay. She'd been assigned from the Terran Marines to teach us something, *anything*, about being soldiers when we'd signed up. We didn't hold that against her, and she'd stayed with us the whole six years, bad times and good.

"You holding grudges?" Bjorn asked her, smiling that smile that could sell vacuum to a spacer. At a premium.

She didn't smile back. "No. The opposite."

She passed on, muttering in other people's ears.

"Sort of an anti-recruiting sergeant," Bjorn said, an unfamiliar frown creasing his face.

For the first time, I saw reflected in his eyes the worry that had been eating away at me.

If a new conflict broke out *before* we were officially demobilized, that small print clause said we would have to stay in the Frontier Brigade. There would be no way to get payments out to Ensylas, let alone get the bio-processors shipped to Calloway. And the way these conflicts went, by the time it ended, it would be too late for Calloway—people would start to die, and then, quickly, the colony itself would die.

E1. Chapter 3

We sweated through the next few days.

Half the brigade decided to sign up for a tour in the Terran Marines, so the transports had to be reassigned. More delays. An ominous notice appeared on our pads, reminding us that we were still in the Frontier Brigade until demobilized and, as per regulations, we were responsible for packing all our equipment onto the transports when boarding.

As if we were being deployed.

Gunny refused to say anything other than that; as far as she knew, the fifty of us from the Ensylas Sector would be demobilized as a group on Ensylas and await onward transportation, as stated in our contracts. She had an expression on her face that would blister bulkheads, so conversations were short.

Did she really know something? At the recruitment show, had she been telling us to get out as fast as we could?

Bjorn and I couldn't decide what to believe.

The Dimitras Incursion had been incredibly unpopular on Earth, with riots erupting every time casualties were brought home. Surely the Council didn't want another war?

On the other hand, the Terran Marines didn't recruit soldiers to stand around and look pretty. They'd taken on a thousand, just from the first transport to return. Was that just because we came back first? Why had they ignored the Terran Volunteers?

While we argued it, transports left for every Sector in the Frontier, and ours kept being re-scheduled.

The day eventually arrived and, maybe because we were the last to ship out or because there were no 1st Frontier officers joining the Ensylas transport, Gunny elected to come with us. In addition, we had a handful of surly military police and a civilian official from the Terran Council's Military Oversight Commission who'd been tasked with officially demobilizing us.

I didn't believe our transport would really leave, until I heard the docking clamps retract.

And even then, I still wasn't sure we'd be released when we got to Ensylas.

The journey itself was agonizingly slow: the merchanter was sound, but the navigation and sensor systems were so old that it had to emerge from

Chang space at every intervening star to check its bearing and velocity. Every recalibration and adjustment took time. Then it had to recharge the Chang generators. Refuel.

Every pause, every day, made me more anxious.

∞ ∞ ∞ ∞ ∞

Despite my fears, fifty-three days later, we disembarked into Orion's Wheel, the space station that orbited the planet of Ensylas.

This system was the Frontier's local sector capital, and they had a welcome for us that was supposed to be an imitation of the ceremonies on the Ganga, including a parade from the Acid Penguins.

Not what we were good at, but this was our last parade and we did our best for Gunny.

Campaign medals. Salutes. A speech from the governor of Ensylas.

The Commission's official took the stand.

My heart was in my mouth.

Surely we couldn't be recalled now?

Blah. Blah. "...and I now declare this troop to be honorably discharged..."

With cheers we broke ranks. To hell with parades and speeches. Suddenly we were civilians again, and it seemed all my worries had been groundless.

I didn't remember too much after that. There were celebratory drinks. Bjorn and I drifted off from the others and ended up in a bar somewhere. Lots of drink. Some dirty dancing.

I may have got a bit short with some stationers who wouldn't take no for an answer.

There might have been some pushing and shoving.

I was doing fine, but then Bjorn noticed, and after that, the pair of us won, big time.

Which meant that when the station police arrived seconds later, we were the only ones standing and of course we got zapped. And, naturally, by the time we came around from that, every other person in the bar had identified us as the people who'd started it.

Sore losers.

Like an idiot, I was expecting to get bailed and put in the brig, before remembering that I had become a civilian a few hours before my arrest. The army had no obligations or loyalty to me.

Stupid. *Stupid.*

I came out in a cold sweat. What had we done? Had the army already booked us tickets to Calloway? Would we miss the departure?

We couldn't get messages in or out. The police wouldn't even talk to us.

A lawyer eventually turned up. He said he would get a message to Gunny, but he didn't seem interested in our situation or our guilt. His job was to explain our options: if we took the rap, we would get a fine or a sentence of one month of station maintenance and cleaning. If we took it to court, given the 'evidence' against us, almost certainly a year *and* a fine *and* the likelihood that the 'victims' would be awarded compensation from our assets.

We gritted our teeth and took the month.

By that afternoon, we were chasing burnt-out circuits in the maintenance tunnels wearing fetching yellow coveralls and necklaces that would deliver a shock if we goofed off or tried something stupid.

They relied on their necklaces and the fact that we had nowhere else to go. We were sent off to work alone with our own keys to access the tunnels. An inspector would occasionally come check on us. We were not allowed to communicate with anyone else.

Long hours with nothing to do but work, eat, sleep and regret.

The lawyer never returned, and after two mind-numbing weeks, it came as a genuine shock to find myself in the meeting room at the jail, dressed in my off-duty fatigues, no prison necklace, with Bjorn and Gunny.

"Sorry, Gunny," I said, while wondering what the nova she was doing still in the system, let alone getting us out.

She looked as pissed as I had ever seen her, and I guessed we deserved it.

"Wasn't us started it," Bjorn said.

"I don't care," she said. "That's the least of your problems. Shut up and listen."

My heart skipped several beats.

Her eyes flicked up to the left and right before coming back to bore into mine.

Got it. The room was not secure. There could be recording devices operating.

What the hell is going on?

"You're booked as passengers on a merchanter, paid by the military as per your contracts. Departure is scheduled tomorrow," she said. "I have opted to pay your fines to the station to allow you to catch that ship, because there's nothing else on the boards scheduled to go to Calloway. The amount of the fine will be deducted from your pay."

Bjorn and I twitched at that, but, hey, I'd had enough of station maintenance and, as she implied, we could spend a long time waiting for the next merchanter heading to Calloway.

It was okay. We had 'til tomorrow to pay for the bio-processors and load them on board. As long as we'd been paid...

"The remainder of your back pay and demobilization bonus has been paid into your accounts."

With an expression like she'd chewed on a lemon, Gunny checked her pad and read out the sums we'd received. In Terran *credits*.

No!

My mouth moved without making any sound. It made no sense. There had to be some mistake.

The Terran dollar was humanity's standard electronic currency, but Earth controlled and tried to restrict it. The Terran *credit* was a promise that if you visited Earth, it would be exchanged for a dollar from the account that it was raised against. It actually was almost as good as a dollar for the closest Inner Worlds, but its value depended on there being constant trade and frequent travel between wherever you were and Earth.

For Ensylas, out in the deep Frontier, credits were only really useful on the infrequent occasions you could catch a merchanter that was heading all the way back to Earth. And even then, he'd know he had you over a barrel.

Gunny's face told me there was no mistake.

There was an utter, chilling silence as it seeped into us how completely we'd been screwed. We couldn't pay for the bio-processors using credits. They'd laugh at us.

People on Calloway would die.

Bjorn was about to go full berserker, but it wasn't Gunny doing this. I gripped his arm, held him back.

"How?" I managed to say, but her eyes flicked up again. Recording devices.

We got out of the jail, stumbling like zombies. My heart was pounding so hard in my ears I could barely hear Gunny's explanation.

The Terran Council had created the Military Oversight Commission and taken the lowest bid to run it, 'saving taxpayers money'. Our pay, in dollars, went into the Commission's account. The Commission issued credits against that, and expedited the demobilization so that the maximum number of troops would be at the wrong end of space when they got paid. Unredeemed credits would become bonuses for the Commission's members.

It was a stinking scam.

At the same time, the Terran Marines were going all out to increase their numbers because Military Intelligence said the conflict in the Dimitras Sector wasn't finished, but the Council only allowed them funding to recruit people from the Frontier. Because Frontier troops dying wasn't as 'politically sensitive' as Terrans dying.

Mad as I was, I was still holding onto Bjorn because he was liable to do something that would get us back into trouble. However little we could do to fix this, it'd get worse if we were back in jail.

"I am also required to inform you," Gunny ground out formally, "that I will be relieving you of any *working* military equipment, which is to be returned."

I blinked. In the time it took my eyelids to sweep back up, I had worked out ten ways to temporarily disable my entire battle kit, right down to the weapons. There would be no working military equipment for her to repossess, and she already knew it.

Gunny, you star!

The kit was worth something, as a whole, or in parts. Nothing like enough to offset my loss on the back pay, but something, at least.

I got Bjorn to look at me and he nodded, grim-faced, to show he understood: do what we could and work from there.

E1. Chapter 4

The next hours passed in a blur.

We marched double-time to retrieve our combat kit from the storage facility and assembled it in front of Gunny.

"See?" I said, flexing the arms manually. "The servos must have blown. And the TAW stopped working during the last assault." I pointed at the disassembled weapon. "No supplies available to replace the mechanism."

Gunny grunted.

Out of habit, she slid a finger across the weapon's internal firing actuator.

I snorted. She'd find enough oil to feel oily, not enough to actually wipe off. It wasn't like I was some kind of raw recruit.

"Worthless crap," she snarled. "If you were still signed up, I'd dock you for poor maintenance."

She turned away to mutter notes to her InfoPad.

"You're booked out on the merchanter *Karakun*, Captain Satybal," Gunny filled in as she started inspecting Bjorn's armor. "Departs tomorrow noon, station time."

She paused to mutter again, reading off the serial numbers and then dropping the apparently malfunctioning armor.

"According to the clearing office, you have one other ex-mil passenger on the *Karakun*. A pilot from the 5th Frontier Wing."

I raised my eyebrows. The 5th was a ground attack wing. To us grunts, the ground attack wings were legendary. Mainly because, like legends, you only ever heard about them in stories from long ago. But the battle for Rhea 4 had been different, and the 5th had been true legends for us then. They'd stopped supporting us eventually, but only when they'd run out of everything. Including most of the pilots.

"Name of..." she checked her pad, "Lieutenant Siriwardene. Traveling on to Yorkham."

That was a surprise. Yorkham was a space station, constructed out of a damaged colony ship by the survivors of an accident. The star that the station orbited was outward of Calloway, and the only planets in the system were too lethal to settle on. Since the accident had damaged their Chang drives, Yorkham wasn't going anywhere.

Any ship visiting that system would be flooded with people desperate to leave. That would have made recruitment easy, but what I couldn't see was why someone would be heading back there.

Especially a ground attack pilot.

They were well known to regard themselves as the pinnacle of all pilots, skilled in null-G as well as atmospheric flying. Lieutenant Siriwardene would be a hotshot pilot jock, quiet as a klaxon, subtle as neon lighting, a man with places to go, things to do.

So why was he heading back to Yorkham?

None of my damned business. I had enough problems without worrying about someone else's.

Gunny ordered us to dispose of our 'waste', so we packed our kits back into the wheeled cases and dragged them out into the concourse.

She finished off telling us what had happened while we'd been in jail.

After the news about the credits broke to the Acid Penguins, the Commission's official had retreated into the merchanter hired to take him back to Earth and wisely hadn't come out again.

Gunny had done what she could for her former troops, and they'd all departed to their individual star systems now. We were the last, and she was due to leave on the merchanter with the official in a couple of hours.

She wasn't looking forward to the company on the flight, so she wasn't in a hurry to board. Instead, she offered us a meal at the little dockside hotel-restaurant she was booked into.

"The room's paid for another day. Yours, courtesy of the Terran Marines." Gunny handed us the keycard.

"Thanks, Gunny," I said.

"Appreciate what you've done," Bjorn added.

She looked out across the concourse, eyes focused on something far beyond the station's curving walls.

"I said I'd see you home," she said shortly. "Those that I could, close as I could get."

She *had* said that. I could remember it: one of the first things she'd ever said to the Acid Penguins, and nothing we'd done since then had changed it.

Later, we walked her down the docks, and only as the last call for her ship was being flashed up on the screens did she unbend enough to give us both a hug.

She looked worriedly at us.

"We'll be okay, Gunny," I said. "I'm making a plan."

"That's exactly what I'm afraid of." She stabbed me with a finger. "*You.* Keep Thorsson from going berserk." She stabbed Bjorn. "*You.* Keep Skelling from coming up with situations where you go berserk."

She shook her head, then the sergeant's face slid back into place. "Hate to think of all my training going to waste."

With that, she picked up her duffel, squared her shoulders and walked up the merchanter's gangway.

∞ ∞ ∞ ∞ ∞

We went back to the restaurant to work.

We were still in shock, but we fired up our pads and started looking at the traders' portals to see what we could get for our combat kit. There was a problem: we were following in the footsteps of fifty other ex-1st Frontier soldiers who had been trying to sell their kit. The market was flooded.

Bjorn was scowling. I could feel his temper rising again like a boiler nudging the red line.

"I have an idea," I said, trying to keep control, even though I wanted to blow off as well.

"Yeah?"

"We need to walk around to the market arc," I said. "You can get us better deals face-to-face."

It was true, even if it didn't qualify as much of an idea.

"They'll know we're desperate," he said. "Won't get good deals on the kit. And nothing like enough to get even *one* of the bio-processors."

"Okay. If we can't sell here—"

"We can't afford a passage back toward Earth," he said. "And if we could—"

"Hold on!" I had a brainwave. "The *Karakun* must be scheduled to make stops before Calloway."

I downloaded the itinerary from the transportation portal.

There was one stop. The *Karakun* was a short-haul merchanter and couldn't make the jump to Calloway without stopping to recalibrate on the way. However, the system chosen to stop in didn't have a name; it had a number, GC 10295-83657. And alongside that tag, it had the Facilities Rating, which told you what you could expect to find there: a zero. Nothing. Not even a traffic or navigation beacon.

Odd. There were some inhabited systems between Ensylas and Calloway. Each system was a chance for the merchanter to pick up some business. It didn't make sense to do your recalibration in an empty system. Even if you didn't want to spend time dropping into the gravity well to pitch for business, an inhabited system would have a nav beacon to keep charts updated.

Unless the *Karakun* had a time-sensitive delivery for Calloway, and the route chosen was the minimum time course.

I was no navigator—I couldn't begin to guess the efficiency of the course—but common sense made me ask myself what possible delivery to Calloway would be shipped on a time-sensitive contract. They were unbelievably expensive. I doubted anyone on Calloway was making those kind of orders.

And if they did... at that price, you went for a long-haul merchanter that could make it in one jump.

My trouble-sense started to prickle.

"Bjorn, why would a merchanter like the *Karakun* be heading out to Calloway?"

"Huh?"

He didn't even raise his eyes from his pad.

I lifted my head, but not to look at him; I'd registered that there was someone who had approached silently to stand next to our table.

"I don't think the *Karakun* is going to Calloway," the stranger said in a whispery voice.

She was untidily dressed and clutching a bag in front of her like it was a shield. For a second, I thought it was a beggar, but stations don't allow them.

She nervously ran one trembling hand through her short black hair. Her face was thin, dark-skinned. Her eyes... she had bruised-looking eyes that couldn't stay still.

"You're Skelling and Thorsson, right?" she said.

How would she know us?

"Siriwardene?" I guessed.

She nodded.

I cleared my throat. *Not* the pilot jock that we were expecting.

"Join us?" I said and gestured at the chair opposite.

I could see momentary panic in her eyes and her nostrils flared.

What the nova? Battle fatigue?

But she sat, hugging her bag on her lap.

Bjorn, who could be a real idiot sometimes, nonetheless caught on that something was wrong. When he spoke, he lowered his voice, and put away that dumb, megawatt smile.

"Would you like something to eat?" he asked. "Drink?"

"I don't," she said. "I mean I don't eat or drink food I don't see prepared."

We stared at her.

"You don't know what they put in it."

"Okay..."

Paranoia in addition to whatever else was going on with her.

If we had to live with her in close proximity on the *Karakun*, none of us were going to enjoy this trip.

I waved off a server who was lurking for an order.

"The *Karakun* came in at the same time as the transport that brought me," Siriwardene said abruptly. "I got a good look at her with the transport's sensors."

She had relaxed the smallest amount.

"Well?" I pushed gently.

"The *Karakun* is a pirate."

I ignored the spasm in my gut and frowned. "Pretty serious allegation, Lieutenant."

"I'm not a lieutenant anymore. And I can prove the *Karakun*..." She stopped and her lips thinned. "I *could* prove it, but we can't get into the dock repair gantries."

I tried not to roll my eyes. How convenient. *I could prove it, but...*

"What use would it be getting into the gantries?" Bjorn asked.

Siriwardene's eyes flicked to him and away again.

"The *Karakun* is in the last berth, next to the repair bays. You can see the whole of the ship from the gantries."

"So they have cannon mounted or something—" I started, but Bjorn interrupted me. His voice had gone all silky, like it did when he had a good hand at cards.

"Just suppose, for the sake of argument, that we could get into the gantries. Have they painted a skull and crossbones on the hull?"

"Don't be stupid," Siriwardene said and got up.

I would have let her go, but Bjorn reached out.

"Wait," he said, and she stopped. "We *can* get into the gantries through the maintenance tunnels."

"What? How?" I had a bad feeling about this. "You gave your access key back. I saw you."

"I did," Bjorn agreed amiably. "But I didn't give back the inspector's backup override key."

For nova's sake! Idiot!

He was right on one thing. We *could* get into the gantries with a master key, but the keys were dual system—an actual, old-fashioned electro-mechanical lock activator twinned with an electronic interface which would report the activity.

"They'll have found out it's gone," I said. "If they don't have someone already on the way to arrest us, they *will* have a tracking program to locate anywhere it gets used."

"Relax. It's his backup key. I took it on our first day and he still hasn't realized. He may never realize."

"It was still a stupid thing to do. Anyway, as I said, there'll be alerts that come up on a monitor somewhere whenever those tunnels are accessed."

Siriwardene sat back down and cleared her throat.

"Actually, I may be able to help with that."

E1. Chapter 5

And she could. Which is why, an hour later, we were in the low-G dock gantries near the ship maintenance section.

The section doors had opened, and according to Siriwardene, *call-me-Shami*, nothing had been reported to central monitoring.

Ground attack pilots were *different*. I knew that. I just hadn't really understood how different.

Apparently, the difficulties of flying their craft inside and outside of atmosphere in combat situations required certain additional abilities, including the capability of connecting directly to the onboard computerized systems. Part of her skull was a freaking electronic interface.

The reason she was twitchy was she *needed* that connection to computerized systems. She was addicted to it.

"Low power," she'd explained, as she rested her head on the door's panel. "I need to be close, but this is fine."

Just using her ability to connect to the monitoring system had calmed her right down.

On the other hand, climbing and crawling through narrow, low-G passages didn't help, and Shami was showing signs of claustrophobia. Bjorn and I were fine; Gunny had insisted we train in ship-to-ship combat from null-G to hi-G, from restricted spaces to cavernous hangars.

This far down toward the center of the station, we were well away from the effect of the artificial G of the main area, and the centrifugal force of rotation wasn't having much effect, so all three of us were floating above an inspection window.

Directly 'below' us, the *Karakun* was nose-in to the dock hub, secured in place with standard grapples, front and sides. It was like any other old, small merchanter—a long steel spine sitting between twin cargo bulges, crew space at the front and engines at the back.

The low gravity played tricks with my mind. I felt as if I were looking up at the ship. It seemed huge and menacing. The glancing sunlight made every shadow deeper, turned every surface shape into something monstrous.

I shook my head.

Concentrate.

"What am I looking for?" I asked.

"The section behind the bridge," Shami said. "The raised flat bit."

There was a big rectangular area which looked like it had been added recently. In the middle were what looked like sealed blast doors. Spread out around those were heavy-duty securing pits and recesses for grappling equipment, similar to the equipment used to secure the ship in dock.

"That," Shami said confidently, "is the latest in deep-space universal couplings. Replicates the docking facilities of space stations."

"It's a way to make a sealed connection with another ship?"

"Yes."

I frowned. Unusual, yes. Suspicious?

"What do you think they trade, out there in deep space, out of sight of everyone else?" Shami said. "What's worth the costs of getting a coupling like that installed on a two-bit merchanter?"

"Maybe it's smuggling rather than piracy?" Bjorn said.

I grimaced. "No. Down in the depths of the Inner Worlds, maybe. Out here? Trading station to station? There's no pan-system smuggling laws that individual systems are going to enforce. If they don't want what you've got, they don't buy it."

Everyone knew ships docked at stations with cargo that was illegal for that system. It was a gray area, but generally, if you kept it on board, the station didn't care.

Shami was right. Such a coupling only made sense for bulk transfers, and only pirates would need to transfer bulk cargo in deep space.

There was a long silence, broken by Bjorn: "And they bid for a contract to take us to Calloway because..."

He and Shami kicked it back and forth between them.

"They get three slaves they can sell into rogue systems and all our back pay that they can convert next time they go inward."

"That ship wouldn't dare enter a rogue system. No weapons."

"No, this is their legitimate merchanter. That means there's at least one other, an armed ship, out there in the dark, waiting."

"Can we cancel the contract to travel and re-bid using the same money?"

"Maybe. Even if we can't, and we have to pay passage ourselves, we have to."

They wound down.

"Jan?"

I was floating there, staring at the pirate.

It all hit me in that moment: The greed of the Commission. The betrayal. The three lives wasted—Solveig, Enoch, Hal. The smirks of station traders as they swindled us out of everything. My family's faces if I turned up after six years with no bio-processors. The despair as the colony faced its own collapse. More deaths from starvation. My uncle's face—*I told you she wouldn't amount to anything. Probably spent it in bars.* Six years of my life, my *soul*, risked and wasted.

And finally anger—white-hot and steady as Sirius, flooding through me. Enough.

I shook my head again. "We can't stay here. We take that ship."

"Ah... I vote to not be a slave," Bjorn said.

"Well, that's given," I replied. "But you know what? I have a plan."

"Oh, shit," Bjorn said.

E1. Chapter 6

My plan hatched in the relative comfort of the Orion's Wheel station looked... different now that I watched the second pirate ship coast in by the faint red light of an empty system's dying sun, surrounded by cold, hard vacuum.

Back on Orion's Wheel, we'd arrived at the *Karakun* acting belligerent in case Captain Satybal wanted to check our luggage for contraband. We didn't have to worry. The crew of the *Karakun* didn't bother to greet us. There was a screen next to the gangway, which demanded confirmation of our identities and then directed us to the 'passenger accommodation'.

That was three rooms. One with a set of bunks, one with chairs and a ReadyMeal dispenser, and one bathroom. As soon as we were inside the short corridor that formed the entrance, the door had sealed behind us.

Ship security and safety were the reasons given when we'd used the comm to query it.

Hogshit.

Even before we'd undocked, Shami had located, identified, and subverted the electronics of the monitors that the *Karakun* had installed to keep watch on us. And while we were outbound from Ensylas, I'd broken into and crawled through the maintenance tunnels. With instructions from Shami, I'd rigged a connection for her into the computer system network.

It made her so happy, she had to discipline herself not to take over until we were ready.

She *wasn't* in control of the much larger, obviously heavily armed pirate ship that was incoming to connect up with the *Karakun*. Getting control of *that* was a job for Bjorn and me.

The newcomer's name was *Tünjorgo*. Both ships were registered to Zilkum, a small Frontier system at the other end of the Parvi Arc. There was almost nothing in the Ensylas databanks about Zilkum. Exactly the sort of setup that spoke of rogue systems and pirate bases.

Karakun was the merchanter that visited systems and learned about rich prizes. *Tünjorgo* was the demon that waited in the dark places to seize them. Goods went to the *Karakun* to sell at the next legitimate system, while slaves went into the *Tünjorgo* to wait until they were sold in the next rogue system. Neat.

What the *Tünjorgo* didn't know was that Captain Satybal had not picked up three helpless potential slaves heading home with currency cards full of credits they couldn't convert, but rather three angry, pissed-off veterans, one who was poised to take over the *Karakun*'s computerized systems, and the other two in fully operational combat armor, waiting to do something less subtle with the bigger ship.

We waited in silence, except for the blood pounding in my ears and the rush of my breath. Knowing Bjorn could see my vital signs soaring in his helmet monitor didn't help calm me down.

Showtime.

"Let's go. When we get there, remember to point your weapon away from me," I said as we launched ourselves into space.

Bjorn's response was rude and crude. It helped take my mind off the thought that we were flying between two ships in deep space using nothing more for maneuvering than a rig made from a couple of cheap, out-of-date fire extinguishers, which were going to run out...

Now.

We were still traveling toward the *Tünjorgo*, but one extinguisher had run out before the other, so we were spinning slowly. The distant stars wheeled above me. We were only three-quarters of the way between the ships, and we needed to hurry.

Theoretically, the danger was slim. Automated scanners would ignore something relatively low mass and slow moving like us, but all it would need would be for someone to get curious.

Too late to change the plan.

We needed to get rid of our exhausted propulsion rig.

Bjorn's countdown came through my helmet. "Three, two, one, go!"

I kicked the rig with the empty fire extinguishers away, in the opposite direction we wanted to travel. Newton be thanked, it helped: equal and opposite reactions. It even slowed the spinning a bit, which was lucky because we crashed into the surface of the *Tünjorgo*, out of control.

Hey, it was our first unsupported EVA.

Newton got his revenge, because Bjorn bounced off the ship and started drifting, waving his arms and legs.

I anchored myself using a magnetic grapple and chased after him in comical slow motion.

Found a second anchor point.

Threw a line.

Too short...

Leaped. Grabbed the end. Reached...

He grabbed hold of my hand.

"Stop playing the fool and come back here," I hissed at him.

"Very funny."

His vital signs were all over the place. Made me smirk.

He reeled himself in and we had five minutes of more slow-motion racing across the surface of the *Tünjorgo*, looking for an access airlock, while the ship shifted beneath us like a restless monster.

"Docking in five seconds." Shami's voice came over the command channel. "Brace."

Three... two... one...

There was a recessed area with a raised lip just in reach.

I felt the servos in our armor gauntlets ramp up just in time. A violent shudder ran through the ship and slapped us hard against the surface.

"Docked," Shami said. "They're checking systems. I'm guessing you have about five minutes before they come looking for us."

"On it," I said. "We found an airlock."

The next step was to get inside. Almost all ships like this were built in the Inner Worlds and they usually built them with standard controls, but there was no certainty the airlock wouldn't be sealed or made to a different specification.

Bjorn was swearing as he worked on the panel.

I felt thumps through the ship as the *Tünjorgo* was clamped in place. That was okay. While they were concentrating on that, they weren't moving around.

Then the vibrations died away, and I started prepping explosives, running through what would be needed if we blew the airlock open.

It would be bad news because whereas an airlock showing it was opening and closing, with no alarms sounding, would probably be ignored by the crew for a while, blowing the outer doors would not.

Bjorn grunted: "Got it."

I heaved a sigh of relief.

The lock cycled open, and the inner door was a simple push button once the lock had flooded with air.

"Inside," I reported to Shami.

"I've frozen the docking bay's blast doors," she said. "They're blaming a faulty installation. It'll give you another couple of minutes until they get down and force them open."

"Good thinking."

Bjorn and I took ten seconds to check each other's suits.

"All okay. Weapons free," he said quietly.

I nodded, with the usual sick feeling in my mouth I got before action. "Clock zero. Go."

We came out of the airlock. Bjorn turned right, I turned left.

From the outline of the *Tünjorgo* that Shami had provided to us from the *Karakun*'s databases, we had three objectives and only two of us.

I headed to the front of the ship. I had to take control of the bridge.

After a long, difficult discussion yesterday, we'd agreed Bjorn should take the prisoners' section. We knew the *Tünjorgo* had some, and we didn't want to face a situation where they were used as hostages.

That left engineering.

We had to hope I could isolate them from the bridge.

We'd run analyses. We estimated we had four minutes and fifteen seconds for both of us to achieve our tasks, at which time Shami could seize control of the *Karakun* and lock the whole ship down through the computer systems.

Then we had another twelve minutes before we had to return and prevent Satybal and his crew from bypassing the computer controls.

If any of that went wrong...

Four minutes remaining.

Passage end. Rung ladder. Up one level. Straight ahead.

A crewman turned in shock at the sight of an armored soldier sprinting along the passage.

No time. I had no police weapons like a stun gun. The guy was unarmed.

Then again, he was a slaver.

I backhanded him out of the way. That was serious hurt, delivered by military armor.

"One hostile down, not dead," I grunted as I accelerated through the door he'd opened. Didn't slow. Slammed into the wall. Turned left. Sprinted down that passage. Then right.

The first major obstacle. The ship had enough safety discipline that they'd closed emergency bulkheads while docking.

A simple lever and bolt. I tore it open.

Three minutes.

"They've switched to using auxiliary power to open the blast doors. I can't stop them," Shami said over the command channel. "You have two minutes."

Shit. Two minutes!

More crew ahead of me. And some kind of a comm panel on the wall.

I hit the crew hard and punched my fist right through the comm panel. Sparks flew out.

"Two more down," I said and kept going.

Another level change.

I didn't bother with the rungs. I just jumped up. My arm was extended to kill my momentum. It went right through the ceiling and some of the cabling above it.

Alarms went off. Something I'd done. Or Bjorn.

"I've sealed off the docking bay and I'm venting it." Shami's voice. "Venting *Karakun* bridge and engineering."

Shit! She wasn't messing around.

"Prisoner area secured." Bjorn's voice. "Three hostiles down. Can't get inside the cells."

We had to hope I could open the cell doors from the bridge.

A security barrier started to slide out across the passage from one side. I dove through, sensed trouble, rolled, came up with the TAW already pointed.

Crew were hurriedly grabbing weapons from a storage area.

No time.

I fired as I ran, wide dispersal, and dropped a fragmentation grenade behind me as I darted into the last passage that led to the bridge.

The grenade exploded behind me. My armor soaked it up, but when the whole ship shook and lurched, I went spinning and sliding.

"*Tünjorgo* trying to disengage docking by force," Shami said.

No time.

"Clamping circuits are being bypassed on the *Tünjorgo*'s side. You have fifteen seconds."

I bounced to my feet. The door to the bridge ahead was sealed. I sprinted, hit it at full speed, dropping my shoulder.

My armor took most of the impact, but I still saw stars. The metal door buckled and bent, but it held.

No!

I stood back, dialed in armor piercing—*only two of those rounds left*—and fired the TAW.

They punched through the door and did who knows what damage beyond. The alarms doubled and lights started flashing.

I tossed a dazzler into the bridge area and took a grip on the hole in the door.

The servos in my armor whined. This was *not* what they were designed for.

The dazzler went off. Intense light and *loud* noise.

"Ten seconds," Shami said.

The door's holding structure distorted.

There were shots from behind me. The armor let me know about it, but it would hold against typical shipboard weapons. I couldn't spare the time to deal with them.

With a screech, the door began to peel open.

"Seven seconds."

I kicked my way through onto the bridge.

There were three of them there, all stumbling about from the effect of the dazzler, their faces blank with shock.

I grabbed the nearest and shoved the TAW in his face.

With my suit's speaker amplification up to maximum, I shouted: "Turn off all power to Docking and Engineering. *NOW.*"

"Four seconds."

The man collapsed against a control panel, his eyes unfocused and his fingers clumsy.

Luckily, the command menu was in English. Once he called up the right menu, I reached past him and stabbed at the options on the screen.

Power. Emergency. Docking bay. Off.

"Two seconds."

A message popped up on the screen: *Power disconnect from docking bay. Are you sure?*

Yes!

Docking bay power disconnected.

I repeated the sequence for Engineering.

Then I found the comms panel. Switched it to ship-wide broadcast.

What the nova should I say?

"This is Lieutenant Commander Skelling of the Calloway Navy Anti-Piracy Unit. The *Tünjorgo* and *Karakun* are now under my control. If there is any further resistance, I will vent these shit-heaps to space and throw your stinking bodies out of the airlock."

∞ ∞ ∞ ∞ ∞

A ring of expectant faces looked up at me.

A dozen men and women, the crews of a couple of small ships that had been captured, who'd been held prisoner in the *Tünjorgo*, knowing the fate that had awaited them—slavery.

Relief on their faces, mainly. Anger, too. And hope.

The pirates, living and dead, were now in the holding cells, and their former captives sat on the seats in the *Tünjorgo*'s mess area.

I was standing, still in my suit, but with the visor cracked so they could see my face.

I'd already told them they hadn't been rescued by the 'Calloway Navy'.

What the nova do I say now?

"There's good news and bad," I started. "You're free and we will get you back to your systems, or any place we get to, that you nominate."

Cheers. Smiles.

"We need some of them to run these damned ships, *Lieutenant Commander*," Shami snarked in my ear through the command channel. "Have you actually thought through *any* of this?"

I ignored her and went on. "The bad news..."

It got quiet.

"These ships don't have enough credit to go wandering all over the Frontier."

"You'll get bounties from handing over the pirates to any system that has signed the Anti-Piracy Accords," one of the men at the back said.

"*We* will get bounties," I replied. "All of us. But if we turn up with the *Tünjorgo* and *Karakun* in the Ensylas System, for example, the ships would be impounded, and your share of the bounty might not get you home."

And Bjorn, Shami, and I would be back where we started, with fistfuls of credit that wouldn't buy what Calloway or Yorkham needed and probably wouldn't even get us passage back home.

Absolute silence, even on the helmet radio. They were all waiting for me.

"But it's okay," I said. "I have a plan."

Episode 2
Problems and Opportunities

E2. Chapter 1

"Problem," Bjorn muttered.

"Opportunity," I replied.

We were in a noisy dockside bar on the Orion's Wheel, eating the sampler platter, which rested on the tabletop between us. We were leaning in, our heads together, looking over each other's shoulders.

"Sounds like an old curse," I went on. "You first. What's the problem? Not enough salt?"

He picked up a spicy hog sausage and dipped it in the relish before chewing appreciatively.

"You know when you catch sight of someone on the other side of a bar," he said between chews. "And he keeps staring at you, really staring, so you can see his pupils? Like you can see white all around them?"

"Oh, yeah. Crazy eyes. Bad news. You been looking at his girlfriend?"

Bjorn snorted.

I'd spent six years fighting alongside Bjorn. As casual as we might have sounded, I knew he was serious.

He reached for the last pretzel dumpling. I batted his hand away.

"That's mine."

He snorted again. "Tell me about the opportunity," he said.

"You know when someone looks at you with their eyes narrowed, like they're thinking hard about some deal they're trying to sell you?"

"Yeah. Anyone we know?"

"The trader we spoke to at the Markt Donnier emporium," I said. "Ross-something. The woman who brought in that planet-wide satellite comms system for the government of Ensylas, and then the deal hit a snag."

He frowned. "Not exactly an opportunity for us. We don't want anything like that, even if we could afford it, which we can't."

"We know that, and she knows that, but she's here, alone, done up in an outfit like she doesn't want to be recognized, and she keeps looking across at us."

He grunted. "Apart from looking, what's she doing?"

"Having a long, detailed conversation on her InfoPad. Something tells me it's about us."

Bjorn ran a hand across his jaw. Since our faces might be remembered from our previous visit to the station, and raise questions we wouldn't want to answer, he'd completely shaved his red hair off and grown a goatee beard. It didn't suit him, but even his family would have trouble recognizing him.

I'd colored my hair like a rainbow with dyes I'd found on board the old pirate ship *Karakun*, dabbed on scarlet lipstick, and I'd painted a black horizontal strip across my eyes. It was the sort of thing that could pass as dockside fashion for spacers.

Hell, even *I* couldn't recognize me.

Not bad for a pair of amateurs trying to stay incognito, but it didn't seem that the authorities were the ones we should be worried about.

"Crazy Eyes is looking down at his pad too," Bjorn noted.

"A paranoid would think he's waiting for orders."

"You think they're working something together?" Bjorn took a long drink of his beer.

"Nah," I said. "It's bound to be a coincidence. Let's cool it, okay? We don't want to spend any more time as guests of the Orion's Wheel correctional services."

Once had been enough. And we hadn't even started the fight. The legal system on this station sucked asteroids.

But, bad as that episode had been, it would be even worse if it happened again.

For a start, they'd discover who we really were and our plan would go up in smoke. For everyone, not just for us. The ship we'd arrived in, which we'd announced as *Acid Penguin*, would be discovered to be the *Karakun*. We'd easily show we weren't the pirates, and that the original owners were, but regardless of that, the Ensylas system would confiscate the ship.

We couldn't afford to let that happen. The whole of our home planet of Calloway depended on that *not* happening.

"Fine," Bjorn muttered. "I'll cool it. But I won't let people piss in my beer."

He was starting to sound surly, and I knew that was a bad sign. The boy had a temper like a volcano on a tectonic fault line.

"Think of what's at stake," I hissed at him. "We can't afford to get into trouble. Come on, let's get out of here."

"Too late."

I glanced over my shoulder. Crazy Eyes was on his way, pocketing his pad. He had two friends close behind, and I shuddered at the sight of them. Gene tricking is illegal everywhere, but that doesn't mean it doesn't happen. This *was* Frontier space. Based on their size and the way they moved those hulking bodies, I suspected those two were mutants bred for street fighting.

Crap.

My stomach clenched as nanos started to pump bio-agents into my bloodstream. Senses went pin-sharp, and muscles suddenly got that loose-tense feel.

Not the physical reaction I needed at the moment. Even if we did fight our way out of the bar, that would only bring the station police down on us.

Couldn't afford that.

Couldn't stop it either, but these three were going to be sorry if they started something.

No. No.

More important to get out of here and back to the ship.

"Just stay calm," I forced out through clenching jaws. "No fighting unless there's no other way."

I palmed my steak knife as I spoke. *Never* fail to bring *any* advantage you can into a fight: Gunny had drilled that into us. It still applied even if I didn't want to rumble.

"This acting civil and responsible is shit." Bjorn looked up as Crazy Eyes arrived, but stayed seated, even though that put him at a disadvantage. His voice probably still sounded all relaxed to others. "Evening, folks. What can we do for you?"

"Cut the crap and keep your fucking junk hauler the shit away from my routes," the man spat, deliberately looming over us, with his jaw thrust out and his thugs close behind him. "That's what you can do tomorrow. And tonight? Tonight, you go back to your ship like a good boy while we party with your girlfriend."

Bjorn stood up slowly, all two meters of him, and Mama Thorsson didn't raise any skinny weaklings. Crazy Eyes went from looming over us to looking upwards.

Bjorn had to do it, but it was a bad move. Whatever had got Crazy Eyes worked up originally, being made to look small got him even angrier, and angry people were less likely to listen to reason and back down.

If that had ever been an option.

But... one in, all in. Gunny taught us that, too. I stood beside Bjorn, my body on that singing line between holding back and going all out, even as my mind searched frantically for a way to calm this down and get the hell back to our ship.

If we fought, whichever way it went, our whole plan was blown.

The mutant thugs spread slightly, blocking other people's view of us. I decided that worked for me, because no one would see me stab Crazy Eyes. I let the steak knife slip down until it rested comfortably in my hand.

"And what routes would those be?" Bjorn's voice had gone all soft and slow. Very, *very* bad sign to those who knew him.

"Ensylas-Ranier, for one."

Bjorn laughed.

Crazy Eyes didn't like being laughed at.

"Look, why don't we buy you all a beer and discuss trade routes," I said, voice hoarse with adrenaline. "Ranier isn't something special for us."

"Oh, they won't serve beer to those two," a voice beside me said. "The bar's not stupid."

It was the woman trader from Markt Donnier. Her hand gripped my arm, hampering me from sinking the steak knife into Crazy Eyes's gut if he moved against Bjorn.

Shit. They *were* working together. We'd been cornered.

E2. Chapter 2

But Crazy Eyes took a step back, jostling his own thugs.

"Who the—"

"Thandi Roskilde of Markt Donnier," the woman said, very loudly, slipping off the hood that had obscured her face and her shock of curly hair. "Greetings. Captain Maykn of the merchanter *Sambuk*, I think, eh?"

"I know who you are. This here is none of your business," Maykn snarled.

"Eh, but it is, Maykn. A restriction of trade between systems? That would affect all of us, in both systems. If you were the only hauler on that route, you could be tempted to raise your prices. Monopolies like that are against the law, for good reason, yes?"

She was speaking loudly enough that people around turned to listen. It was a dockside bar, full of traders and merchanters, and this *was* something they were interested in.

Maykn's eyes got even crazier, but he wasn't stupid. If his original intention had been to start something and then claim it was us, he couldn't do that as the center of attention.

He got into Roskilde's face.

"You're gonna regret getting involved, bitch," he said, and shoved past her.

His thugs followed him, the threat of violence still swirling around the three of them like a chilling fog.

And Maykn's brown coat... the way it moved and hung heavily told me what it was—a popular item of clothing in some of the rougher parts of the Frontier: a stab-proof coat.

It was clear to me, Roskilde's interruption had come just in time. Another few seconds and we would have been fighting. There would have been no way to stop it.

Maykn probably didn't realize what he was up against—a couple of ex-soldiers with boosters flooding our bodies. He would have been the first dead, within a second, fancy coat or not. On the other hand, I didn't know what boosters the thugs with him might have. Bjorn and I had the standard military set which would be more than enough for normals. But those guys...

I glanced at Bjorn and saw he'd gone a bit crazy eyes as well. Useful in a battle, not so much now. He'd take some time to come back down, so I spoke first.

"That was kind of you, Trader Roskilde," I said, my voice still sounding creaky. "But I'm not sure it was wise."

She raised her hood over her head again, even though everyone who'd heard the argument would know who she was. She was wearing one of those robe-dresses made of fabric that changed color dependent on temperature and pressure, so she was a one-person lightshow that rippled distractingly whenever she moved.

I could see the theory: with the hood up, everyone's eyes would be drawn to the lights and maybe they wouldn't see or remember her face. But she'd ditched all that when she'd come to help us.

Why had she come to help us?

She was inspecting Bjorn with a thoughtful look. And she hadn't let go my arm.

Not that she was strong enough to stop me pulling free, but I still wanted to de-escalate everything. Struggling with her could set Bjorn off.

"Why don't you join us," I had to force myself to say. I wasn't nearly as close to blowing my top as Bjorn was, but with all the adrenaline pumping through me, I wouldn't be good company for a while.

She ignored that. I could see gears turn in her head. She put her free hand on Bjorn's shoulder and carefully leaned closer.

"We are not out of this yet," she said quietly.

"What's with this *we*?" Bjorn's words came out clipped.

"You need *me* to get you out of here," she said. "And I need *you two* for the same sort of reason. *We* need each other."

"You're not making sense," I said.

I moved her hand from my arm.

She turned to me. The light from her hood made her dark skin seem even darker, but I could see her eyes clearly.

"You're not going to go berserker on me, are you, *soldier*?" she whispered.

Nova!

We thought we'd hidden our identities well. Bjorn and I exchanged glances. He'd calmed down enough that the shock of hearing our secret spoken brought him down another level.

Good. We *needed* to understand what was going on here.

"I'm not going to lose my temper," I downplayed it. "And thanks again for your help with Maykn, but I don't see why we need more help from you, or—"

"Because he hasn't gone. He and his thugs are waiting outside. There are station police who 'happen' to be half an arc away, just waiting for the fight to start."

This was getting better and better.

"Assuming what you say is true," Bjorn said, "what help are you going to give us, and why?"

I took a decision to ignore the conversation and pulled out my pad, intent on calling for help from the ship.

"Whatever you're thinking with that, don't do it," Roskilde said quickly, hand on my arm again. "All your comms are routed through the station datanet."

"You're saying the station *itself* is after us?" Bjorn's voice was rising.

"No. Not the whole station. Just enough of them, with enough in management positions. A gang." She looked around. "Eh, we don't have time for this. Trust me, or take your chances outside. And believe me, you will lose your ship if you go out that door."

That hit my gut like a punch.

We couldn't lose the ship. There were people on Calloway who were depending on us. Depending on my plan. And without the ship, they were dead.

"Wait here," I said.

I trotted to the main doors. As with all ones that opened onto the station's main concourse, they were twin iris doors, separated by a ten-person space, so they could be sealed and used like airlocks for emergencies. Through the view panels, I could see men gathering outside. Maykn and his two mutants at least—maybe others were joining them.

I hurried back and nodded at Bjorn.

We'd worked together so long, we both knew how the other thought. We silently agreed we couldn't put a lot of trust in Roskilde yet, but she was a better risk than brawling on the concourse.

Probably.

"We're going to trust you," I said. Not quite the truth. Not yet.

She didn't waste time. With an upward jerk of her head, she said, "Come with me. Quickly."

She led us to the back of the bar, where the manager gave her a tiny nod and looked away.

She waved at us to follow through swing doors into a kitchen and storage area. A couple of heads turned toward us as we walked through, and then turned away. Deliberately incurious.

Interesting.

Roskilde hurried us to a service entrance at the back, and peered out through the view panel cautiously.

"*Izuri*," she muttered to herself with satisfaction, unsealing the door and sliding it open. "Into the first trishaw. Hurry."

A trishaw?

When engineers designed stations, they expected goods and people to move around the hub by hissing monorails, or silent mag-lev cabs. Orion's Wheel had a monorail on the next level down, but it had a cost, and there were lots of people keen to supplement their incomes by providing a cheap alternative for those too lazy or too drunk to walk. Cycling cabs was one popular way.

In the gloom of the service ringway, two trishaws waited for us. Bjorn and I got into the first, Roskilde in the one behind.

"Pull down the canopy," the driver hissed as he set off.

I pulled it. The canopy only came down part of the way and it was translucent.

The driver looked over his shoulder and grimaced. "Don't just sit there like crash dummies," he said. "They'll send someone around the back as soon as they realize you're not in the bar. Hide your faces. Make out or something."

Crashing down off my adrenaline high, I started to giggle.

Okay, it *was* a good idea for disguise. Making out would hide our faces.

But, *nova*, it was awkward. Six years' military service with Bjorn. Six years on the same team. Six years of 'off-limits'. It would be like kissing my brother, wouldn't it? And our working relationship was important. Far more important than enjoying this, for even a moment.

We weren't in the military anymore, but my thoughts hadn't changed: Bjorn was a good man, but not necessarily a good bet. He probably thought something similar about me. So, because we weren't a good bet for each other, and because we didn't have intentions towards each other, getting involved would be a *bad* idea for our working relationship, and that would be a bad idea for my plan.

Still, we wrapped our arms around each other and pretended, while using the pose to look both ways, like we had in the bar.

There wasn't a lot to see.

Orion's Wheel was a classic, old-fashioned station: a torus with spokes — essentially a wheel spinning in space. The main habitat and services ran around the outer hub, with the spokes providing the spaceship docks, automated production and resource storage. Everything else was centered around the habitat zone, the level we were on, which in turn centered around the main concourse, the broad ringway which ran around the hub. But at that moment we were scuttling around on one of the smaller service ringways, and there was little traffic until we turned off and went through an unlit conduit alley onto the main concourse.

Smaller stations like Orion's Wheel created station-time night and day. By that clock, it was evening now, with the wide regulator tube that made up most of the concourse's ceiling turned from bright gold to pale silver, casting a moonlight effect. Between the reduced light and getting disoriented in the service ringway, I couldn't recognize the shops and businesses the trishaw was gliding past.

But as we went through the restriction of one of the emergency isolation junctions between arcs, I could read the glowing sign. We were entering Arc 16. The dock where the ship was berthed was between Arcs 15 and 14, and the bar was in Arc 15.

I untangled myself from Bjorn and stuck my head underneath the canopy, which had jammed into place.

Unfortunately, all I could see of the guy pedaling was his backside, and his pumping thighs.

"Hey! Wrong way," I said to the backside. "Where are you taking us?"

"It's dangerous close to the bar. We're going to a safe place to talk," he replied. "Just ahead. Stay inside."

Dangerous?

Bjorn and I scanned around us again. The concourse curved up gently to the next junction. Advertisements for bars and restaurants lit up the sides with lights and low-power holograms trying to tempt people inside. Some shops were still open. People were strolling: there were stationers in Ensylas's planetside styles and merchanters either in functional ship clothes or weird fashions.

Other trishaws weaved through the loose crowds. It was a clever idea to spirit us away, and faster than walking, but still, it felt so slow.

Especially when I saw a squad of four police walking the other way — toward the bar. Not strolling, not looking around.

Looking for us? Or was it all just a typical station evening?

I sat back and willed myself to calm down.

"You okay?" I asked Bjorn.

"Yeah. Of course." He straightened his jacket, scratched his chin and looked out at the other traffic on the concourse. His mouth twitched and his eyes glittered. "Being hunted by a gang of criminals working for the station's ruling elite, putting our trust in some other gang, who have their own agenda, but who are helping us escape from a trap in slow motion in a damned squeaky trishaw, and..." He stopped abruptly and began shaking with laughter. "Why wouldn't I be okay?"

Still coming off the adrenaline high, we both started to laugh, making our trishaw driver look around in puzzlement. We always had this reaction after our military combat nanos quit pumping us, but he couldn't know that.

"Well, he's going as fast as he can without appearing unusual," I said when I could. And the guy was traveling quickly for a trishaw, but without apparently attracting attention.

The man pedaled us into another conduit passage and then onto a secondary service ringway, the opposite side from the first, so we were on the other side of the main concourse, and more than an arc away from the bar where it had started.

Far enough.

I decided I trusted Roskilde this far, but no further.

"Ready for anything?" I nudged Bjorn, who had sobered too.

He nodded.

"This is enough." I leaned under the canopy and spoke to the backside again. "Stop."

"Just here," he replied, waving at the anonymous service entrance of a building a short way ahead. It looked closed, with a metal roller shutter for deliveries pulled all the way down.

Our driver cycled straight for it, speeding up. Someone heaved it open at the last moment. We rushed inside and skidded to a halt with Roskilde's trishaw slithering in right behind us.

We struggled to get out of the seat as the shutter slammed down, trapping us in a dark storeroom, with a group of people staring hungrily at us.

E2. Chapter 3

"We're safe here for a very short while," Roskilde said, with a half-smile pulling at her lips. "Even though your efforts to disguise yourselves in the trishaw were hardly convincing."

"What the nova is going on?" Bjorn asked. His voice had gone right back to dangerously soft and slow.

Our adrenaline had started pumping again. Not so much as when we'd been confronted by Maykn in the bar, but we didn't like the feeling of being trapped. We didn't like the roller shutter coming down and the looks we were getting.

I still had the steak knife and it was back in my hand.

"We don't have time for big explanations." Roskilde shook her head, standing tall and crossing her arms. "Eh, so. Short version: you're not merchanters, and your ship's registration has never been seen by anyone on station. Orion's Wheel isn't the busiest stop, but there are merchanters here from all over the Margin and Frontier. Long odds against *no one* knowing anything about you. Too long. First guess was you were pirates."

"If the station thought we were pirates, we'd have been arrested," I said.

"The station doesn't work like that. Not unless you were dumb enough to come in on a recognized pirate ship. No. People in Docking Control sell information to people in the Traders' Combine. They all do it, all the time. Who's inbound. Where from. What cargo. And anything odd, like a merchanter no one ever heard of before. Then people talk in bars. Then they watch what you do in the trading arc. You buy a whole planetary bio-processor, eh? But only one. Then enough ship supplies to get a little hauler like yours halfway across the galaxy, but... so strange... *no* trade goods. None. And no crew out drinking and eating in the bars. Just you two."

I could feel Bjorn look at me. It was my plan, and it hadn't had enough leeway on the financials for us to buy trade goods just to look more like merchanters. Not yet.

The plan also didn't have any leeway for us to be caught up in some stationer turf war. Especially on what appeared to be the weaker side.

Bjorn and I were tensing up for the second time that evening. Military nanos were once again ramping up our bodies to fight, while we struggled to restrain ourselves. These people weren't trying to attack us, *yet*, but their expressions... I'd got it right when we came in; they looked *hungry*. As if we were the first food they'd seen for a week.

Our nano systems were reacting as if they were a threat.

This was something we'd been warned about when the news came that we were going to be demobilized. The nanos will fade away eventually, they'd said. Until then, you just have to work hard at stopping your body from railroading you into a combat response in civilian situations.

It *was* hard.

"So when you came into Markt Donnier, I talked to you," Roskilde went on calmly, seemingly unaware of my struggle. "Even though it was obvious you had no interest in a planetary satellite comm system."

Her mouth stretched in a slightly bitter smile.

I snorted. "No money for luxuries like that. No clients either."

"New colony?" Roskilde asked. "You have found some little paradise off the star charts you want to keep secret?"

"No," I said. That sort of thing did happen. The Frontier got expanded little by little, mainly by marginal groups thinking an uncharted and unknown world was going to be easier than trying to fit in with an existing colonized world.

Dumb.

Bjorn and I exchanged looks.

It seemed Roskilde had worked out a lot about our story, and hadn't told the station authorities. There didn't seem to be a downside to listening to her, at least until we worked out what she wanted in exchange for keeping quiet and helping us.

"So... five minutes of talking to you about my problems selling satellite systems and I had you down for military," she was saying. "Former soldiers?"

"Yeah," Bjorn said. "We were heading home. Decided against being turned into slaves by the merchanter who sold us passage."

She snorted appreciatively. "You turned the tables on slavers? And took their ship? Now *that* will be a great story to tell."

"Later, maybe," I said. "If you say we're short of time, we need to get back to our ship, so tell us who's after us, why, and then why you're helping us."

"And what you meant by *you* need *us* to get you out of here," Bjorn added.

Roskilde nodded at Bjorn. "On that one, it's simple. I have to get off Orion's Wheel, and the same people who want to seize your ship, want to stop me." She squinted and wrinkled her nose expressively. "Eh, they wouldn't mind me going, so long as I leave the satellite comms equipment behind. But no, I want to be on your ship, *with* my goods *and* my family."

"How do you think they're going to seize our ship?" Bjorn said, at the same time as I said, "Who's behind all this? Why are they after you?"

"This gang who wants your ship is a group within the Trader's Guild." Roskilde answered me with a sigh and ran her hands over a face that looked suddenly tired. "They made a deal with the planet's Communications Ministry for a satellite system to give Ensylas planet-wide comms. Then they persuaded me to handle the purchase and shipping. Now that the system's here, they changed the deal."

"They're preventing you from selling the comms system the planet wants until you give them more money?"

"It has gone beyond that. I actually factored in that they'd gouge me for an extra 10% or 15%. But they got greedy. They started at 40%. I'd just break even on that, maybe. When I refused, they forced the financiers to start pressuring me. My company is fifteen to twenty days away from going bankrupt and having everything seized."

"You owe money on the satellite system? It's not yours?"

"No. I had to fund that up front, but to do that, I borrowed money for my normal trading while the satellite system was shipping here. Eh, they can seize the rest of my goods, I don't care, but I am *not* giving them the satellite system. I'll destroy it before I do that."

That got through to Bjorn. He relaxed enough to chuckle. "Woman after my own heart."

I shook my head at the distraction. My plan needed changing. But how much time did we have? Or was it already too late?

"And what about seizing our ship?"

"They will think you cannot prove legal title to it." She stared at me, one eyebrow raised. "You can't, can you?"

She was right. That's why we'd tried so hard to hide from the authorities.

"We didn't steal it," I pointed out. "We confiscated it from pirates."

Roskilde snorted. "The Piracy Accords say only planetary systems can do that, and you know it."

"We're going to get it sorted out," Bjorn said, and we were. That was all part of my plan.

"But you haven't *yet*. So they'll confiscate it. It will be completely legal."

"*They*. You mean the station," I said. "I don't care how powerful this group is, they aren't the station itself. *They* can't do that."

"No, you're right. But they will find a way. So say you'd been arrested by police for fighting at the bar. The ship wouldn't have been allowed to leave. Then the police find it's not your ship and the system confiscates it. But mooring charges and service fees would mount up, and by the time it gets through the arbitration, the outstanding fees and fines would have compounded so much, the station would just hand the ship over to the creditors. Obviously, the ship would still be worth more than the debt, but whatever else happens, you can't prove you own it, so you'd get nothing."

"But they didn't arrest us, thanks to you," Bjorn said.

"Which means they'll try something else," I said. "How long have we got?"

One of the men in the room waved urgently at us. He was watching a monitor and had one earpiece of an old headphone set pressed to his ear. "No time," he said. "They've worked out you have escaped and they've split up their teams. Some looking on the ringways, some heading for Markt Donnier, thinking we'd take you there."

"Then we've got to go now," I said. "You and your people can come with us, Roskilde, no charge, but you'll have to leave your satellite system behind."

I knew as soon as I said it, that wasn't going to work. She had that sort of gleam in her eye.

"We are prepared, and your holds are not full, I think. Let me worry about getting the satellite system down to the loading bays," she said. "However, the one thing I cannot do is get you back on board. They'll have people watching the docks for you trying to sneak back."

"It's worse than that; we need to get aboard before you get there," I said. "Standing orders on the ship are to let nothing in that we haven't spoken to the crew about. You leave enough containers for a whole satellite system blocking the mag rail and someone is going to get suspicious. And as you say, we can't just walk up to the ship in plain sight. They'll have some plan to stop us if they see us."

A ring of worried faces looked at me.

"They won't see us," I said. "It's okay, I have a plan."

E2. Chapter 4

At every junction, along with the arc number, the concourse had a digital clock, big enough to be visible for fifty meters or so.

It blinked and changed to 21:07.

We had fifty-three minutes left to get to the ship.

Through Roskilde's eavesdropping, we'd heard the people after us had searched Markt Donnier. They were now all concentrating on the concourse. There were a lot of bars and clubs to check out and they still wouldn't find us, but in Roskilde's estimation, that wasn't going to be the limiting factor. It was the length of time she had estimated it would take for our enemies to get some kind of a bogus legal challenge through the Orion's Wheel legal system at this time of night.

A challenge that would allow the station to prevent our departure and start demanding documentation from us, including proof of ownership.

22:00 was the first target we had to meet. At that time exactly, Roskilde and her team would arrive at the gates for cargo loading, with a tug dragging a train of goods containers up the mag rail. Bjorn and I had to be on the ship by then. We had to get one of the crew to alert the dockside security that we had a shipment inbound, so there was no holdup or call from the gate to docking central. We had to have the ship's loading bay open, with the cargo area reconfigured, to board them in the least possible time.

If we weren't clear of the station half an hour after that, 22:30, Roskilde's estimates were that the station police would be on our dockside with a warrant.

And we'd just lost seven minutes, lurking in the shadows, because there were a couple of station police idling in sight of the maintenance junction. Maybe not looking for us, but it wasn't a risk we could afford to take.

They finally turned and started strolling away.

Bjorn and I slipped out. We'd changed disguises while we'd waited. We now both wore the hated yellow coveralls that identified us as prisoners on maintenance duty. Maintenance ran all day, every day, so it wouldn't appear unusual. Stationers ignored anyone in yellow coveralls. Usually. My makeup was cleaned off and an old scarf covered my hair. Bjorn had a stained wool cap pressed down on his distinctive shaved head and he'd hastily shaved his beard off. His face looked as if he'd been fighting a cat.

But he still had the supervisor's key to the maintenance tunnels from our last visit to Orion's Wheel.

We were *so* screwed if we got caught now. Like if someone had actually noticed he'd stolen the key, for instance, and set an alarm on its use.

"Here goes," he muttered. The key engaged. The access LED flickered. Red. Amber.

Green.

He twisted and pushed.

The maintenance access door opened. No sirens went off.

There was still a log of the key's use somewhere, and the chance that someone was looking for it. Hopefully, not until tomorrow.

No time to worry about that now.

We were one station spoke away from the dock where the ship was. Far enough that there was no one watching this access. From here, we had to get all the way to the inner hub, cross over to the next spoke, without being seen, and descend that spoke until we reached the bay where the ship was. Then exit the maintenance tunnels and make it across the docking area and into our ship. Again, without being seen.

In fifty minutes or less.

"Stop gawking and let's go." Bjorn closed the access door behind us.

"Wise guy." I was already climbing. "Try to keep up."

There were no elevators in the maintenance passages. We had to ascend a ladder, and it was a climb of more than a half-klick to the inner hub. Two thousand rungs, give or take. The good news was the gravity dropped slightly for every rung we climbed. The bad news was that there were five mechanically sealed hatches on the way up this spoke, and there would be two on the way down the next till we reached our ship's bay. Every hatch had to be unsealed, opened, closed and resealed, otherwise alarms would sound and the whole spoke would seal off.

We'd had well over a month of space flight leading up to this visit to the space station, and we'd been too busy recently to keep up military levels of fitness.

The first hatch was painted shut and hadn't been unsealed in years. It took ten minutes to open, with both of us on the levers.

That put us way behind schedule.

I raced ahead to the second hatch. Looked back to check he was done sealing. Couldn't have two hatches unsealed at the same time without setting off alarms. He forced that locking lever closed. I gripped mine and heaved. Not so gummed shut as the last, luckily. Opened the hatch.

Climbed through and up the next few hundred rungs while Bjorn closed and sealed the hatch behind me.

Checked he was done.

Unseal and repeat.

We managed to make up four of the lost minutes. Still six behind.

Not good enough.

After the third hatch, I waved Bjorn through and stayed to seal the hatch, lungs heaving and my breaths pluming in the cold, thin air.

"I did the hardest ones," I panted as he passed me.

"Eat my afterburners," he replied.

He swarmed up as I swung the hatch closed and heaved on the sealing lever.

It was 21:37.

We had eight minutes to cycle through the next two hatches to get back on schedule, let alone ahead of it.

Bjorn was quick. He had his hatch opened a second after I sealed mine.

My boots slipped as I scrabbled after him.

He gave me a push through and in the lower gravity it was enough to fly me most of the way to the next hatch.

"Beat you!" I yelled as I braced to open it.

He snorted, slamming his hatch shut and sealing it in one motion.

I heaved, expecting this one to have been painted shut as well, but it popped open.

We were in the inner hub.

21:47.

Two minutes behind.

While Bjorn sealed it, I kicked off and floated to the next spoke. Checked the hatch designations. It was the right one. Opened it and jumped in, not bothering with the rungs. It was the sort of maneuvering I'd learned in the military, but that had been in my combat suit.

My boots banged against the hatch and the shock went through my whole body.

Worse, the air was thin, but not so thin it would stop the booming noise. Anyone in the maintenance tunnels, or close by in the public areas of the spoke, had to have heard something. Stationers get twitchy about unusual noises. Someone would report it to Environmental Security. But, late in the evening, I was betting, *hoping*, it'd take a while for them to come check.

We cycled through one more hatch, then at exactly 22:00, we eased open the maintenance access door onto the docking bay for the *Penguin* and peeked outside.

No!

One of the gate security guards had come up from the concourse and was standing right in the way, in front of the ship's personnel access tube, talking to an agitated crew member. Heston. The guy we'd left in command.

E2. Chapter 5

Roskilde had given us an illegal, unregistered comms account, and her pad was running another. They were for 'last resort' types of problems. It was an offense to use unregistered comms, but the sort of thing the police would follow up in normal working hours. The gang that was after us had infiltrated the police, but not the whole police force. They had a finite number of people. They'd have someone watching for communications to and from the ship, but not monitoring messages between random, unregistered accounts.

Well, that's what I hoped.

I hadn't wanted to use it, because until we made that call, we hadn't done anything illegal on the station. Now, we were out of other options. This was already a disaster.

I sent her a message. "Delay 10."

Delaying ten minutes meant we wouldn't have enough time to load all her containers. Each one had to be de-coupled, ramped and maneuvered into the hold. Each task had a certain length of time it took, and they couldn't be done any faster. We were already on the critical path before this delay.

Could we leave some containers?

I knew she'd be furious, but maybe getting the most valuable parts of the satellite system off the station would be something she could agree to.

Bjorn eased the access door shut and we retreated into the maintenance tunnel.

"We can't stop now." He shook his head. "Too much riding on it. Let's rush the guard."

"No," I said. "This gang isn't the whole station. That guard out there... he's just some guy doing a job. He's only where he is because Heston got worried about us and is asking where we are."

We'd left Heston with strict instructions, including that no one was to leave the ship, not even him, except to help load cargo we'd specifically informed him was coming, and then only on the dockside itself.

"I feel sorry for the guard already," Bjorn said sarcastically. "But time's wasting."

"Not the point," I said. "So far, we haven't done anything illegal..."

Bjorn's eyebrows twitched upwards.

"...that they can actually prove," I went on. "We're technically in good standing with Orion's Wheel as a station. We got one bio-processor this trip, but that one on its own isn't going to save Calloway. We need to come back here for the rest of them. We can pay a fine for making an illegal communication. We can't start assaulting guards."

"We could get bio-processors somewhere else."

"We'd need to hunt for them, and we'd probably end up going all the way back to the Inner Worlds. We know they have them here. And even better, those merchants are already nervous because they've been sitting on them for two years. It's looking to them like Calloway isn't going to come up with the money, and where else are they going to sell expensive items like that? Lot of investment sunk and they can't afford to count on odd merchanters like us turning up and buying."

Bjorn nodded in reluctant agreement. We'd got a good deal on the one we'd bought. We needed to be able to return and buy the rest. We needed to do this by the plan I'd made back when we turned the tables on the pirates. Or come up with something better, and no one had.

"All fancy words," he said. "Doesn't get us back into the ship, and we can't afford to get caught with an order to stop us leaving."

"Come on," I said. "I have an idea. Next bay. No time to explain."

We launched ourselves down the ladder and dropped through the hatch to the next bay in double quick time.

As I'd known it would be, the bay was empty and silent as we emerged from the maintenance access door. The separations between bays on old stations like this were set up for in-system ships and shuttles. All inter-system merchanters, even a small one like ours, were big enough to need several bays cleared on one side of the spoke.

I raced over to the cargo handling equipment store and extracted a small, wheeled trolley with a flat bed.

Bjorn knew how my mind worked, and he'd seen similar things in our time with the 1st Frontier.

He laughed and shook his head. "You are either pure genius or pure evil, Skelling."

"Shut up and put on your best performance, Thorsson."

We stripped off the yellow coveralls and hung them on hooks where they probably wouldn't ever be noticed.

There was a dispenser on the wall with an alcohol-based cleaner.

I squirted some on my hands and sniffed it. Not ideal, but it did give off a chemical sort of smell. I wiped it on Bjorn's face and neck, then we wrestled the trolley out of the bay and into the elevator.

As it always turned out, the trolley we chose had a sticking wheel. It squealed and shuddered and made straight lines impossible.

Five minutes gone. No time to get another.

When the elevator doors opened on the ship's bay, Bjorn was sprawled over the trolley with a tie-down strap loosely across his chest. He was shouting incoherently about being thirsty and waving his arms like an underwater swimmer.

"Skip!" Heston had turned at the sound of the elevator's doors and immediately raced across, worry twisting his features.

"No questions," I whispered at him. "Play along."

Heston had been a good choice to leave in command. A blink, a moment's hesitation and he reared back, waving his hand across his face as if the smell of drink was overpowering.

"Nova! Some evening out that must have been, Skip," he said. "We were getting worried."

"So was the bar," I replied. "They said it would be free if he could empty the whole barrel. Damn, but he got close."

The trolley squealed and swerved as drunkenly as Bjorn was acting.

The guard was trying not to laugh.

Heston left off helping with the trolley to shake hands with the guard and apologize for disturbing him on his watch. He casually placed himself between the guard and the trolley. The man had some skills at this kind of thing.

Was that just good to know, or should I be concerned about his past?

We hadn't had time to get to know our 'crew' well, all the people we'd rescued from the slave pens on the *Tünjorgo*. All the people we'd pressed into service with my plan. All the people we were depending on.

And the whole of Calloway was depending on them. Every man, woman and child on our home planet.

All of us were in danger if we didn't depart the station before someone appeared with an order to hold the ship.

Which would happen in around twenty minutes.

Heston and I lifted Bjorn up and into the personnel access tube. As soon as we were inside and out of sight, Bjorn 'recovered'.

"Well done," Bjorn said to Heston. "No time to explain. Open the cargo bay. We have a big delivery and passengers to get on board in less than twenty minutes and then we're gone."

The worry was right back on Heston's face, and I couldn't blame him, but he turned and ran down the passage. I sprinted back out after the guard who was waiting at the elevator.

He turned at my call.

"Sorry about that," I said. "We were celebrating."

He laughed. "Yeah. Got that."

"Look, there's a big delivery coming in any moment," I said casually. "That's actually what we were celebrating. I'll get the full authorization to you, but it's on my second's pad. The delivery team will have all their side of the papers. Could you just wave them through on that, please, and we'll finalize later?"

He shrugged. "Sure. Not like everyone has everything they should have at the right time, especially this late."

"Thanks."

He left in the elevator, talking to his colleagues back at the gate.

As I dragged the trolley clear of the loading ramps to secure it, I could hear Bjorn's voice through the open access tube on shipwide repeat broadcast: "All hands. All hands. Cargo bay."

A minute later, his voice was drowned out as the shield doors to the ship's cargo loading bay rolled aside. Red warning lights began spinning and the ramp inched out.

Ten meters below the platform, an orange light began to pulse above the delivery ramp doors and I could feel the hum of the train on the mag rail.

On the display above the entrance to the platform, the time flickered to 22:12 and a message came up.

"Warning. Remain clear of mag rail. Cargo train inbound for *Acid Penguin*, bay 3."

E2. Chapter 6

Loading cargo was a scary process at the best of times. Loading a train's worth of fragile electronic and photonic equipment, in a hurry, in a giant vertical hopper configuration...

Roskilde and her team appeared from the elevator and stood beside me. For a minute there was nothing we could do except watch the train get into position.

The ship was berthed alongside the spoke, and rotational gravity acted down the spoke. The dockside platform we were on, and the loading bay itself, were oriented to be level, so the first thing the train had to do was slowly climb up the mag rail, past us, continuing until the tug itself was in the next bay.

Finally, we had a vertical stack of ten connected containers towering nearly a hundred meters above me.

22:17 the clock said.

Cutting it too fine.

The process of loading was theoretically simple. A powered grab came out of the ship and positioned itself underneath the rear container. The tug eased down until the container contacted the grab surface. The container was disconnected from the train and mag rail. The train then moved up half a meter, allowing the grab to return into the ship with the first container.

Regulations said each step in the process had to be given the green light by a handler. Get it wrong and 54 cubic meters of container weighing anything up to 20,000 kilos could ruin your whole day.

Roskilde's people seemed to be competent enough; the six of them raced backwards and forwards quickly, giving sharp clear signals.

Grab positioned—container contact—container disconnected—train clear—grab and container retracted.

The clock display moved on to 22:23 as the first container disappeared into our cargo bay, where it was shunted down to the securing points by another powered grab.

Roskilde was looking at the clock as well. She didn't have the skin complexion that would go pale, but I could read the tension in every line of her body.

"We're running out of time," I said. "But maybe they're running late with the warrant. Maybe the judge they woke up is actually asking questions."

She gave a single, jerky shake of her head.

"We know the judge they've gone to. He has to be able to show he's had it long enough to read it, and I estimate he got it just as we pulled up. There's no secure datanet points on the docks, so we've stopped surveillance for now, but I know he'll finish reading and message back their authorization within minutes. Then it's a matter of how long it takes them to get here and persuade the gate guards to lock down the mag rail."

"Best guess?"

"Ehhh... We have no more than fifteen minutes. Less if they are already moving and counting on getting authorization through the datanet. How quickly can we undock?"

"Ideal circumstances? Ten minutes. I need to start..."

My voice trailed away as I looked at the train hanging onto the mag rail above me. All those steps...

"Stop!" I yelled.

Roskilde's crew froze and they looked up, confused. They were about to disconnect the second container.

"What are you doing?" Roskilde shouted.

But I could see in my mind the picture of how the train had got here and what we were doing now. There was a quicker way.

A train had started off on the mag rail in the service ringway. It had to come off that to climb up inside the spoke. In fact, it had to turn through a complete 90 degrees, from horizontal to vertical to do that climb. And the tug was capable of holding the entire train while it had done that maneuver.

Prasad, our cargo bay boss, came out at my urgent call and joined Roskilde's crew around me.

I explained what I was thinking.

"All we need to do is guide the connected carriages into the bay horizontally one at a time. The tug can hold them up for that. Then, inside the bay, we guide the first one down into the cargo bay. We've got enough grabs to hold them steady at least inside the hold. The tug will feed them in. Only the last one needs to be disconnected from the tug, and then it can be held by our dockside grab."

Prasad's eyes were wide, his voice choppy. "You can do that, yes. I guess. It will be quicker. But Goddess look down on us, it's dangerous.

And even if there's no accidents, they still won't be secured inside. You can't maneuver the ship with them like that. They'll come free and tear the cargo bay apart."

"The cargo shifting grabs will hold up to 1 G," I said. "That's all we need to get clear of the station. We need to do this, Prasad. We can secure them when we're underway. Then we can even go inertial, if you want, while you move them into place. We'll have as much time as you need, but only if we get off this station in the next fifteen minutes."

He still wasn't sure, but I slapped him on the shoulder. "Go do it!"

He and Roskilde's crew began to work at it.

Her crew.

She'd said she wanted her *family* off the station. All I could see she'd brought were men that I guessed were her employees.

No time. Not my problem.

"Make sure everyone who's coming gets on board before the last container," I yelled at Roskilde and ran for the bridge. "I'm closing the doors and undocking as soon as it's inside."

The bridge was silent and empty except for Heston.

He was the only qualified pilot among the group of prisoners we'd freed. That he was only qualified for in-system work was something we'd had to overlook.

We'd had to split up, and our fully qualified pilot, Shami Siriwardene, had taken the *Tünjorgo*, which she'd renamed as the *Dark Shark*, to her home system, where the damaged and stranded colony ship Yorkham waited. We'd been able to make the jump into the Ensylas systems with the *Acid Penguin*'s consoles slaved to the *Dark Shark*, with Shami essentially flying both ships.

But now she'd gone on to Yorkham and the next time we engaged the Chang field, Heston would be on his own.

I shivered. If things went wrong in Chang space...

The Dark takes fools. It was a dockside saying throughout the whole of human space, a mantra.

But that was something to worry about later. Several jobs needed to be done at the same time now, but I would need to do most of them, to let Heston concentrate on flying the ship.

"Start the checks, Helm," I said to him. "We're moving in ten minutes, and we're restricting maneuvers to 1 G until I say otherwise. We're going to be flying with an unstable load in the hold."

I could see the gears grinding in his head. We'd saved him from becoming a slave, but his gratitude would have a short half-life if I forced him to do things that compromised his future career as a pilot.

Like being caught flying a ship with unstable cargo.

Of course, if my plan worked, no one else needed to know.

If it worked.

And if it failed, it might be that no one else would ever know. Accidents in space are like that.

I didn't want to explain that to Heston, but I was still in credit with him apparently.

"Aye, Skip." He turned back to his console and started waking the ship up.

I sat down in the captain's seat. The controls were still unfamiliar to me and it was a couple of minutes before I was able to open all the files, connections and feeds to my consoles that I needed.

I could see in one video feed that Prasad and Roskilde's crew had worked a miracle. The last container was inching around the corner, and Prasad was poised ready to hit the disconnection sequence that would free the station's tug. Everyone else had cleared off the dockside.

Good. What else?

I scanned video feed from the dock gates on the concourse. Nothing out of the ordinary. I could see a couple of guys lurking nearby. They'd probably been posted there to intercept us if we'd come in that way, but they were just leaning against the wall, talking and checking their pads. No instructions to interfere with cargo loading.

Again, good.

On the operational journal, I could see Bjorn had already taken the documentation that Roskilde had given us and passed it through our purchasing system to create the ship's matching entries. Although it gave no details of the commercial arrangements, that shipment we were just about to finish loading was now at least legitimate in the eyes of the station. I sent the appropriate forms to the gate guard so he wasn't in a difficult position for letting the cargo train through without completed documentation. A matching set went to the station's Excise department.

Another quick scan of the visual feeds. *Nothing happening*. I started to hope we were going to get clean away.

Rushing on, I checked the current outstanding amounts of all docking costs, station fees and taxes.

How much?

Still, nothing unexpected, so I took a deep breath and triggered the automatic payment of them.

Then I connected my main comm to Docking Control and put on my best bored, authoritative voice.

"Docking Control, this is merchanter *Acid Penguin*, CSS701, berth S7-03, activating flight plan file GJU5926 to Calloway for immediate departure to the planar nadir."

The main comm screen flickered and brightened as the night shift in Docking Control hurriedly pushed his personal pad to one side and looked up at the data flows suddenly pouring onto his screens.

"Ahh... *Acid Penguin*. CSS701. Docking Control. I... ahh..." He stumbled and blinked. "I have your status. Say again? Departure? I have your captain shown as on station? And... I have you still loading?"

"I am the captain, and I am on my bridge. System verify."

The ship system spoke to the docking system and I saw the statuses change. They confirmed I was on-ship, I was authorized to make a departure and there were no bills outstanding.

"Roger that, CSS701, flight plan approved, departure not approved."

My outside monitor showed Prasad complete the disconnect and scrabble inside, hugging the sides of the loading bay as the cargo grabs rotated the last container.

I hit the door seal command.

"You have cargo in process—"

"Cargo loading is complete, Docking Control, and the tug is now returning to you. *Acid Penguin*, CSS701, requesting *immediate* docking clamp release. Expedite please; our payload is time sensitive."

The man's mouth worked silently for a second and my hand hovered over the emergency release command I had prepared. It was a very bad move to blow your docking clamps. Illegal and very expensive should we ever return to Orion's Wheel, but I'd do it rather than be kept here and lose the ship.

My gut told me this man on Docking Control wasn't part of the gang trying to steal our ship. He was, however, still a traffic controller, and like most, it had gone to his head.

"Roger the loading completion," he said slowly. "This is highly irregular, CSS701. There are forms for urgent departure."

"Which, typically, don't get filled in for really urgent departures. We haven't had time to fill in your forms, but the ship is ready to move, you're on Docking Control, you're not doing anything else, our systems have cleared and confirmed. I'm requesting immediate clamp release."

"Very well, CSS701." He looked irritated, but I could see him working his boards and my feeds now showed the red alarm lights spinning in our docking bay. Pressurization doors sealed it off. After an agonizing, minute-long delay, I got greens on all seals.

And on the visual feed from the dock gates down on the concourse: movement, figures running, police.

Shit.

Still red on the clamps.

"Helm, confirm maneuvering status," I said, my hand back over the emergency release.

Come on!

"Positioning jets operational. Engine status all greens. Good to disengage." Heston couldn't keep the tension out of his voice. Mistakes while ship and station were actually touching, even small mistakes, were costly.

"Docking control..."

"Yes, yes, yes, CSS701. Patience. I'm releasing the clamps now."

I felt rather than heard the docking clamps releasing, and finally the green lights came up on my displays.

We were held against the station by nothing other than our own magnetic buffers.

"Helm, transition to flight at your discretion."

I could see Heston wipe his hands nervously together and then gently grip the maneuvering controls.

The trouble was I could also see more frantic activity at the dock gate. I also saw the man in Docking Control twitch as one of his other monitors showed him a message.

"Now, Helm."

The magnetic buffers clicked off and I could feel the ship tremble.

"CSS701, hold position," Docking Control said, his voice unnaturally even. "I am reapplying docking clamps."

"Negative, Docking Control, we are disengaged and under our own power now."

"CSS701, this is Docking Control, you are required to return to dock immediately."

"Negative. Thank you for your assistance, Docking Control. This is merchanter *Acid Penguin*, CSS701, outbound to the planar nadir for onward to Calloway, and switching channel to Space Traffic Control. Good evening."

I cut off his impotent squawk.

I didn't even get a chance to speak to the woman who appeared on the Space Traffic Control channel before her manager pushed her aside.

This man was part of the gang; I could smell it coming off him.

"CSS701, Space Traffic Control, return to berth S7-03. Negative on flight plan GJU5926. You are not approved. Return to docking immediately."

"Space Traffic Control, my flight plan has been logged and accepted. Your only function is to provide separation from other ships for safety on that route."

"Negative CSS701. Your flight plan has been cancelled. Return immediately to—"

"You have no grounds to cancel a flight plan, other than safety."

I muted the mike and spoke to Heston. "Get us on track, Helm. No more than 1 G and give Prasad warning of the acceleration."

"CSS701, there are traffic safety issues," Space Traffic Control was saying.

I activated the mike again. "There are no other ship movements, Space Traffic Control. What traffic safety issues? Asteroids? Comets?"

The man went an interesting shade of red.

Conversations between ship and station were recorded, and were on broadcast frequencies. With any luck someone else was awake and watching what was going on. This gang's power had limits so long as others were watching.

Predictably, the next thing he said was: "CSS701 switch to encrypted channel—"

"Not going to happen," I cut him off immediately. "Anything Space Traffic Control has to say affects the safety of all ships in the system. Everyone should get to hear it."

His eyes flickered to his pad. Someone had just messaged him more instructions.

"If you insist we remain on this open channel, fine," he said. "The real reason you're being called back is that you're attempting to leave without paying taxes on your last cargo. You're sneaking out like a common thief. Return to your bay, settle your bills and we'll officially ignore your actions. Your standing among others might not be so clear."

I flicked feed controls, and the station's confirmation that I'd paid my bills was beamed out on the broadcast instead of my face.

"Doesn't look like it to me," I said. "No more true than your claim that there are traffic safety issues."

I sensed someone behind me. It was Roskilde. She sat to one side, out of range of the pickups, and she was clearly focused on what I was doing.

She wasn't supposed to be on the bridge, but I couldn't take the time to kick her off.

"That's a misrepresentation," Traffic Control shouted. "You have just loaded a cargo, and export duty hasn't been assessed."

"The cargo loaded this evening was not purchased. It's the private property of my passengers. No taxes are due."

I switched my image broadcast to the Roskilde documentation, showing that the containers in the hold remained Roskilde's.

"Theft—" he started to say, but Roskilde leaned into range of the videocam.

"Not theft. My property."

His eyes bugged. "*Acid Penguin*, you're helping criminals escape the station."

"Ehh. There are no judgments or court cases, against me or Roskilde Trading," Roskilde replied. "But I see I will have the basis for one against you, for slander. And before you try any more claims, all outstanding bills are paid to date, and rentals cancelled. My affairs are in order. Any further claims can be made against remaining assets at my former premises in Markt Donnier. I will deal with disputes on my return."

"There you have it, Space Traffic Control," I said, as Roskilde sat back. "We have left your orbit, and I have a ship to run, so I'm closing this channel. We will monitor your data channel for any genuine traffic advisories. CSS701 out."

I switched the feed off and leaned back with a sigh.

"Well done," Roskilde said warmly.

I snorted. We were very slowly heading out toward the planar nadir, and by law and precedent, the *Acid Penguin* was effectively a sovereign state once we cleared the station's vicinity. Ensylas system didn't have a space navy, and even if they did, the gang that had been trying to steal our ship had no basis for getting us arrested and brought back. Their attempts to catch us had resulted in no more than some interesting recordings. With any luck the Ensylas government would work out something bad was going on aboard their space station.

In the meantime, flicking video feeds, I found Bjorn in the hold. Working with all the hands we could spare and Roskilde's crew, we had seven of the ten containers successfully secured already.

We'd escaped the Orion's Wheel, and the ship would soon be ready for the next obstacle.

That was waiting at the planar nadir, where ships engaged their Chang fields and switched to FTL flight. Heston's entire experience with that part of piloting consisted of watching as Shami had piloted both ships through the last jump, into the Ensylas system.

It wasn't so much the piloting in FTL itself, as the transition into and out of Chang space. If he got that wrong, we'd be dead. If we were lucky, we wouldn't even know about it. If we weren't, we'd end up in the Dark with no way home.

Shami wasn't available. Heston *had* to do it.

It was probably *not* a good idea to bring this up with Roskilde at the moment. In fact, I might not tell her at all. She'd only worry.

The woman herself was talking on her pad to one of her men. "Meson, don't forget, the tenth container must be accessible."

I could hear the response, good-natured and exasperated: "Yes, Sithandwa, because it is where our supplies and clothing are. I know this."

I had to smile, but the tone Meson used had brought back a topic that I'd pushed to one side earlier.

"I thought you said you had family to get off the station," I said to Roskilde.

She sat back and gave me a beaming smile. "Yes, indeed. We are all safely here, thanks to you. Such cleverness to sneak yourself into the docks, to load the containers so quickly and then to rebuff that Traffic fool with such firmness. I am very pleased to be on your ship, Captain Skelling, and so are my family."

"Ah. I see. Sorry; I thought those were just your employees. They're brothers? Cousins?"

"Oh, no." The smile became even broader and more cat-got-the-cream satisfied. She made a gesture at the figures on the video feed from the hold. "They are employees too, of course, but these are all my husbands, every one."

E2. Chapter 7

Dinner was as bizarre as it was funny.

I gathered everyone the ship could spare into the rec room, the central crew space that could be configured to what was needed. We set it up to be a cafe. Roskilde, *call-me-Thandi*, organized her husbands. Two in the galley cooking, the rest serving tables.

"I must sit here, in the center, and supervise," she announced grandly.

"We're only doing this once," Meson warned me, with a laugh. "But we do have to do it that once, to thank you all for taking a chance with us."

I hadn't had the opportunity yet to investigate exactly how big a chance that was, or how much it impacted my plans. Those complicated plans that needed a crew for the *Acid Penguin* and the *Dark Shark*, and luck, and compromises, and flexibility, and sheer hard work before it all came together and paid off.

And they wouldn't pay off until Calloway had all the bio-processors it needed, the stranded colonists on the Yorkham were rescued, and every crewmember was delivered to the place they wanted to be. Including Shami, Bjorn and me.

And now Thandi and her merry husbands were added to that list, because, sure as gravity pulls down, they'd want to be delivered somewhere as well.

As soon as I could get her to one side with Bjorn, we'd need to find out what kind of a commitment we'd taken on in exchange for her help escaping Orion's Wheel.

Bjorn wasn't here for the dinner. The bridge could never be left unattended, even in a 'civilized' system like Ensylas, so he'd taken first watch. Which was why my heart rate leaped when my pad pinged a message from him saying we needed to talk. *Urgently.*

I decided it was probably more in keeping with my plan to take the call openly in the rec room rather than to go up to the bridge.

"Problem," Bjorn said when I connected a video call.

I was aware people were looking over my shoulder, and *problems* might be something we wouldn't want everyone to know, but it was too late for second thoughts.

The image on the pad screen split and Bjorn fed data from Orion's Wheel Docking Control to my screen.

Bjorn tapped something and highlighted a row.

"That's the *Sambuk*," he said. "The guy who wanted to pick a fight in the bar is her captain."

Alongside the ship's name, I could see Maykn listed as the captain. And alongside that, the status showed the *Sambuk* getting clearance to undock.

"Check the flight plan—" I started, but Bjorn had already drilled down into the data.

The *Sambuk* claimed it was en route for Calloway.

"I don't believe in coincidence," Bjorn said.

"I agree. Have we got the specs on that ship?"

Bjorn shrugged. "As much as they have the specs on us, which is as much as either of us wants other people to know. It's newer and bigger than the *Acid Penguin*. Probably faster."

"Fast enough to catch us?"

Thandi spoke over my shoulder before he could answer. "Even if they could, they wouldn't dare. If they attack us in Ensylas system, they show that they're pirates to everyone here. Their gang may be powerful on the station, but they couldn't hide something that obvious."

"They can see our flight plan," I said thoughtfully. "They can see we've nominated a dead rock as a midway point."

The *Acid Penguin* wasn't capable of reaching Calloway in one jump. Shami, Heston and I had chosen what we thought would be the best compromise. It happened to be the empty, dead system where we'd originally taken the ships from the pirates.

A lonely place.

The sort of place where things could happen that no one else would ever see.

"Skip."

It was Prasad, his eyes gone all wide again, like when I'd told him what I wanted to do with the cargo.

"Yes?"

"After you rescued us, and we shifted cargo off the *Tünjorgo*... I mean, off the *Dark Shark*. The cargo was in containers labeled with ships that carried them. We thought they were all victims of the pirates." He licked his lips. "But one of those containers is labeled *Sambuk*."

"Can you tell how old that container was?" Thandi asked.

Prasad nodded. "About a year."

"Maykn's been captain of the *Sambuk* for ten years or more," Thandi said. "The *Sambuk*'s no victim. So he's part of this pirate fleet, and that means the gang on Orion's Wheel is as well."

"A damned pirate chasing us and we can't jump all the way to Calloway," Heston said. I could see beads of sweat forming on his head just thinking about it. "We'll have to change direction, and go through inhabited systems to keep them from attacking us."

"None of which we know for sure *aren't* pirate systems," I said. "This *is* the Frontier."

It was a complex puzzle. We didn't have the capability to outrun and outjump the *Sambuk* for any length of time, and I didn't think Maykn was going to give up. We had to face him sometime. We had one weapon: a small plasma cannon the pirates had installed in the *Acid Penguin*, hidden beneath the ramps of the forward loading bay, but it was for scaring merchanters. I didn't think Maykn would be scared by it. Since the *Karakun* had belonged to the same pirate gang, he probably knew we had the gun, and as he had the newer, bigger ship, he would no doubt have more powerful weapons.

Nothing would happen in Ensylas system. Nothing *could* happen once we were traveling in Chang space. When we emerged...

What were his options?

The *Sambuk* could over-jump us, emerging in front of us, and between us and the vector we needed for the onward jump to Calloway. They might also be able to travel faster than us in Chang space, arriving before us. Of course, trying to predict exactly where we'd emerge and what our velocity would be was a risky business. Ships had smashed into each other before.

Or he could under-jump. Emerging before us, but well behind where we would come out, and giving him time to pile on speed.

But...

I became aware the room had fallen silent. Everyone was standing around the table, looking at me.

"It's okay," I said brightly. "I have a plan."

Episode 3
The Dark Takes Fools

E3. Chapter 1

The Dark takes fools.

It was a mantra. The first thing any spacer learned. The first warning a spacer would give to anyone boarding a ship.

The Dark takes fools.

Say it again. Remember it.

Which was all fine, but if I had to choose between the infinite number of *possibilities* of dying by foolishness, and the stone-cold *certainty* of what would happen to me if Maykn caught us, I'd rather play the odds.

We couldn't jump to anywhere we *knew* would be safe, so we were going to have to take a chance at a dead system for a waypoint. The same dead system where Bjorn and Shami and I had captured the *Tünjorgo* and *Karakun*. So, our lucky system. I hoped.

Maykn would overjump us. I knew it. It was the sort of hyper-aggressive thing he'd do.

At that waypoint, Maykn's ship, *Sambuk*, would emerge somewhere in our path, blocking our way. He would want to be close enough to reach us before we had enough time to recharge the Chang field generators. Close enough that we wouldn't have time to run anywhere. Probably close enough we wouldn't even have time to recalibrate the navigation system.

So use that aggression. Make *him* the fool. Let the Dark take Maykn.

It had been a long hard argument. Bjorn hadn't supported me. I respected his opinions, and so that hurt. In the end, what won was the lack of other options.

Heston and I had locked ourselves onto the bridge and earned our fools' stripes messing with the navigational computer.

Even after he'd committed to the course, Heston had muttered: "Navigation rules are there for a purpose."

And my only response had been: "Pirates don't obey rules. But they think we do. They're *relying* on us to obey the rules."

There were two sets of coordinates entered for any jump, *base* and *compensating*. Get either of them wrong and bad things happened. You emerged inside a star. You emerged in the Deeps with no way of getting home. Or you just emerged as a rainbow smear of trace elements spread across an arc of a million klicks.

Base coordinates set the vector between one system and another. You deserved your cold grave in the Deeps if you got *those* wrong.

Compensating coordinates were the tricky ones. They determined if you were close enough to the system's mass for your sensors to function, and not so close that the mass distorted the readings and you emerged in the wrong place, or even closer so the mass interfered with the exiting of Chang space and you emerged in very small bits.

An interstellar ship needed to roll those dice every trip, but even the most experienced of pilots did it cautiously, and only after checking the results three times. But Heston wasn't an interstellar pilot, he was an in-system pilot. Shami Siriwardene, who was qualified as an interstellar pilot, had locked in the base coordinates for this jump, set a semi-automated process for calculating the compensating coordinates, and told us not to deviate from the instructions.

We'd deviated. We'd completely recalibrated the compensating coordinates.

Since neither of us really knew what we were doing, we'd calculated and re-calculated the Chang field parameters for the jump I wanted. At one stage the computers had started producing wildly different numbers, and we'd sat there in uncomprehending shock until we realized that Maykn's ship was crowding us and they had their Chang field generators spooled up.

Even that minor distortion had changed the parameters beyond recognition. It was a vivid reminder of how sensitive the entry and exit from Chang space was.

We'd complained about Maykn to Ensylas Space Traffic Control. There had been no response, but the *Sambuk* had eased back.

Finally, once the numbers had been stable for five reruns of the calculations, I'd made Heston engage the Chang generators and we'd slipped into Chang space, committed to the numbers we'd entered and the plan I'd made.

Now, sixty hours and change later, it was approaching time to find out if my gamble was going to pay off.

We were sitting silently on the bridge, trying not to watch the countdown clock. Bjorn was in the forward loading bay, in full combat suit. Plan B.

Heston was sweating. My heart was skipping beats.

We'd made our decision and it was far too late to do anything about it.

E3. Chapter 2

The countdown timer was only a few minutes from zero when we heard angry footsteps in the corridor, and then Thandi burst in. "What is going on with the jump?"

I hadn't included anyone outside of Heston and Bjorn in the final navigation decision, and everyone else had been working too hard on maintenance issues to quiz us. The *Acid Penguin* had needed fixing more than we needed a discussion on a navigational science that none of us was expert in.

But that made me feel guilty, so I hadn't prevented access to the navigation data either. Apparently, Thandi had found time to look at it.

"You're just in time to find out," I replied. "We're about to come out of Chang space." I pointed at a folding seat against the rear bulkhead. "Sit down."

She looked daggers at me, but it was my bridge. She obeyed.

I tapped a comms icon and gave a warning on the shipwide broadcast. "All hands, stow everything, sit down and strap in. We will emerge from Chang space shortly and this might be rough. Stay put until I give the all-clear."

"Why are we strapping in?" Thandi asked. "And why has Bjorn locked himself in the forward loading bay?"

Heston just looked at me. *He* wasn't going to answer her.

"All for the same reason." I sighed. "Look, the coordinates are fixed, and we're just waiting for the countdown to switch the Chang generators off." I pointed at a decreasing timer on one of the screens and then went on, "You were part of the decision that we had to travel to this system as a waypoint."

"Yes." She waved her hands. "We don't know which places we can trust, and besides, this dead system is where your other ship *should* come back and help us."

I nodded. "But we don't know *when* the *Dark Shark* will arrive. When Shami gave us the jump coordinates, she naturally didn't take into account that we were going to be chased."

Thandi still looked puzzled.

Our bridge didn't have a fancy holodeck where I could display everything in three dimensions to help with my explanation. And there wasn't time anyway; the countdown showed a couple of minutes left.

"Short version," I said, "Shami set the original coordinates for outside the standard transit point for any mapped system, the planar zenith, at the equivalent of about 5 AU out from the star."

"Yes, I understand that. That distance is for safety."

"Yes. The zenith, or alternatively, the nadir, are the only two places where anyone following us would expect us to enter our target system. And they'll know which system we're targeting. When a ship enters Chang space, it leaves an imprint in the gravitational fields that sensors can trace for up to ten minutes."

There was less than a minute left on the countdown.

"The *Sambuk* is going to read where we've gone, our speed, our direction, and they'll follow us," I said.

"But that's dangerous! The jumps could interfere! We could collide!"

"Shocking," I agreed, nodding solemnly. "We'll be sure to file a complaint with Ensylas Space Traffic Control next time we're in the system."

I could feel the evil eye from Thandi, but I had no attention to spare.

"So if the *Sambuk* is faster than us, and emerges near us, we can't get away," she said. "Changing the coordinates makes no difference."

"Unless we cheat." I tapped the comms and broadcast again. "All hands, thirty seconds till we emerge from Chang space. Repeat: this one might be bumpy. If you're not sitting down and strapped in, anything that happens to you is your fault. If you die horribly, please try to avoid damaging the ship. Thank you."

Thandi rocked in her seat as much as the straps allowed her to. "How can we cheat physics?"

"We don't. We use Maykn's stupidity to cheat him."

As we raced toward our destination, the sensors were picking up distorted gravity and electromagnetic readings from the system. The navigation computer tried to represent it as a visual display. I hadn't had time to ask Shami why it bothered with this. The distortion meant everything was presented as a blur, and what little information there was made no difference to us. Well, *theoretically*, if we saw something was wrong, we could override the controls, but that would almost certainly kill us.

"The Dark takes fools," I said. "But I hope today, it's satisfied with the bigger fool."

Twenty seconds.

Heston muttered a prayer to the Goddess and a brief apology to me. Then he wiped his hands and rested them on the controls. If we survived emerging, our lives might depend on some fine piloting from him.

At that point, the sensors got a good enough fix on where we were going. The display filled with a big, red fuzz to represent a serious navigational problem on our course after emergence, and the navigation computer's mandatory alarms went off.

"Goddess of Mercy!" Thandi gasped. "You're diving into the sun!"

"No," I said. "That's an unformed gas planet about 2 AU away from the star."

"But..."

The lights dimmed and went to emergency backup as the main power diverted to reverse the Chang field with the precision we needed. The closer the proximate masses, and the finer the precision, the more power required to flip the generators.

"It's nowhere near as massive as a sun," I said, as much to convince myself as anything, "and we're well short of it, but the closer we get, the more its mass affects the actual point we emerge from Chang space."

I broadcast shipwide again: "Ten seconds to emergence. Brace yourselves."

"And Maykn will try and overjump us on the position and velocity coordinates he read from his sensors," I went on. "He won't have had the patience to check our coordinates. He'll have assumed we were aiming for the nadir. Which makes him the bigger fool. Five seconds."

I patted the console gently. You can do it, *Acid Penguin*.

The ship started to hum. Then vibrate. Then plain shake.

The old Chang generators didn't like reversing the Chang field in the best of conditions, but while coming in under the safety distance on a massive blob of whirling gases? They made their displeasure known; the whole ship shook so hard I couldn't focus my eyes on the counter.

"Emergence!" Heston yelled.

There was a final shudder, a blissful moment of null G and then a crushing acceleration as the normal physical universe took over.

We were dead. Surely. The navigational display was completely swamped in red. The lights stayed on emergency power as the acceleration compensators struggled against the demand that Heston was putting on them.

At the same time, sensors went from making guesses through the distortion of the Chang field to actually detecting real masses and radiation; displays blanked and returned with hard information.

The unformed gas giant was still displayed as an angry red circle in the middle of our screen.

The navigational alarm was still going off.

But this time when I stabbed the icon to mute it, I succeeded.

"Footprint!" I shouted, as another emergence displayed on the navigation screen and the alarms immediately went off again. *Warning! Collision alert.*

The *Sambuk* had emerged as I'd predicted. He'd overjumped us, in the position he'd thought was between us and our next jump point.

But nova, he was close!

I connected to Bjorn in the forward docking bay. "Bjorn! *Sambuk* is in front of us. Relaying navigational data."

I read the numbers being transferred to Bjorn.

Shit!

Either Maykn decided to overjump us by a very small, very risky distance, or the interference in his emergence position caused by our emergence and the mass of the unformed planet had worked *against* us. We'd pulled him out of Chang space short of where we wanted him, which would have been deep inside the gas giant.

"Range 2,500 klicks, dropping. Hold. Hold. You get two shots. Hold for my command."

The plasma cannon in the docking bay had a dual cell magazine. After two shots, it would need recharging, and *all* our power would be going into getting clear of the gas planet and away from the *Sambuk*.

"Locked and holding." Bjorn's voice was clipped.

The distance between ships was shrinking alarmingly. The *Sambuk* probably had more powerful cannon than we did and we were already too close, but I was betting Maykn and his crew were completely disoriented from emerging where they did.

Bjorn needed the front cargo bay to be pointed at the *Sambuk*, more or less, to get a shot with the plasma cannon. The *Acid Penguin* needed to peel away onto a path to skim out of the gas clouds.

As close as I dared...

"Fire!"

On-planet, plasma bolts made for pyrotechnic displays. In space, the electric blue plasma was normally gone before you could see it. But here, in the outer reaches of the swirling gas clouds, the flash on the visible spectrum monitors was like lightning.

Bad news. All that interaction with the gas had reduced the power of the bolt and out cannon was a relative popgun.

The *Sambuk* was too far away for the visible spectrum monitors, but the targeting computer on the cannon linked up with the situational display monitor, and the icon displaying the other ship pulsed twice.

"Two hits!" I yelled.

Heston had already spun the *Acid Penguin* and was accelerating hard to change our vector. The ship groaned from where the acceleration compensators' coverage flickered and the ship's hull strained against itself.

"What is happening?" Thandi demanded.

I ignored her while I killed more navigational alarms and pulled up ship statuses showing the effects of our flight through the thin gas. Temperatures were rocketing up on the outside of the hull.

Nothing that would kill us. Yet.

"I was hoping that *Sambuk* would overjump us right into that ball of gas," I said. "But it didn't happen. Plan B—"

"They didn't crash?" Thandi interrupted.

"No. And it wasn't so much the possibility of a crash as a burn-out. If the *Sambuk* had emerged a few thousand klicks deeper into the gas clouds, their surface temperatures would have gone crazy from the friction. Even if the ship didn't melt, we could have expected all the sensor arrays to be burned off and he'd be blind."

"But it didn't happen," Heston said. "He was only about 3,000 klicks closer in than we were. Gas density ten times higher rather than a thousand. Friction effects dangerous but not crippling."

"So, it didn't work," Thandi said. "Plan B?"

"Shoot him with the plasma cannon," I replied. "Bjorn hit him with a couple of plasma bolts."

"But not hard enough to disable him," she said.

"No," I had to agree.

"Plan C?"

"Well, Bjorn still hit him, and that will have damaged the ship. Emerging where he did also would have done some damage through friction heating."

Heston chipped in. "Even once he's recovered, he's got to get out of the friction effects of the cloud before he can chase us at full speed."

Bjorn came in, still in his full combat suit, but with the helmet under his arm. I reached out and we bumped fists, but his heart obviously wasn't in it.

He locked the helmet into a secured storage bin and took one of the spare seats.

Thandi looked at the three of us, sitting silently and staring at the displays. "Eh! We have survived. You have tricked Maykn. Every second takes us further away."

Heston shrugged and nodded. It was a fair summary, as far as she understood the situation. "All things being equal, we could probably get to a point where it would be safe to load up the navigational computers and try the jump for Calloway. Of course, I'm still not qualified, but we managed the last jump. Sort of."

"And yet you look like you're attending a funeral," she said. "What problem are you not telling me?"

I sighed. "For a start, there would be nothing to stop Maykn from following us to Calloway. And home has no space defense systems."

Thandi frowned. "Nothing?"

Bjorn grunted. "Pacifism. One of the Holy Pillars of the Church in Exile. The reason Calloway was set up in the first place. There are no defenses, not even for protection. That's why we should have fought the *Sambuk* here."

"We discussed this," I said.

"I'm just saying, we took the wrong decision."

Thandi looked angrily from one to the other. "You argued about this and yet you took decisions without consulting the rest of us?"

"My fault." I put my hands up. "We were running out of time for a decision and no one on board has relevant experience in this sort of thing."

"We *have* experience in boarding hostile ships and taking them over," Bjorn said.

"Not the same situation."

We'd thrashed out this argument before the jump. In the end, Heston had sided with me. Taking over the *Tünjorgo* and *Karakun* had depended on three things: Shami's ability to hack into their control systems, our having full combat suits and, most importantly, almost complete surprise.

Maykn didn't know about our combat suits, but without Shami we couldn't hack his control systems and if he closed with us to retake the *Acid Penguin*, he'd be on the alert for tricks.

Now my alternative of getting him to overjump had only half paid out, and hadn't disabled the *Sambuk*.

In the meantime, we'd upset Thandi and probably the rest of the crew by taking decisions without consultation.

And I'd argued with Bjorn.

I couldn't fix that in a hurry, but it was past time to be open with Thandi.

"It may get worse," I said to her.

"It can? How can that be?"

"We captured the *Acid Penguin* and the *Dark Shark* from a pirate group. The same pirate group the *Sambuk* belongs to. The *Karakun* and the *Tünjorgo*, as they were called then, formed a team. A merchanter to visit the places where other merchanters visited..."

"And a reaver to wait in the Dark," Thandi finished. "So you think *Sambuk*'s reaver is coming to this system?"

Bjorn nodded somberly. He'd had to concede that point. Whatever we did to the *Sambuk*, it seemed likely that one other pirate would know about it.

E3. Chapter 3

We got everyone but Heston into the *Acid Penguin*'s tiny mess area, and he was on a comms link from the bridge.

It was cramped.

I'd apologized for not bringing them in on the full situation earlier. Then I'd explained what we had tried and why it hadn't worked, finishing up with the big unknown, that there might be a second pirate—the equivalent of the *Dark Shark*—out there, waiting to see what we were going to do.

"We must return to Orion's Wheel immediately," Prasad said. "Whatever this gang has done there, Ensylas is not a pirate system. We can broadcast our recordings."

Those recordings included incriminating evidence from Maykn, in an open comms broadcast. He'd spent the last hour screaming oaths at Bjorn and me, mixed in with what he intended to do to me personally for daring to fight back. In the course of his rant, he effectively admitted to being a pirate and slaver.

I held a hand up. "Several problems with that suggestion, Prasad. Firstly, Ensylas can't help us. They have no space navy. Let's say we emerged into the system with *Sambuk* and its reaver companion right behind us. They would have no reason to disguise their true nature anymore, and the pair of them could just blow us out of space. Following that, they'd know they couldn't ever return to Ensylas, but they still have conspirators on station, as we found out. So... they'd probably attack the Orion's Wheel, steal all its goods, take all remaining stationers as slaves and maybe pick up a couple of the ships in dock as a bonus."

There was a disturbed restlessness as they took that in. They knew I was guessing, but some of them had actually been taken captive to be sold. They knew what the pirates were capable of.

"Secondly, even if, somehow, we got away, I wouldn't trust Maykn not to take it out on Calloway. You heard what he said, and they have no defenses."

Nods from the listeners. Maykn must have been a borderline personality at the best of times, and being fooled into a near-catastrophic jump had sent him over the precipice. The *Sambuk* probably had the same sort of plasma cannon we did, but if there was a companion reaver out there, with more powerful cannon, it would be devastating against a planet that couldn't dodge or fire back. Or the Sambuk could just push a couple of

The Dark Takes Fools

largish asteroids into Calloway's atmosphere. Not accurate but effective. Both actions were against every law on every planet in human space, with an automatic death penalty, but who would witness it?

"Thirdly. If that second pirate is out there, it's highly likely we wouldn't make it. We're in a trap."

Shocked silence.

The bulkhead behind me was covered in a bare expanse of plastic. I took marker pens out of my pocket and started to draw.

"Okay, remember this is all in three dimensions of course. This is the dying star at the center of the system." I drew a small circle. "And here's the safe distance from the star that you can engage the Chang field." Around the star I drew a large dotted circle. "All this volume inside that distance is the zone where you can't enter or exit Chang space without the mass of the star distorting your ship. That's breaking it into little pieces, people."

So far, so obvious. Anyone who even thought of going into space knew that much.

"Here's the huge gas planet we're skimming past. Here's the same zone around that. Much lower mass for the planet, so smaller zone size, same restrictions."

I drew it, showing the zones overlapping.

I traced out the overlapping zones with a different colored pen.

"Together, this is called the Mez, the Mass Effect Zone. And we're in it, somewhere here." I marked a spot inside the gas planet's zone. "We emerged from Chang space as close as we dared to the gas planet, hoping that the *Sambuk* would overjump us by enough that it either came apart because of the effect of the planet's mass on the Chang space transition, or it would burn up through friction."

My mouth turned down. It hadn't been a great plan, but it'd been a plan.

"Didn't work that well," I said. "Friction will have done some damage. Bjorn fired a couple of shots from the plasma cannon in the docking bay and hit, so we did some more damage, but if you listened to the broadcast channel, the *Sambuk* is still chasing us."

"How close did we get to the *Sambuk*?" One of Thandi's husbands, Meson, was looking puzzled.

"1,000 klicks when we fired. It was down to a couple of hundred klicks at closest point, but by that time we were pointing away."

"And yet Bjorn hit," he said, frowning. "This is not a military ship. You cannot fire a plasma cannon and hit something you can't even see."

"You can if you use a powered military combat suit and feed it targeting information from the navigation computers."

Meson's face cleared. "Clever," he said, nodding. One person on my side, maybe.

"Not clever enough, unfortunately. So now we're putting as much distance as we can between us and the *Sambuk*. Because we're in the smaller part of the zone, around the planet, we could make it to the outside of the critical distance in a day or so, probably before the *Sambuk* could get close enough to fire on us. But..." I let it hang in the air. "If there's another pirate out there working with Maykn, and he's halfway smart, he's waiting outside the Mez and watching."

Thandi caught on immediately.

"If he is outside the critical distance, he can use Chang space to jump to anywhere else in this system that is also outside the critical distance."

"Exactly. He just needs to see where we're going. That information reaches him at the speed of light. As soon as he knows where we're going, he enters Chang space and emerges where we're headed. At these sorts of distances, he can move from one side of the system to the other almost instantaneously, as long as he keeps just outside the Mez. We're restricted by the physics of flying sub-light through a system."

"But we could take a chance," Prasad said. "Engage the Chang field while we're still inside the Mez."

"We *could*, though there's still the issue we have nowhere to go. We would probably end up as dust, but I'd rather that than let Maykn get his hands on me, *if* that were the only option. But there are slightly better odds..."

"We wait for the *Dark Shark*," Thandi said.

I nodded. "We keep our distance from the *Sambuk*, we make sure we're well inside the zone, so the other ship can't get us, and we wait for the *Dark Shark* to turn up. The reaver doesn't want to come inside the zone, because then they can't jump either. The *Sambuk* will try and herd us towards them, or panic us into making a mistake. It's a sort of two against one, three dimensional board game using the gravity of the planet and the star as slingshots."

"But the *Dark Shark* won't know what's happening," Bjorn pointed out.

"That's problem one," I agreed. "Problem two: let's just say we and the *Dark Shark* coordinate and destroy *Sambuk*. The reaver runs. We can't afford to chase it. There's a good chance that Calloway remains a target, and he might come back with friends."

"Problem three," Prasad said. "*They* destroy *us*."

"Then it's not our problem anymore," Bjorn said with a twisted smile.

E3. Chapter 4

Bjorn's practical but gloomy comment closed the meeting without much in the way of resolution.

I told everyone I'd keep them posted, and they should keep close to seats where they could strap in, in case things got rough.

Thandi organized preparation and distribution of meals, so people didn't need to mill around in the mess area. She wasn't happy with us for not talking sooner, but that wasn't going to stop her from doing what she could.

Which made it a mixed reaction from our crew and passengers. About half of them thought my plan had been criminally irresponsible. No alternatives offered though.

Back on the bridge Heston had some good news. "*Sambuk* has damage, Skip. They're making about half their normal speed at best."

"What do you think's the likely cause?"

He shrugged. "Acceleration compensator damage would limit their acceleration, not their speed, so I'd guess they lost one of their in-system engines through overheating when they emerged."

"Fixable?" Bjorn asked.

"Maybe. Long job, best done in dock."

"Okay," I said. "Let's take it that we have a temporary advantage in maneuvering speeds. Good enough for us to fight the *Sambuk*?"

Heston was an in-system civilian pilot with no experience of combat. I didn't expect him to say yes, but he was opening his mouth to reply when an alarm on the navigation board lit up.

"Footprint," I said. "Ship transitioned from Chang space at the planar zenith. Two AU out."

The radiation burst telling us that was about twenty-five minutes old.

Although he'd shut up now, twenty-five minutes ago Maykn had been shouting at us over the radio. Whether it was the *Dark Shark*, or *Sambuk*'s reaver companion, whoever it was would know what was happening in-system.

"It could be the *Dark Shark*," Heston said.

I shook my head. "We'll know in a minute anyway, but I'm sure Shami would have transitioned further out."

The rules for a system without navigation beacons or a lot of traffic were simple.

The planar zenith, chosen by the direction of the system's spin around the star, was the point for entry at 2AU to 3AU, that was 300 to 450 million klicks 'above' the star. The other side of the system, the planar nadir was the exit point, 'below' the star.

If you were only in transit, navigation rules expected you to enter and exit at the zenith, but at 4AU to 5AU.

Neither the *Dark Shark* nor the *Acid Penguin* had originally intended to enter the system, so we'd expected to meet somewhere around the transit point.

A minute after the radiation burst announcing their arrival, the new ship's ID registered with our comms system.

The *Jahazi*.

And since it'd been the way we knew that the *Sambuk* was a pirate, I'd had Prasad list every name on every container in the *Acid Penguin*'s hold. There had been one from the *Jahazi*. I could only think of one reason for the new arrival to turn up here: it was the *Sambuk*'s reaver companion.

I had tried searching the database of ships, but there was no information. Data maintenance hadn't been the pirates' top priority when this was the *Karakun*.

Barely a minute later, there was another burst of radiation in the same direction, from a ship entering Chang space.

"He's gone," Heston said in disbelief.

"No such luck." I nodded at the sensors.

Sure enough, seconds later there was a third burst of radiation, from the other side of the system. The side we were closest to.

"He's quick, this one," I said. "Took it all in, and moved to the point closest to where we are. He'll be staying just outside the Mez, so he can jump again."

"How quickly can he recharge his Chang field generators?" Bjorn asked.

"For short, in-system jumps, quickly enough," Heston replied. "Quicker than we can get outside the zone."

I sat and watched the screens while Bjorn went on ship broadcast to tell everyone what was happening, as we'd promised to do.

Heston tapped the options on the comms screen. We'd been recording the open channel, but not listening to it—Maykn's ranting had gotten old quickly. Someone new was talking now.

Heston put it on speaker.

A woman's voice. I'd thought I'd heard every variant of common English while I fought in the 1st Frontier, but I couldn't place her accent.

"*Acid Penguin*, this is Comara Corzey of the ship *Jahazi*."

Bjorn swiveled his chair back to listen.

"I will not insult you by pretending to be other than what you probably have understood already. We are hunters. We wait in the Dark and we take ships. We're very good at it, and you will not get away from the *Jahazi*. How that turns out for you depends on your ongoing behavior, so I advise you to listen carefully to me.

"Your actions to arrive at this point make me believe that you are a clever and resourceful crew, with a bold captain and excellent pilot-navigator. Hunters are always looking to grow our operations with good men and women like that. Join us and become part of our success. You'll be split up among ships in groups of three or four, but so long as you remain loyal, you'll be treated exactly as anyone else is. You'll rise or fall solely on your ability. With us, you have the chance to command your own ship and gather more wealth than you could ever expect as a merchanter.

"But in the same way, failure will be dealt with harshly. The captain of the *Sambuk* has made a fool of himself and damaged his ship. You can ignore his rantings as the impotent raving of a condemned man.

"The Frontier is not your friend, *Acid Penguin*. The more a Frontier system claims to be civilized, the more trade it handles, the more corrupt and dominated by Earth it is. Don't be part of that. Be part of the group that opposes that.

"If you choose to remain part of the Earth-contaminated disease, we'll still take your ship, but we will deal harshly with you, and you will lose everything.

"The Dark takes fools, *Acid Penguin*. Do not be fools."

The voice stopped and the sound from the channel returned to space noise.

Heston's ship had been taken by the *Tünjorgo*, and every survivor on board locked up to be sold, as far as we could make out.

"Did they offer you that when you were captured?"

Heston shook his head. "Not that I was aware of, but we were kept in groups and moved around a few times. Plenty of opportunities for some of them to be offered a chance to join. And we met up with other ships, people were transferred." He shrugged. "About the only question they asked me was what my skills were. Maybe they didn't want in-system pilots."

"You've impressed Corzey," Bjorn said. "'Excellent pilot-navigator', she called you."

Heston smiled faintly, but he was pleased.

"It would be in keeping with our 'open' policy if we shared that with the rest of the crew," Bjorn went on. "You think there would be a problem?"

Heston shook his head. "The crew's already been captured by these people. No one is going to want that again."

Bjorn looked across at me and I nodded, but I was distracted.

Corzey's message had started repeating, and Heston was changing the options on the comms panel. The open channel went straight to recording. He set up a scanner for the other channels.

He saw me looking. "For when they start talking to each other. They'll probably do it in code, but we might get lucky. We might be able to find a decoder in the computer somewhere from when this was the *Karakun*. If we do, it'd give us a heads-up on what they're planning to do."

"Good thought," I said and scratched my chin. A plan began to form. Half a plan. "Tell me, what channels does a ship scan first as it transitions from Chang space?"

"Nav beacon. Then Space Traffic Control. Then ID broadcasts. Then I guess whatever's on the list of procedures for the place it's arrived at, or the open channels."

"What if you arrived at a place where there was no nav beacon and no Traffic Control?"

"I've done a total of two inter-system jumps, remember."

"Bear with me on this."

"Pilot-navigators I've spoken to work with checklists. It's like a religion. You *always* listen out on the navigation frequencies when you arrive, even at a dead system like this, so you'll never forget to do it when you enter a busy system. New ships probably have it as a built-in sequence so you don't even have to think about it."

"And then you'd turn the nav beacon and Traffic channels off? Like we have." I pointed at the comms board.

"Well, yeah. No information on those bands, no point in listening."

Bjorn finished talking to the rest of the crew and swiveled his chair back. "What're you thinking, Jan?"

I stared at the displays for a minute before speaking. "You know, neither of those two pirates out there know that the *Tünjorgo* is now the *Dark Shark*."

E3. Chapter 5

"I have a plan."

That got a smile on Bjorn's face, which was a welcome sight after we'd argued so much about the best options to survive *and* protect Calloway.

I was typing as I talked—a message for Shami. Heston would code it and transmit it on the band assigned for the nav beacon. I'd transmit something similar as plain text on the Space Traffic Control band. If Shami jumped in with those bands active on her comms panel, surely she would look to see what was being transmitted on two bands that were supposed to be empty in this system.

With any luck Corzey and Maykn had switched them off and wouldn't even realize we were transmitting. If they did, what would they suspect? Maybe our transmissions were a last desperate and garbled attempt to communicate the danger we were in on the chance that someone might hear.

I kept it as clear as I could about the two other ships in the system and said nothing about the *Tünjorgo*. I added the text of the speech that Corzey had made to the transmission and then ended by saying that pirate crews couldn't be trusted, and they were going to murder us all.

We started transmitting those.

There was no change in the speech coming from the *Jahazi*; no indication she knew we were transmitting.

That was step 1 successfully completed.

Step 2. I had to admit to myself, there wasn't a step 2 yet. There was no way I could accurately predict where Shami would enter the system and what she'd do *if* she noticed the messages. *If* she thought that she could play at being *Tünjorgo*. *If* she thought that would give her enough advantage.

If she came.

She should already have been here, surely.

I didn't want to follow that line of thought; the Dark takes fools and Shami was no fool, but the Dark also takes others, from time to time.

And it was all a matter of time and resources, now. With the amount of supplies we'd taken on board at Orion's Wheel, and the damage to the *Sambuk*, we could zig and zag around this system, keeping ahead of the *Sambuk*, and far enough away from the *Jahazi* that they couldn't corner us.

We weren't set up to refuel from the gases of the giant planet, but it could be done.

They'd run out of supplies, or the *Jahazi* would run out of fuel, or they'd run out of patience.

At which point they would have to change the stakes. The obvious one was *Sambuk* could threaten to jump to Calloway and bombard the planet unless we gave up.

So maybe we'd need to keep them focused on us.

I commed Guillaume, down in the engine room. He wasn't qualified as a spaceship engineer, but he was the closest we had.

"Yeah?" He answered the call cautiously, already on the defensive.

"Hi, Guillaume, I just want to ask your advice about engines. Specifically, what our emissions would look like to another ship if they started developing a fault."

He hummed and hawed a bit.

"The in-system engines are damned reliable and kinda self-correcting for minor problems," he said.

"And major problems?"

"The engine blows up."

"Okay. What about the damage to the *Sambuk*'s engines? You and Heston came up with the explanation that they overheated when he emerged into the gas clouds."

"Yeah. I guess if you want to focus your scanners on the *Sambuk*, you'd be able to pick out a different quantity or temperature for the engine emissions."

"Okay. Call you back in ten."

I'd timed it well. The *Sambuk* had emerged from the swirls of gas surrounding the giant planet and I could get good images on the scanners. I ran them through temperature and radiation analyses and called Guillaume back.

"You're right. Every minute or so, their left-hand engine loses power and they have to compensate by reducing the thrust from the right one. You can see the changes in emissions and even the temperature of the engine housing."

"Oh." He seemed pleased.

"We need to be able to mimic that sort of thing," I said. "An engine losing power every now and then."

I left him to work out the best way to do that without actually damaging the engines.

"Play the lame duck?" Heston said.

"You know, I've no idea what a duck is," I replied. "We don't have them on Calloway. But I get the meaning. Pretend to be damaged."

Bjorn squinted. "Lure the *Jahazi* in?"

I nodded. "If the *Jahazi* stays outside the Mez, it would be difficult for Shami to close with her."

"But if they think the *Dark Shark* is actually the *Tünjorgo*, and we have an engine problem, maybe they'll come chasing us. That's your plan?"

"Basically."

"You bet on long odds," he said.

"I'm coming to the conclusion that everything in space is long odds," I replied. "You two take a rest. Nothing will happen until it all happens and then we'll need you fresh."

Bjorn got up. He and I had done this a hundred times or more in the war. One to keep watch while the other took a break. It had kept us alive. And despite our arguments over the best way to get rid of the threat of the *Sambuk*, he still trusted me. That felt good.

When he went, Heston followed, moving stiffly from his long hours at the console.

Bjorn sent Thandi up to give me a hand, or maybe to keep me awake.

E3. Chapter 6

Thandi brought snacks as a meal for us both.

"Those are like pork wrapped in vegetable leaves. Those ones are beef grilled on a spike and coated with melted cheese. Those are plum dumplings. And these," she pulled a small container with little pastries closer to her, "they will be too spicy for you. They are a favorite from my home planet."

She took one and closed her eyes as she bit into it. "These are Meson's best dish. I would marry him all over again, just to have him make these."

I laughed. "I have the palate of a garbage disposal system. I'm amazed I can still taste things." I took one of her favorites. It was a little brown roll with a crispy, flaky cover and it looked innocent enough.

Thandi poured me a long drink. It was something called Frucht Sprudel we'd bought in crates on Orion's Wheel.

"You said your homeworld is called Rundi," I said, waving the snack around. "Which arc is that on?"

"The Lauma arc. Spinward of the sector capital at Bourke." She was eyeing me and the snack carefully. "It's one of the early seedship colonies that jumped too far out."

I didn't know anything about the Lauma arc, but that wasn't unusual. Most of the Frontier systems were known only to their neighbors.

I pulled up a star map overview on the console and absentmindedly bit into the snack.

Inside the pastry were little strips of meat. Crunchy vegetables. A sort of bean sauce. And fire ripped straight out of the heart of a nova.

"Oh..." I barely managed to stop myself swearing and Thandi handed me my drink. "That is evil," I choked.

"I warned you. Try the plum dumplings. They will help soothe your mouth."

Between the drink and the dumplings my mouth recovered slowly. Fortunately, the rest of her snacks weren't so violent.

Thandi seemed intent on distracting me as an apology, and the conversation drifted as I kept an eye on the positions of the pirates.

"Can I ask a rude question?" she said suddenly.

"Ask. I might not answer."

Thandi nodded. "You and Heston have been working together a lot, so he obviously knows things about you that the rest of us don't."

"What are you getting at, Thandi?"

"You've stopped swearing. Not only that, when he swears, or calls on the Goddess, if you're near, he apologizes to you."

"Oh. That." I pressed down on the twist of anxiety that returned to my stomach. "It's a religious thing. Bjorn and I... well, we're nearing home. Hopefully. We need to examine ourselves, our behavior."

"Eh, I understand the swearing. But the Goddess..." She paused and rethought what she was saying before going on. "I never heard of any other religion taking offense at the Goddess."

"Well, there aren't many congregants of the Church in Exile. You may not have met us. There were other Churches still running on other planets when Calloway was settled, but I guess we're few and far between. Didn't find a single one in the whole of the 1st Frontier except the five of us from Calloway."

"Very strict?"

I nodded.

Very strict didn't cover it.

I was reluctant to talk about it, but there was nothing happening on the screens, and she was asking very politely, so I eventually responded as we ate our meal.

"Calloway is a colony set up by the Church in Exile, to be a beacon in the darkness."

As I spoke, I felt the patterns of my voice change, and the me from six years ago returned to use the style of language that she had grown up with.

"All are born into the Church. I was confirmed as a teenager and reaffirmed as an adult, but I remain a mere Initiate. When I have borne children into the Church and they are confirmed, I become an Elder. As an Initiate, it is normally forbidden to walk among the Unknowing, in case their darkness steals the light in me."

Thandi frowned.

I didn't know what to say, but I remembered the Judge's words to us: When the mind falters and the voice must speak, fill your mouth with the words of the Scriptures.

One of those phrases came, making me feel guilty that it had been so long unused. "Gather together, for light calls to light, and the uncertain lamp is quenched in darkness."

"But they *did* let you out, five of you, to earn enough money to buy those bio-processors and save the colony."

"Yes. We were desperate. Without those bio-processors, we knew the colony would die. Literally, we'd starve to death in twenty or thirty years. We couldn't afford to move to another planet, even if there was one willing to take us. We couldn't even communicate with the head Church, and anyway, Calloway was the planet they'd assigned to us. You could say it was our duty to make a success of Calloway, and the Church in Exile is big on duty. The Judge—that's the senior of the Elders and leader of the Synod—he made a ruling. He said because we would be doing the Church's work among the Unknowing, even though we broke the Church's rules, if we supported each other in the path, we could be shrived on our return."

"Eh? Shrived? Forgiven?"

"A ceremony." I'd never spoken to anyone outside the original five of us about these things, not in all the six years I'd been in the 1st Frontier. And now, talking seemed a way to keep my anxieties about our return at bay.

"The Church gathers to listen. We confess to all we've done," I explained. "Fighting and killing mainly. Not keeping regular services. Listening to the Unknowing. Swearing and sinful thoughts... and so on. Everyone in the congregation prays to take a share of the sins, so no one person is burdened."

Thandi looked thoughtful. "Just the two of you now to go through that."

"Yes, but two who spent six years away. Double the time that was authorized. And we must bear witness for the other three who died."

The familiar pain made me turn my face away and check the screens again. Solveig. Enoch. Hal. Bjorn and I had to bring them home. It had seemed so much less heavy a burden when there had been three of us bringing two home. Before Hal had died in the assault on Rhea 4.

I could tell I wasn't explaining it well to Thandi, but I didn't want to get any deeper into the details about the Church in Exile, our duties and the painful results of self-examination.

It was bad enough that we would be the ones to break the news of Hal's death to his family, because it had happened too late for official channels. Worse, because our duties would include, right after giving the news of his death, bearing faithful witness to his failings.

And against Solveig and Enoch.

Against each other.

And, finally, against ourselves.

Such was our duty to the Church.

Bjorn and I had not spoken about it, but the closer we got to Calloway, the more it shadowed every word that passed between us. I knew Bjorn was examining himself, as I was myself, using the process that the Church called the Mirror of the Soul.

I had known all along some of what I would have to say before the Congregation of Shriving.

But it went far beyond the obvious major sins of fighting and killing. Those had been anticipated by the Judge when we volunteered. I felt I had carried some measure of absolution already to shield my soul as I went into war.

It was beneath that. I realized, in the words of the Church, the darkness had stolen much of my light. I had become 'immodest' in inner thoughts and surface appearance. I'd constantly flouted authority. Become argumentative. Hedonist. I'd brawled and partied. I'd *enjoyed* it.

I'd turned my face from the ways and teaching of the Church in Exile.

Worst of all, I had not supported Bjorn. I had not supported any of the others. In fact, by my bad example I had *encouraged* them to turn away from the Church.

Those were what *I* could see, and I knew I would need many sessions in front of the Mirror of the Soul to truly understand all the damage I'd done. What else would I find Bjorn had seen?

Would my family see I'd led the others astray by going so wild as soon as I had gotten away from the protection of the Church?

So much to deal with.

"I know this is difficult for others to understand," I said. "It would be hypocritical or even counter-productive to try and explain the fullness of the Church's creed while I am so poor an example."

Thandi finished the last of her favorite snacks before speaking again. "I hear a lot of guilt in what you're saying and *not* saying. Guilt is double-edged. It can be used *for* you, but it can also be used *against* you. Maybe that's why I'm hearing anger, too."

"I am angry, but that's not productive," I said. "I was taught by the Elders that anger against the Church is what I would feel when I examine the darkness that has seeped into my soul."

Thandi huffed. "I think your Church sounds full of..." She stopped and changed what she was going to say. "Of itself. Too dependent on this Judge and Synod."

"Like all human systems, it's not perfect, but the path is clear, and the Judge is good."

"Good while he's the Judge."

Which made me think about the six years that had passed. Judge Yevenst had been elderly when we left. What if...

"Well, at least you will have the support of your husband when you return," Thandi said, as she collected up the empty food containers.

I knew immediately what assumption she'd made and I laughed. "Bjorn's not my husband. He's my partner, I guess."

"Eh, so the Church isn't strict in that—"

"No, no. I didn't mean that kind of partner. Sorry, Thandi. It's just that we were so often referred to as partners in crime while we were in the army."

"But you share a cabin," she pointed out, eyebrows raised skeptically.

"It just seemed easier." I shrugged. "With this number of crew, we don't have a lot of cabins on the *Acid Penguin* and, well, we've had to share accommodation for the last six years. It doesn't mean anything."

Of course, it *would* mean something to the Church, despite the fact that the sharing had been forced on us in the army.

Thandi gave a little smile. "Well, we need—"

"Emergence!" I yelped as the long-range scan showed the telltale flash of a ship appearing.

All the concern about how things would go back at Calloway had to be put aside. We were still a long way from home.

And that flash on the scanner... it was reading as right up against the Mez, the Mass Effect Zone.

Far too close for Shami and the *Dark Shark*.

E3. Chapter 7

Heston was back on the bridge in less than five minutes. Bjorn trailed in a few seconds behind him, still pulling on his clothes.

"ID?" Bjorn said.

"Came in dark," I replied. "Like you'd expect a pirate to."

"We can't escape two reavers." Heston's voice betrayed an edge of fear, but he settled back into the pilot's seat.

The new arrival had emerged from jump at the nearest point of our current trajectory and the edge of the zone.

Heston began to ease the nose away and the projection of our path moved on the screens.

"Wait," I said. "Hold steady."

"What?" Everyone turned to look at me.

I silently chewed on a nail for a moment, frantically trying to work out the distances and times involved. There were too many variables; I had to make a decision on gut instinct. I commed the engine room.

"Guillaume? Time for the lame animal routine."

"Duck," Heston provided.

"You got it," Guillaume said. "One lame duck."

The acceleration compensators masked slight variations, so we didn't feel anything, but the displays showed the projected path veer off to one side, then come back. The acceleration and speed dropped.

Not a lot, but maybe enough for the *Jahazi* to notice.

I switched the broadcast comms channel back on.

Static.

I wound back through the recording until I picked up Corzey's voice again. While we'd been ignoring it, the original broadcast had changed to something much darker. Corzey had ended by trying to persuade the crew to mutiny, and finally promising lingering death to all of us.

I switched the recording off and went back to listening to the live broadcast.

With the distances, 'live' was ten minutes old from the new arrival and about the same from the *Jahazi*. Maybe five or six from the *Sambuk*.

That delay was going to make time crawl.

"You're gambling on the new arrival being a better choice than the *Jahazi*?" Thandi asked.

"No," I said. "I'm betting that's Shami and the *Dark Shark*."

Bjorn frowned. "How are you working that out?"

I tapped on the navigation display and rotated it until everything I needed to show fell into a straight line, more or less.

"We've been broadcasting on the nav beacon and traffic control frequencies for a couple of hours."

I made the display show the volume of space that our signal had reached in those two hours.

"We arranged to meet Shami in the vicinity of the transit point, here, at about 5 AU 'above' the star, okay? Because she's formally trained, she'd have arrived with *Dark Shark* showing on her ID, and she'd have the nav beacon and traffic channels open. That's what pilot-navigators do, right, Heston?"

He nodded.

Bjorn got it. "She heard our signal. So she switched off her ID, like a pirate, and jumped again, right down to the limit of the Mez."

"Yes!" I stood up and paced the bridge. "Now, what we have to do, in the time remaining..."

Bjorn tapped at a calculator app. "The radiation from her initial emergence, when she had the *Dark Shark* ID showing, will reach us in, say, thirty minutes, and then reach the *Sambuk* five minutes later. *Jahazi* would get it five minutes after that, give or take."

"In that forty minutes, we've got to lure the *Jahazi* deep enough inside the zone, while keeping far enough away from the *Sambuk*."

"Which is the lame duck plan," Heston said. "But how can we—"

"ID," Bjorn shouted. "Yes!"

The display now showed the new arrival as *Tünjorgo*.

Moments later a voice came on the broadcast channel: "Merchanter *Acid Penguin*, this is Captain Kenkul of the merchanter *Tünjorgo*. We see you're in deep trouble with this scum, but we can assist you. We have defensive weapons at the ready. Maintain best speed to our position and we will cover you while we both jump out of here."

The voice made my heart skip a beat, but I knew it wouldn't be Kenkul.

"Heston, respond back. Make like you believe it. Say we're having engine trouble."

"Thank the Goddess!" Heston blurted into the comms. "*Tünjorgo*, we're coming as fast as we can. We damaged one of the engines in the jump."

I gestured at him to go on, and he babbled about a crazy captain jumping in too close to the planet and now trying to make the engines run past their safety limits.

I had to smile at that while I pulled Thandi aside.

"Shami has a way with computer systems. Direct interface." I tapped the side of my head and Thandi shuddered. Normal people didn't like that sort of augmentation any more than they liked gene tricking and the other practices that flourished out in the Frontier. "She'll be synthesizing his voice from the ship's records."

"Eh. And the ship ID is completely valid, because that *was* the *Tünjorgo*. So the pirates see the ship, they hear his voice and they believe. Clever."

"But it's not a magic gun. Shami can't sneak up on the *Jahazi*." Bjorn was frustrated. Stick a weapon in his hand and put him in the middle of a planetside battle, he would be in his element. Out here, where it took hours or days to get somewhere, and every movement had to keep in mind gravity wells and the Zone, he felt useless.

"If the *Jahazi* comes into the Zone," I said, "and we keep the *Sambuk* busy, Shami will be able to take them both. She flew—"

"Ground attack fighters," Bjorn interrupted me. "She flew ground attack, not space combat."

"Okay, not her specialty, but you know that ground attack candidates get picked from the top space combat pilots, just the same as space combat go through the full pilot-navigator training."

But I conceded the general point. The *Dark Shark* wasn't a space combat fighter, much less a ground attack variant. What could she do? How powerful was the *Jahazi*?

It took ten minutes from the time we'd seen the *Tünjorgo* ID for that signal to reach the *Jahazi* and another ten for the information about the effect that had had to reach us, but it was immediate.

The *Jahazi* fired her engines and dived into the Zone, at full acceleration.

"Yes!" I shouted. "Come get us, Corzey, you..." I bit off what I'd been about to call her.

The trap was sprung.

Twenty minutes later the signal from the *Dark Shark*'s first emergence appeared on our sensors. With her *Dark Shark* ID showing.

I had to assume the *Jahazi* and the *Sambuk* would be watching their displays, and they'd know in under ten minutes that there was something wrong. That was going to be too late. There was nothing *Sambuk* could do, and the *Jahazi* would be half an hour at maximum acceleration into the Mez. No way Corzey could enter Chang space there, and even turning around would take time.

I commed the engine room. "Back to normal operation, we need full power, Gillaume, please."

Bjorn knew what to do. "I'll suit up and get down to the docking bay," he said, retrieving his helmet and exiting the bridge.

Heston looked up inquiringly.

"Swing back and raise the flag," I said.

Shami and I hadn't worked out any method to talk in code. I had to hope I knew what Shami was doing, and she would anticipate what I would do.

Heston keyed the ID screen. Our ID was still showing *Acid Penguin*, but in place of the merchanter designation Parvi-Merchanter-Calloway Space Ship-701, we were transmitting a naval style designation: Parvi-MILITARY-Calloway Navy Ship-701.

Time for my persona again.

From the corner of my eye, I caught Thandi looking at me, and our earlier conversation came to mind. Not that she would understand the nuances of what I was about to do in terms of the creed of the Church in Exile, but my agreed exemptions with Judge Yevenst had been entirely to do with my service in the army.

Once that service was complete, the creed would say everything I'd done was taken on my soul's own account. Including lying and contemplating murder.

There was no other way; my personal salvation weighed nothing against the lives of everyone on Calloway.

I opened the broadcast channel.

"This is Lieutenant Commander Skelling of the Calloway Navy Anti-Piracy Unit. *Jahazi*, *Sambuk*, we have you bracketed in our trap. There is no way out. There is no negotiation. Signal your surrender by the following actions: Decelerate to rest with respect to the primary star and completely power down your engines. Close down *all* power on your ships except for life support. Discharge your energy weapons in a neutral direction. We will be scanning for your actions."

I let that hang there for a second.

"If you choose to comply, you will be boarded by suited marines. Any resistance will instantly be met by immediate, overwhelming and lethal response. No care will be taken to protect the integrity of your ships or the lives of others on those ships. Should you comply with the arrest, once you have been taken into custody, you will be handed over to the competent authorities in the Ensylas system for legal processing."

Another pause.

"If you choose to not comply with any of that... the Dark takes fools. Do not be fools. Skelling out."

E3. Chapter 8

Even with the closer *Sambuk*, the signal took five minutes to get there, and so it would be ten more minutes before we found out what they were going to do.

"We're probably outgunned just by the *Sambuk*," Heston said in the silence on the bridge.

"They don't know that." I had retrieved my combat suit and was strapping myself into it.

"Like *they* don't know *we* know that they have collaborators on the Orion's Wheel," Thandi said. "They may be thinking it would be good to be handed over there. This is also clever. You would make a good merchanter."

I raised an eyebrow at that, but I was too focused on what we had to do, too tense about how the pirates might respond.

"Thandi, we don't have suits for everyone," I said. "Maybe it would be better for you to take your husbands and wait in one of the sealed compartments."

She snorted and waved my suggestion away. "If it goes badly, we do not want to be captured by pirates. I know my husbands' minds on this."

There wasn't a great deal to do, but I took over from Heston while he got into his emergency suit.

We had spun around to reverse direction and the in-system engines were on full power. Heston kept muttering how inefficient it was, but there was no way I was letting *Jahazi* and *Sambuk* out of my sight by orbiting the planet and using its gravity to boost us.

Bjorn reported in from the docking bay, once again open and exposed to space. I fed him the navigation output and his suit targeting computers used his servos to rotate the plasma cannon. It wasn't exactly a naval solution, but it probably gave us the teeth to take *Sambuk*.

What the *Jahazi* was capable of was anyone's guess. We hadn't even had time to work out what the *Dark Shark* could really do.

"*Sambuk*'s trying to run for it," Heston said as the signals eventually reached us.

I tuned out the electromagnetic spectrum apart from infra-red and focused on the *Sambuk*'s engines.

"That's not good," I said, as Thandi leaned over my shoulder. "It seems Maykn can fake an engine problem just as easily as we can."

The odd cycle of heating and cooling that indicated a malfunctioning engine had gone. The *Sambuk* was taking the minimum path to get outside the Mez in the direction furthest away from both us and the *Jahazi*. And his acceleration was higher than we counted on.

This was going to be a chase we would lose.

"That ship is *much* quicker than us," Heston said.

"Not faster than a plasma bolt," I replied. "Bjorn, you copy?"

"Got it. Not going to get any closer," he said. "Just fine tuning the targeting solutions for their new velocity."

"Fire when you can and keep it up," I said.

"Recharging the plasma capacitor cells will lower our acceleration as well," Heston pointed out.

I nodded.

Outside of the upper bands of the planet's gas clouds, there was next to no visual clue that Bjorn had fired, only the small drop in acceleration.

Ten minutes later, the infra-red signal from the *Sambuk* flared up before reducing again.

"Hit!" Heston yelled.

Bjorn had already fired again, but the *Sambuk* started to weave. I knew he'd miss now. We had no way of predicting exactly where the ship would be in five minutes' time.

"Hold fire, Bjorn. All power back into the engines. Maybe we've damaged the ship enough that we can catch up."

"What's happening with the *Jahazi*?" he asked. He had no navigation displays down in the loading bay, but there was a general announcement screen.

"Running as well," I said, and sent the bare figures down to the docking bay screen. "On a minimum time route to exit the Mez, given her starting vector and velocity. It would be safe for her to jump in about an hour, which is plenty of time for Shami to prevent it, if she thinks she has the firepower. We have to leave them to it. We can't get there in time to make any difference."

"So much for the call to surrender," he said. "But it sounded good to me. I'll stay here just in case."

"Thanks."

Heston was tapping at the display options again and he cut into the conversation. "We're closing on the *Sambuk*," he said. "You did some damage, Bjorn. Look at the trace."

He copied his screen output to the docking bay as well.

He'd overlaid the image of the fleeing *Sambuk* with a filter to show that the ship was leaving a spreading trace of gases and debris as it raced away. He'd added a sidebar, showing the distance between the two ships was counting down slowly.

"Awesome," Bjorn said. "Maybe I'll get another shot in if we get close enough."

"I'll keep the targeting numbers live to you, but Maykn is still weaving," I said.

I wasn't paying much attention to Bjorn and Heston. There was something about the damage and the debris from the *Sambuk* that didn't look right. In total we'd hit the ship four times—twice after we'd just arrived in the system and the power was reduced by traveling through gases from the giant planet, and twice at extreme range.

I wasn't a real naval officer, but I'd been in planetside battles. I'd seen plasma cannon damage. I'd seen combat vehicles with entire sides of armor melted or holes punched straight through. We hadn't done that kind of hurt to the *Sambuk*. The scanning resolution at this distance wasn't good, but there didn't seem to be major damage.

So why was there this much debris?

"Heston, feed into your nav computer where the *Acid Penguin* and the *Sambuk* were when I called on them to surrender. Okay? Now add in the course that the *Sambuk* has taken since then."

He tapped and selected options, then looked up at me.

"And now ask the nav computer how many best time options there are for an intercept."

He wrinkled his brow.

"I'm not doubting your course, I'm interested to know how predictable it is."

A few moments passed before the computer showed him the results. "It's the only one, Skip."

"I thought so. I don't like being on a predictable course," I said. "We have radar sensors, don't we?"

"Yeah." He quickly tapped up some options on the control panel and took over one of the screens to display the radar returns along our path. The picture built up as the radar pulses began to come back from further and further ahead of us.

"Cut off anything beyond the *Sambuk*, and I want higher resolution images of anything we're pinging near our path. Especially anything that appears to be debris from the *Sambuk*."

"No can do, Skip. That's military tech. I could separate out strong reflections from metallic objects..."

"Do it. Bjorn, standby with the cannon for some targets."

"You think there's something aimed at us?" Bjorn asked calmly.

"A self-positioning mine," I replied. "Or a missile. Got to hope it's dumb if it's a missile."

"You're thinking the gas emissions from the *Sambuk* were just there to mask maneuvering jets to get the fake debris into our path?"

"Yeah. You hit the *Sambuk*, and some of that debris may be the result, but some of it is moving too far and fast."

"Gotcha. I'll fire at half power. It'll be enough to take out a missile or a mine and it'll give me four shots at a time."

"Go for it."

Heston directed the radar analysis down to Bjorn. There was a delay, as he had to reconfigure his targeting computer.

The first lump of debris seemed to be rushing towards us and Heston's hands hovered over the control panel, ready to pull us up.

Four flashes from the loading bay.

Our acceleration dropped.

Four small flashes in the visible light spectrum as Bjorn's bolts hit.

Heston eased the ship's nose up a little. "He can't hit that many in the time, Skip. I can fly around the debris trail, but we'll lose time."

"If Bjorn misses, we'll have to, but hold steady until the last moment."

The four nearest blobs on the radar display had disappeared.

Four more flashes. Three answering flashes on the visible spectrum and then a bright and silent explosion that maxed out the display.

"Goddess!" Heston muttered.

On the display Heston had made of the *Sambuk*, the sidebar showing the distance stopped coming down and went back up.

"That was a good spot, Skip. He was trying to get us to chase him and fly straight through that debris."

I looked at the numbers.

"We can't catch him. Let's just give all the debris a wide berth and keep watching it. Bjorn, free fire on the *Sambuk*. Try bracketing his position and maybe we'll get lucky."

E3. Chapter 9

We didn't get lucky; after another hour and a half, the *Sambuk* made it outside the Mez. The ship was clearly damaged, but there was no evidence that had affected the Chang generators. There was a flash to show it entering Chang space, and then nothing.

Captain Corzey and the *Jahazi* didn't get lucky either.

Trapped inside the zone by Shami, and believing the *Dark Shark* was a military ship, she engaged her Chang generators in a desperate attempt to escape.

We watched silently as light an hour old reached us.

There was the flash as the generators opened Chang space, but it wasn't the single, sharp flash of a normal transition.

Everything was over in seconds. Heston captured it, cleaned the picture up and played it back in slow motion.

The body of the *Jahazi* twisted and tore apart like wet paper. The actual generators seemed to make it into Chang space, but then reappeared as a spreading arc of glowing fragments.

Heston pulled up the frequencies for emergencies and distress beacons.

Nothing.

Thandi left the bridge looking ill. I knew what she was going through, and I felt guilty I no longer had those sort of reactions about people like the crew of the *Jahazi*.

Shami's voice broke my thoughts. *"Acid Penguin*, this is the *Dark Shark*. We're all greens. What's your status?"

"Hi, Shami. We're fine. I guess you saw the *Sambuk* got away. Scanners show you heading towards the wreckage with shuttles. We'll join you there."

∞ ∞ ∞ ∞ ∞

There were no survivors, but lots of wreckage.

A broken plasma cannon. Twenty-five shipping containers. A shuttle that seemed only slightly damaged. An entire sleeping accommodation unit.

Bodies.

"No survivors, and this stuff isn't going anywhere in a hurry," Shami said, close enough for no delay in the transmissions. "I think heading for Calloway is more urgent than scavenging."

Now that we had checked there were no survivors, we had time to speak.

"How did the proposal to the Yorkham go down?" I asked.

She laughed. "How did you think? Jan, the *Dark Star* is *full*. I have the first two hundred of us and as much baggage as we can fit in. You're a nova-class heroine. I have people I have to introduce you to."

My eyes prickled unexpectedly.

My plan had seemed so simple to me, back after we captured the *Tünjorgo* and *Karakun*.

We had ships. We had some money—not enough, but genuine money. We had lots of Terran credit. And we had a sort-of, temporary crew, about enough for both ships.

Calloway needed bio-processors. The sooner the better, so Bjorn and I had set off to buy the first one from Ensylas and take it home. The rest would have to wait until we worked our way deep enough into the Inner Worlds that we could change our Terran credits for dollars, and come back to buy the remaining bio-processors.

But while all this was going on, what were we to do with Shami's people, the survivors of the damaged colony ship, Yorkham, stranded in a hostile system?

Back then, it had seemed so obvious to me.

Calloway as a planet was nearly empty and, even if there was an environmental problem that we needed more bio-processors to fix, it was immensely more hospitable than the poisonous planets in the system where the Yorkham was.

It seemed clear to me that we should offer to move them to Calloway.

Great plan. It was only now that I was starting to worry about the reaction of the Elders. Calloway was a religious retreat. People from the Yorkham would be 'Unknowing'—as anyone outside the Church was. Unwelcome would be another way of putting it; a source of potential corruption to the soul of the Church.

Shami wasn't hearing any of those doubts. Shuttles brought the senior Yorkham staff across to *Acid Penguin*, and they shook hands, clapped backs, hugged everyone and spoke so enthusiastically about what they could do for Calloway that I got carried along.

That feeling of buoyancy carried me all the way through the journey until we emerged from Chang space at the planar zenith of the Calloway system, a regulation 2 AU out from the star and about five days away from orbit over the planet at a fuel-conserving cruise speed.

"Emergence," Heston said. "And the *Dark Shark* footprint is about fifty thousand klicks behind us."

That wouldn't be a problem. The *Dark Shark* was much quicker than us. I patted the worn control panel housing on the bridge to apologize to the *Acid Penguin* for thinking such unfaithful thoughts.

"You are my favorite spaceship, little *Penguin*," I muttered, too quietly for the others to hear. "I don't care if you're not as fast and don't have as many cannons."

Bjorn looked at me with an oddly neutral expression on his face.

"Home, sweet home," he said.

We couldn't see anything without enhancement, but the display was showing a representation of the Calloway system, six planets in their serene dance around the star.

"Thought any more about what we say to the Elders?" he went on.

"Yes. I have a plan."

Bjorn laughed. Thandi and Meson were sitting with us on the bridge, and they joined in.

Heston didn't.

I frowned as I watched his hands skating across the comms options on his panel.

"What's up?"

The first icicle of doubt formed in my guts as I saw his face, pale with shock, turn towards me.

"Skip... there's nothing."

"Of course," I snapped back. "This isn't Ensylas. There's no traffic through here."

"No. *Nothing*. No nav beacon. No radio. No electromagnetic emissions on any channels. Skip, there's no one here."

Episode 4
Home is the Hero

E4. Chapter 1

Once a ground attack pilot, always a ground attack pilot. Shami flipped the shuttle on its side and we dropped through the stratosphere like an arrow on fire.

Somewhere down here, there *were* people on Calloway. Scanners could see the evidence.

But there were no communications of any kind in the system.

Unknown situation: assume hostile had kept us alive in the war, and good habits die hard.

"Solar array's still there," Bjorn grunted as Shami leveled us out twenty klicks later and we thundered over the vast fields of panels that covered foothills well away from the settlements.

"Something's wrong with it," I replied.

We were flying at a height of a klick, but even at that distance I could see the panels weren't being maintained. Their color should have been a uniform matte gray, but they looked dull and mottled.

"No threats identified. Five minutes to landing," Shami said as she curved north and began to lose height. "I'm going to come in VTOL. Not going to trust that surface 'til I walk it."

In the forty klicks between the solar array and the landing area on the coast, there were some of the Great Farms in the Lord's Eastern Reach. They were widely spaced, each with a distinctive patchwork of crop and stock fields surrounding them. I could see the fields were being worked. There *were* people down there, but the look of it all was wrong. Like it had all shrunk.

"No tractors," Bjorn said suddenly. "The array's not working, so no solar power, no charging, no tractors. Nova! They're working everything by *hand*."

"What the..." I stopped myself swearing. I was back home. *An Initiate is always modest in looks, modest in words, modest in deeds.* "No communications either. No electronics? What happened?"

Bjorn just shook his head. There was little value speculating. We'd find out soon enough.

The last of the Farms passed beneath us. Calloway town, visible mainly because of the Great Church and the wide-armed stretch of the docks into the sea, passed on the left side, too far away to see clearly.

Shami dumped her speed, making the shuttle shudder.

Ahead of us was the rocky promontory that had been used as a landing area for shuttles back when the colony was founded eighty-five years ago. Shami rotated the jets and dropped the shuttle gently on the vitrified rock surface.

"I'd give it a few minutes for the heat to dissipate," she said as she powered down the engines and sent a status report to the spaceships in orbit.

I looked out at the bleak and empty landscape. "You promised me crowds, Bjorn."

He snorted. "I exaggerated."

"Exaggeration would be calling a small group a crowd. You can't really exaggerate zero to anything."

"Picky, picky."

There should have been around seven thousand people on Calloway. Even when Bjorn was telling me they would all turn out to welcome us back, I knew it wouldn't happen. Farms needed to be tended. Fish needed to be caught. I could almost hear the Elders: *the Lord's Work must be done first.* Add all that to everyday issues like babies and youngsters to look after, urgent domestic emergencies, lack of enough transport, the distances... there would have been reasons for the welcome to be no more than a delegation alerted by our messages.

I'd never imagined arriving back in silence, to be greeted by no one.

Bjorn and I got up and our eyes met.

I raised an eyebrow in question and he nodded. We'd traveled down in ship's coveralls, but until we *knew* what was going on, he and I would be in combat suits.

The decision taken, we started the awkward dance of suiting up in a restricted space. It wasn't so bad, really. We hadn't always had the luxury of a dedicated suiting room in our six years of fighting Earth's war. And even after a break of not wearing the suit every day, everything felt so familiar, down to the squeeze and release as the armor recalibrated itself on my body.

We hadn't wanted to wear the suits. Not back on Calloway.

"We are so—" I started.

"Alert to risk," Shami cut across me. "Yes. And we keep it that way. I'm staying here, in the shuttle. I will not even open the doors to anyone but you two. I will also take off if I consider the shuttle to be in any danger, even from you."

"Agreed," I said.

She watched us finish off preparing. "Anywhere else, in these circumstances, suits would be an obvious safety precaution. Are you *sure* you're going to be in trouble for wearing them?"

"The pacifism of the Church in Exile is complete," Bjorn said. "These suits are weapons. We're bringing weapons to Calloway. Sin, basically."

Shami snorted and shook her head in irritation.

"How long is your List of Sins?" I asked Bjorn, with a twisted smile. It wasn't really funny.

"So long, I had to store it on my InfoPad. Do you think they'll allow reading from it at the Shriving?"

I laughed bitterly.

I'd attended Ceremonies of Shriving—once or twice a year from puberty right up until I'd signed on for the 1st Frontier. The Appellants at the ceremonies had been folk who'd 'strayed'. But there had never been a list longer than two or three sins.

The Elders were *good* at catching sin early.

And there were no pads allowed in the Church. We both knew it. Bjorn and I were just going through our pre-mission routines, which including joking and teasing.

While Shami powered up our ATV, we started checking each other's suits. With a twitch of guilt I realized it was a ritual far more familiar to me than any Church service now. *Seals. Movement. Comms. ID beacon. Weapons. Ammunition. Suit Diagnostics. Charge. Reserves.*

Green. All green.

Good to go.

It was just the stuff *inside* the suits that wasn't ready. Couldn't be ready.

"Good?" I asked through the suit comms.

"Good. Just remember to point your weapon away from me," Bjorn's voice came back clearly, and I hit him.

It was tight getting down to the bay where the ATV was stored, and it took five minutes for us to ease through and clamber aboard.

"Ready to deploy," I commed Shami as the bay sealed itself from the rest of the shuttle.

"Yes..." she said, and paused. "Look, guys, I want to say something."

Bjorn and I exchanged glances. We knew what had been bugging Shami, and everyone else. But there was nothing she could say that would make it better. She didn't get the Church in Exile. She didn't get that, officially, she was one of the 'Unknowing'. She *really* didn't get that, officially, just listening to her talk about the Church was a sin, much less agreeing with anything she said.

Her voice through the comms was quiet, but she couldn't hide the trace of anger.

"I met a pair of soldiers on Orion's Wheel who could take on the universe and everything it threw at them. We got together. Earth betrayed us, but we didn't give up. The military abandoned us, but we didn't give up. Together the three of us beat two pirate ships, and took them over. Then those two soldiers went back to Orion's Wheel and outfoxed the pirates' allies on station. We got back together and beat two *more* pirate ships, out in the Dark by a dying star, with little more than attitude and bluff. Because we didn't give up.

"Then there's you two."

I couldn't fault her view. The closer to home we'd come, the more I'd felt crippled with self-doubt about returning, and I knew Bjorn was the same way. The shock of arriving to find no nav beacon and no transmissions at all from Calloway had somehow precipitated all that, and I'd been a miserable wretch for the days it took to get from our arrival point outside the Mass Effect Zone into orbit around the planet. I was a different person, one going through the motions.

"You've been six years away," Shami went on, her voice rising. "Nearly a quarter of your lives, doing what had to be done, and *no one* gets to take that away from you. What you did and why you did it should be a source of *pride*. You should look any person on this planet in the eye, and you shouldn't take *one* step back. You've come back. You have some of what they sent you to get, and a plan to get the rest. They should be pinning nova-cursed *medals* on you. That's all."

She dropped the front ramp and Bjorn drove us out.

We were silent. She was right, and she was wrong.

The ramp sealed behind us, and Shami would be starting the process of decontamination of the bay. Just to be certain. Military procedures.

The same kind of hard-trained habit made me eyeball my mission counter. It told me I could remain completely protected from the environment for twenty hours. After that, if there were no dangers in the atmosphere, and I breathed the air straight, the suit had enough charge for another hundred hours or so in non-combat mode.

I couldn't think of a scenario where we'd need to fight, but if we started fighting, then everything got used up in half the time, or less.

But Calloway was a completely pacifist planet. Outside of farm tools, there shouldn't be any weapons. A couple of combat-suited veterans were invincible.

But what was it Gunny used to say? The battle is decided in the mind.

I put it all aside. It wasn't the time to think of what-ifs. We were following through on the military protocols for potentially hostile environments. What if there was some terrible airborne contaminant that attacked electrical equipment? Or some virus had killed off so many of the people here that the colony was unable to carry out even the most straightforward of functions, like solar array maintenance?

That was what I needed to think about first. Not what to say to the Synod of Elders.

"Home is the hero," Bjorn muttered as the ATV bobbled across the uneven, deserted ground towards the distant town.

E4. Chapter 2

"Stop!"

"What?" Bjorn brought the ATV to a juddering halt.

"Over there. Someone's working a field."

"Here? There aren't any Farms."

We jumped off and trotted up the gentle hill.

There *was* someone there, where the ground leveled out. He had to have seen and heard the shuttle, and ignored it, but I guess the sight of a couple of combat suits coming for him was a whole different thing. He took off, running as fast as he could.

We could have overtaken him in seconds, but neither of us wanted to scare him even more.

We stopped where he'd been working and I had a look at what he'd been doing: tilling the soil by hand, with an old wood and steel hoe, row by painstaking row.

There was a bag of seed abandoned, but I didn't recognize the plant.

"Got to be a punishment of some kind," Bjorn said. "He's working alone, a dozen klicks from the Farms, and the soil here is lousy."

I looked at where he'd run. There were scrub trees that hid him from us now, but I'd got a good look.

"Yeah. His clothes..."

I didn't want to say. There was no cotton on Calloway, and clothes were made of synthetics. We had coarse cloth we made from a fibrous native plant, but it was only used for sacks, and one of its less pleasant uses had generated a nickname.

"Made of shitsacks," Bjorn said, and it was so ridiculous we laughed.

"Not really funny," I said. "No solar energy, no new fabric. But they can't all be wearing shitsacks."

"Foul language." Bjorn mimed writing it on a list.

We sobered up. To bear full witness against ourselves, we should include things like foul language. It was only that we'd die of old age before we finished listing all that level of sin.

"It supports the idea that he was here as a punishment," I said.

At the Ceremony of Shriving, and sometimes afterwards, those who'd sinned showed their repentance by wearing the uncomfortable local fabric.

"Maybe. Let's get to town."

∞ ∞ ∞ ∞ ∞

There were no Farms along the coast path we used. No one lived here. The families and combines who fished lived in the town by the docks. Farming families lived on the Great Farms in the Western and Eastern Reaches.

My family was out on the Western Reach. Without vehicles, it would be a four-hour walk to get to town. I wouldn't see them for a while, unless there was someone in town collecting or delivering.

Bjorn's family was closer, and he had some relatives down in the docks.

Apart from the Great Church and the docks, Calloway town was the hub for warehouses and manufacturing. What little administration was required also had offices in the center. It was the highest concentration of people on the planet.

Yet we saw no one when we reached the edge of town half an hour later.

Warehouses and workshops were empty. They didn't look as if they'd been used in years. Some had been partially disassembled.

Everything looked *smaller* than it had six years ago.

And it looked dirty. Unmaintained. There was litter. The road had holes.

Had it been like this when we left? Was I misremembering? Had my memories become idealized?

There was no one to ask.

In fact, we didn't see anyone until we reached the center: Founders' Square, in front of the Great Church. There was a group of five people standing in the middle of the square, obviously waiting.

Everything looked wrong somehow. Without needing to discuss it, Bjorn and I stayed in military mode; we turned the ATV around before we got off, and we walked separated by ten meters, scanning everywhere as if we expected an ambush.

"Feels odd not having our TAWs out," I said on the comm.

The Tactical Assault Weapons could punch holes in the buildings surrounding the square. Again, we didn't discuss it, but the weapons would be a degree of overkill we didn't feel was justified. Whatever had happened here didn't seem to have involved fighting, so the TAWs stayed in their holsters.

"Movement," Bjorn said suddenly, and his targeting computer shared data with mine.

Just people. Watching from the shadows. Not standing in plain sight, but peering nervously.

Someone opened a door, saw us and shut it again.

"I guess full combat suits are scary," Bjorn muttered.

We stopped ten meters from the group in the square.

All five wore clothes made from shitsack fabric. They couldn't *all* be doing penance, and anyway, why would penitents be sent out to greet us?

I didn't recognize a single face. They all looked old. Shrunken.

My mouth dried out. I'd thought of all sorts of things to say and now that I needed to say them, my mind went blank.

Bjorn seemed the same.

Old teaching saved us. When the mind falters and the voice must speak, fill your mouth with the words of the Scriptures.

"Blessed is the gathering," Bjorn said from his suit speakers, "that the light shall not die in darkness."

"The Lord be praised!" the woman on the right said, voice quivering with emotion and her bony hands clasped in front of her. "Light calls to light. The Church has come."

"We are saved," said another. "The Lord has delivered—"

"Silence!" The guy in the middle, apparently the leader, was not happy. "Leave us, both of you two. Go to the church. Pray, and consider the ways of darkness and the folly of your pride."

The two who'd spoken lowered their heads, bowed and backed away, stumbling as they went toward the Great Church.

The leader looked at the two remaining and intoned: "The Church does not come wrapped in sinful technology. The Church's people do not bear weapons."

Pompous ass.

At least his attitude helped me finally find my voice. "It's okay. The combat suits are just precautions. We're back," I said, my eyes prickling. "It's Janice Skelling and Bjorn Thorsson. The war ended finally. We've come home."

"We're wearing the suits because we don't know what's happened down here," Bjorn said.

"Bjorn? Bjorn?" The old man on the left took a hesitant step forward despite the leader. His hand reached out and his voice was feeble. "It's really you? It's Lars."

"*Cousin Lars*? What..."

Bjorn's suit speakers clicked off and his voice came through the comms to me alone. "Jan. Stay sealed."

I blinked. Bjorn's cousin Lars was fifteen years older than him, not fifty. Was there another Lars I didn't know about?

Bjorn reached up and cracked his visor open, then thumbed open the release springs to lift the helmet off.

"You shaved your hair, boy! But by the Lord's grace, it *is* you." Lars grabbed Bjorn by the arm of his suit, ignoring the protests of the delegation leader.

Then he fainted and collapsed on the ground at Bjorn's feet.

E4. Chapter 3

Hunger. Long-term.

Everyone was on starvation rations. People expected to faint all the time.

That much we learned while we carried Lars to the old town hall, but no more.

Elder Tuominen, the leader of the little delegation, refused to let others speak to us.

Once he'd worked out who we were, he grudgingly accepted we were 'of the Church', but clarified that our status was 'Excluded'. That was the same status we would have if we'd been caught by the Elders indulging in some terrible sin like murder.

But he was an Elder; his word was law. Other than designated Elders of the Synod, we were not allowed to talk to people. We couldn't set foot inside the Great Church. Couldn't have us tainting everyone and everything. We needed to go through the Ceremony of Shriving before we would be accepted back.

It shocked me so I couldn't think straight.

We'd gone away knowing we would return from the war as sinners, but somehow the practical details like not being able to talk to people hadn't really occurred to us.

There was no point trying to discuss it with Elder Tuominen, or to find out more of what had happened. He felt his argument about our exclusion was irrefutable in Church logic. It meant he had no duty to explain anything to us. He told us we had to wait for the Judge and the Synod to arrive.

He then pointed out this was all a 'grave inconvenience to the community' and left us alone in an empty office.

I had to turn down the gain on my suit amplifiers because of the trembling of my muscles. I was shaking with anger; so angry, the anger seemed to feed on itself.

That anger had been building and building on the journey. Every time I had sat and listed another thought or action I knew would be regarded as a sin in the eyes of the Church in Exile, it had risen another notch. A tiny notch for each, but many, many sins.

The thing was, I'd been warned that I would feel anger on my return.

The darkness that will have crept silently into your soul over the years amongst the Unknowing will struggle against the return of the light. You will feel this struggle as a great anger, so powerful it will strike you dumb.

Maybe.

Or was it a perfectly normal response to the thought of returning to the claustrophobic confines that wrapped themselves around the whole community of Calloway? A normal response to the thought of returning to a regime so strict it would feel like I couldn't breathe? That had gotten unfathomably stricter in our absence?

It didn't strike me dumb, but contemplating returning to live here now felt like I would be deliberately drowning myself.

"This is shit," I said. Another sin for the list, but I was beyond caring. "We went to war for Calloway, at the risk of our lives and our souls, and now we're pariahs."

"We were always going to come back sinners," Bjorn said.

"Sinners. Not *outcasts*."

In a way, we'd come home, and yet we weren't home at all. Home was a memory that no longer existed. In the same way, in the minds of the people of Calloway, we were memories. We weren't the people who'd gone to war for them.

The anger unlocked something in me that I'd been suppressing from the moment Heston told us there was no nav beacon. I'd been going through the motions without thinking about what I was seeing.

Now, it was all coming down like an avalanche. I started *seeing*, and not just looking.

"Maybe it's just Elder Tuominen misunderstanding," Bjorn was saying. "I mean, I can't even remember him from before we left. They all look old, but I think he's new into the Synod. Hasn't had time to really—"

"You're making excuses."

"I guess I am a bit." He put his helmet down on a rickety handmade table. "It's not just the welcome, is it? What's eating you?"

I opened a shutter to the square. The breeze blew in. I knew it would carry the smell of the sea, but as agreed with Bjorn, I was still sealed in my suit.

"The town hall used to have neo-plas windows," I said, gesturing at the empty aperture.

Bjorn frowned. "I don't get your point. If they're starving, everyone's concentrating on food production. They wouldn't have the capacity to repair things."

"We've been away six years, Bjorn. Things don't fail like this in six years. You don't get every window in the town hall broken, let alone every window in Founders' Square. And they replaced them all with shutters, so there *was* work being done."

"What are you saying?"

I pointed at the furniture. "That table and those chairs were handmade to replace manufactured goods. And look out there." I pointed at someone staggering across the square pushing a cart. "That's a handmade cart. Don't tell me every single manufactured cart in town fell apart as well. Those things last generations."

Bjorn sat down. Apart from the helmet, he was still in his suit and the chair creaked alarmingly.

"Then there's the solar array," I said. "There's almost nothing to go wrong with that tech, short of a meteor strike. We didn't see that. It looked like it had just been abandoned."

"You're saying the colony's done this to themselves? That's crazy!"

"Is it? Bjorn, the nav beacon to this system didn't fail. We pinged it with a maintenance override and it came back up working just fine. You understand? That means someone actually switched it off using a communication device from down here, on the planet surface. Then once they'd done that, they switched off their comms. This is deliberate. The colony's gone primitive."

He couldn't deny my argument, but he was still reluctant to follow it. "Why would they?"

"The Church—"

There was a noise outside in the passageway. An argument. Elder Tuominen telling someone that they couldn't talk to us.

A voice answering. Having none of it. *I knew that voice.*

I knew who it was. My stomach clenched.

No!

I wasn't ready for this.

She burst in, ignoring Elder Tuominen stumbling after her and threatening retribution.

Bjorn leaped to his feet. Even though I was sealed in my suit, I cracked my visor's reflector shield so she could see my face. Which meant she could see the tears I could not stop.

My mouth had gone dry. "Mrs. Osmundsen," I whispered.

"My Hal? My boy?" She could see the answer in our faces. *"No! No!"*

All the desperate strength went out of her, and she slumped to the floor like a cast-off coat.

"No. No. No." She cried the word over and over.

We knelt and raised her up. Even if we hadn't been in the suits, she would have weighed nothing. We set her down on a chair, and knelt beside her.

"I am so sorry," I said when she fell silent.

"When?" Her voice was tired.

"A couple of months ago."

She shook her head, tears dropping from her cheeks. "So close. So long since we heard about Solveig and Enoch. Such a precious hope we held."

"You cannot be speaking to them," Elder Tuominen hissed from the doorway. "The Judge is almost here. *Go.*"

"You think I care now?" Hal's mother said and raised her face to look at the Elder.

He gaped in astonishment, and then looked over his shoulder, hearing a noise behind him.

Obviously, the Judge had entered the town hall. I could hear him as he made his displeasure known: "Darkness needs only the slightest weakness to exploit. I see such weakness here."

This couldn't be happening.

But it was. The Judge strode into the room, pushing Tuominen aside. He wore the same clothes as everyone else, but around his neck was the chain of office, and on his fingers he wore the great gold ring.

"Uncle Nikolai." My lungs felt as if they'd seized up; the words escaped from my lips on their own.

"You will address me as 'Judge'," he sneered.

E4. Chapter 4

That evening, I sat in the *Dark Shark*'s larger shuttle which had joined us on the landing field.

Whatever I thought about the risks, they'd insisted on decontamination, and I'd been through the complete routine. Despite that, it felt good to be out of the suit, sitting in a chair, showered and changed into fresh coveralls.

"It's not some airborne pathogen," I repeated.

We were in the cabin, and I was talking with Captain Kumara of the Yorkham colony ship. Shami was with us on a comms link from the *Acid Penguin*'s shuttle.

Kumara nodded. "It seems most unlikely. We've brought environmental test equipment down with us and it can't find anything that would have caused behavior of this nature." He grimaced. "There are, of course, many trace deficiencies on this world, and from what you tell us, the Calloway people aren't getting supplements."

"It's impossible to get a straight answer on things like that from the Judge," I said. Even saying the title and knowing it meant Uncle Nikolai left a sour taste in my mouth. "And, as I said, no one apart from a couple of Elders is supposed to talk to us."

"But Bjorn believed he could get a better feel for what people really think out on the farm where his main family is?" Shami asked.

"We hope so. The Synod can't be everywhere. If they're not around, surely someone in his family will talk to him. But until they do, all we have to go on is what we heard from people like Mrs. Osmundsen."

Kumara poured us more tea. The Yorkham scientists had found a way to cultivate the bushes, even trapped in space as they had been for the last ten years. It was delicious.

"We'll see if Bjorn has more to add when we hear from him," he said. "In the meantime, we have to suppose that this... behavior of the people in the colony is caused by..."

Kumara, normally so smoothly spoken, stumbled over how to phrase his thoughts. He didn't want to insult me.

"It's okay, even Bjorn and I have to agree it's madness," I said, shaking my head. "Can't deny it looks like the Church is to blame."

"A mass psychosis rather than madness, I think, but I still can't quite see how they got from the religion that you described to me before we arrived, to this..." He waved a hand to encompass everything outside of the shuttle. "There's surely nothing in standard religious scriptures that would lead to this."

"Not in the basic Bible, but the Church in Exile has a set of clarifications, called the Meditations." I ran fingers through my wet hair.

"I read some of those," Kumara said. "It seemed to be a lot of aphorisms. I can't say it clarified anything for me."

"I guess it's the way they're taught. But the bit that's important at the moment is the last section. That's the guidelines for the 'Exile' part of the Church's name. The way to spread and prosper through human space."

Both Shami and Kumara kept their silence respectfully. Even in the 1st Frontier, insulated from what was happening in human space, I knew the Church had *not* spread and prospered. Certainly not the way they thought it would back when the Calloway colony had set out.

"You have to understand, most of this is based on what Bjorn and I knew before, what we could see, and a hurried, whispered conversation with Mrs. Osmundsen, who's grieving."

Kumara nodded.

"The guidelines in that last section were always going to be loose," I said.

"Of course," Shami said. "It would have been impossible to anticipate all the various environments which colonies would find themselves in. What did you and Bjorn think happened?"

"Start about seven years ago, before the army recruiters had even arrived. We had been seeing the direction of the atmospheric cycle for a few years. The scientists had been running analyses on the soil and they came out with a report. Basically, the atmosphere changes linked to chemical changes in the soil."

"Which was why you needed to join the army to get the money to buy bio-processors to reverse that change," Shami said.

Kumara looked about to say something, then turned away and frowned.

What was that about?

Something to discuss later.

I continued, "Yeah. What we didn't think about back then was an appendix in the scientist's report saying that our farming methods were accelerating the change."

"By a lot?"

"No," I said. "Almost nothing. I'm sure the old Judge, Yevenst, understood and dismissed it. But after we left to join the war, Yevenst died and my uncle, Nikolai, took over. He'd been clear when we debated it that he didn't agree to the idea of us joining the army, but what no one realized, until he took over, was he was against the whole idea that we should fight this using terraforming tech."

"And his position became more extreme?"

I nodded. "To justify his position against the bio-processors, he started to use part of the Meditations which says basically *don't put your faith in technology, put your faith in the Lord*. But it was never meant like that. Then there are other passages about the environments of planets being different, and having to adapt to them, about not relying on things that come from hi-tech planets."

"All taken out of context and exaggerated," Kumara said.

"Exactly. But the situation on Calloway now is that all off-world tech is banned. In fact, anything that can't be made with what they can build themselves. Even some things built on world using off-world tech are banned. They actually started to tear buildings down, but then they realized everyone has to work full time for food just to survive. They farm by hand, they fish using sails and nets. They're eating more and more local plants."

"Which don't have the right nutrients," Shami said.

"Yes. They're starving, but they won't even accept food from us because it's *tainted*."

Kumara shifted uneasily in his seat. "He must be promising them something at the end of this."

"Oh, yes. When sin is eliminated from the world and the people truly accept the truth of the way, the Lord will provide, then magically everything will be fine."

"I've read up on situations like this, with cults..." Kumara glanced at me to see if I was going to argue the name, but I wasn't. It was the stupidest thing that had finally broken my instinct to defend Calloway—the appearance of Uncle Nikolai with the Judge's chain around his neck. And the ring on his finger. He'd wanted me to kiss it. I hadn't responded the way I'd wanted to: if I was going to be able to do something for everyone on Calloway, then I couldn't tell the leader of the colony to piss off. Instead, I told him I was sealed away under an agreed protocol in case I had an off-world infection.

Bjorn had played along, saying he'd been in isolation. Bjorn had even kissed that ring.

But in those few minutes, I'd realized that coming home was harder than I thought. Either I had darkness in my soul, or I was finally seeing things as they were.

"With cults like these, the outcomes are generally not good," Kumara said. "We need to proceed with a great deal of caution. And I think we should assume that Bjorn will not get much even from his family."

"Why?"

"I understand you all live communally on large farms. The way these cults work is that every farm will have someone who reports to the Synod."

I wondered what would have happened if Bjorn and I had reversed our roles. If I was at my family's Great Farm. Would they refuse to talk to me?

I shook my head to clear it.

"I agree about moving carefully. I guess that means we should find another place to land your people, out of sight of the settlements around Calloway. Shouldn't be hard. There's a whole planet to choose from."

Although only a couple of hundred of them had arrived on the *Dark Star* this trip, the Yorkham colonists were keen to get down to the ground and start building. The Yorkham had been a colony ship, so they had everything they needed. It would just have to be transferred to here from the inhospitable system where their Chang drive had failed. Which meant the *Dark Star* would need to become a ferry.

"You could get the basics going now. We'll ship more of your colonists across as quickly as we can. In the meantime, the colony here and the station at Yorkham need to be viable the whole time. The Yorkham has its hydroponics. We bought enough food from Ensylas to keep you going until the first harvest."

I was thinking aloud, running through my plan with the minor change that the new colony would have to be out of sight of Calloway town and its surroundings.

"We'll obviously have to install the current bio-processor at your colony site," I said. "And we'll have to hope that we can convince the Synod to allow the same tech before everyone there starves."

Kumara was frowning and shifting on his seat again.

"What?"

"We've been examining the bio-processor and my engineers will have no difficulty installing it," he said, speaking reluctantly, "but there's a problem."

"What kind of a problem?"

He looked like he'd bitten a lemon.

"You were originally told you needed eight processors to cover a sufficient area for the existing settlements around Calloway town..."

"Yes?"

"And you doubled up the requirement for a new settlement for us."

"Yes, and even with the Terran credits changed to actual dollars, we don't have enough money for sixteen, I know, but I've created a plan with Thandi, and I'm sure we can do enough trade to cover the additional costs before the soil cycle reaches the point where the bio-processors are essential. Anyway, we'll bring your entire hydroponics section across eventually. And we'll rebuild your station in orbit here—"

"Jan, we can do all of that, but it's not enough."

"I understand," I said. I felt the pit of my stomach fall, but I steeled myself. It was only a spaceship. Nothing against the lives of the colonists. "We'll have to sell the *Acid Penguin*. We don't need two ships, and with that money we'd be able to fill the entire cargo capacity of the *Dark Shark* with bio-processors."

He shook his head, his eyes full of sympathy. Maybe he'd realized what it'd cost me to say that about my ship.

"You don't understand, Jan. It still wouldn't be enough. You'd need a thousand times that amount, a million. Calloway was sold a lie. Those bio-processors, they'll work just fine, but they're not the specification for open planet terraforming. They're designed to work in *biomes*. For the twenty or thirty years this atmospheric cycle lasts, we'd have to do all the farming in huge, sealed biomes. We can't construct those in the time we have, not for two colonies. Certainly not, if after all that, one colony won't eat the food because it's 'tainted'."

E4. Chapter 5

The day after Kumara rained on my parade, I walked into town from the landing strip to meet Bjorn.

Driving the ATV would have been another sin on my list. So was using the comms to talk to Bjorn, wearing my clothes, eating the food in the shuttle, sleeping in the shuttle. Breathing filtered air was a sin, too. I found there was a point where the addition of sins became mathematically insignificant in comparison to the total as far as I was concerned.

But the real reason I walked was I needed the time to think.

Bjorn was waiting in Founders' Square, sitting on one of the fabricated benches that no one had found time to dig up and discard. He looked tired and upset.

"Light calls to light," he greeted me formally, but the words came out dull rather than ironic.

"Gather and prosper." I gave the appropriate response and snorted. "You know, nothing in all my plans over all the years ever came close to the shitshow of coming home."

I'd explained to him the shortcomings of the bio-processors over the comms.

"We were stupid," he said. "Misguided."

"We were *duped*, but that's a different topic. You think we can turn it around?"

"That's really tough, Jan."

"That's why they're paying us so much."

He laughed out loud, briefly. It was a strange sound in the bleak square.

"Are you going to bring Captain Kumara and a delegation to meet the Synod?" he asked.

"No. It'll only get their backs up and they'll stop listening to us."

"They aren't going to listen anyway."

"Maybe. Or not until enough people talk to them like Mrs. Osmundsen does."

"Yeah. That." He leaned forward and rested his elbows on his knees. "They're going to Exclude her."

I shook my head in disbelief. The Excluded had to fend for themselves, like the sole farmer we'd seen on the first trip into the town. The way things were, it was a death sentence.

"All the more reason to get moving sooner," I said. "They can't Exclude everybody. They can't even Exclude a group as small as a single family, because the whole food production process is balanced on a knife edge. If output drops, people would actually die of starvation. Most people know that, so the Synod can't scare everyone."

Bjorn grimaced.

"They managed to scare my family. Apart from Ma."

Mrs. Thorsson didn't scare easily. If they Excluded *her*, they'd lose the whole family. It was the kind of weakness we needed to exploit, if we could explain it to enough people quickly. But they'd got the rest of his family. That was a shock.

But Bjorn sighed. "They need me," he said. "Grandpa can't handle the work any more, not on the rations."

Suddenly my gut went into free fall. He couldn't mean...

"What are you saying?"

"I have to go back to the Farm."

He stood up.

"There's a field needs ploughing. Fruit harvest to preserve. You know. They need me," he said again.

"I need you, too." The words came out before I could catch them. I didn't mean it. We both knew I didn't mean it. "I mean..."

He shook his head.

"It's their *planet*, Jan. Calloway belongs to the Church. They control it. We can't even talk to people without their permission. If we want to live here, to return to our families, we have to accept the Church, and it's all or nothing with them, good and bad. Even Ma has to admit that. We've always known the choices."

He began to walk slowly to the western exit of Founders' Square. He'd be an hour on the road to get home.

I walked with him across the square in a daze.

Yes, we'd always known the outcome of the choices we made six years ago. Back when it was supposed to be three years and it was all theoretical anyway.

The late Judge Yevenst had called us aside on the landing field, and spoken to the five of us just before we boarded the recruiters' shuttle. As always, his speech sounded to me like he was climbing stairs: up one flight, pause, up another, pause, then a third. Rest. Repeat.

"You're going off-planet," he'd said. "You'll be away from the security of the Church, from the eyes and ears and arms of those who would protect you. You have humble hearts and I know you're not too proud to admit you will sin. This is a good start. You must always remember that mercy and forgiveness await on your return, when you will pass through the Shriving and become one with the Church again."

I'd listened quietly, but I was impatient. The shuttle was waiting, and he was going on about stuff we knew. We'd spoken of it.

But then the Judge went on a different tack: "Now, I have a warning I must add. A burden; a heavy truth I must reveal to you, so you should be prepared for what will come."

He walked to and fro with his hands behind his back for minute, gathering thoughts as he did.

"This is hard to understand, I know. The Lord's mercy is absolute, that we may not measure it, yet the Elders must also be vigilant to ensure the safety of the whole community, for we are not individually of the quality that deserves the Lord's mercy."

We stirred and glanced worriedly at each other. What was he talking about?

"You are a good potter, Hal," Judge Yevenst said, stopping in front of him. "Should a pot break, will you repair it?"

"No, Judge."

"Why? Would the pot not be as good?"

Hal squirmed. "No. It can't be completely repaired. It's too difficult. It'll always have a weakness where it broke."

The Judge nodded and threw in a quote from the Meditations as he went on. "*We are of the same clay, yet we cannot be cast aside and another made.* This is the burden I must place on you: you will return, you will be Shrived, you will be accepted back into the Church." He stroked his beard before continuing sadly, "And yet, always, you will bear the scars of your battle with darkness. The fault lines of your human weakness. Your sins that you bore for the good of the community as a whole."

We were stunned. None of us was stupid; we could see what he was saying. The open doctrine of the Church in Exile was that Shriving cleansed the soul as new, and he was telling us that this wasn't true. Our sins would remain, invisible to others maybe, but still there, forever. It was like those stories in the old forbidden books we'd read, how the weapons of evil could wound you such that you were never fully healed.

But the Judge was not finished.

"I pray you are individually stronger than your weaknesses, but as light calls to light, my children, so darkness ever seeks that same darkness in others. You will return and be accepted back, and I pray to the Lord that you will live blameless lives afterwards, but as Elders, we must make rules that help protect you, and ensure that you do not, unwittingly, bring evil to Calloway. After you return, when you seek to marry, to bring children into the Church and to take your place as Elders, I shall assign those you will marry. I make this promise: that I will ensure your spouses are from the most virtuous among us, that they will bring only light to your union, and help protect your soul, and the soul of the community."

My mouth was open. It was too late to back out.

"As the only five from Calloway, it is inevitable you will be thrown together. And you may fall into sin with each other. But always remember this, my children: you will return to the arms of the Church, and here, you are not destined for each other."

He ended with a blessing over our dumbfounded heads and then we were marched onto the shuttle still gaping at each other.

There was no time that day to process that for ourselves. From the moment we set foot on the shuttle, the 1st Frontier began to program us to be good little soldiers.

I never really processed Judge Yevenst's last shocking revelation. I'd come to think of Bjorn as a partner, but always telling myself he could never be anything more than a friend. Always telling myself a relationship with him wasn't a good bet. It couldn't last. Not once we were home. Pretending it was my decision, that he wasn't right for me.

But now we were here, and he was going to leave me to walk back to his family's farm because a field needed ploughing.

If I had always known we would be parted when we returned to Calloway, why did I feel I couldn't breathe?

As it happened, I didn't get the chance to ask Bjorn what he felt.

Uncle Nikolai, *Judge Nikolai*, came out of the Great Church with Elder Tuominen, and called me over.

E4. Chapter 6

He clearly knew about Bjorn's decision. He didn't have to say anything; I could tell by his smug expression.

"We have a lot to discuss," he said. "There is much to be done."

"Yes, Judge."

He'd learned some of that speech pattern from Yevenst.

But, aside from that one last bombshell on the landing field, I remembered Yevenst as a good man. I couldn't remember *any* positive thing about my uncle. How could the one succeed the other as Judge and effective ruler of the whole community on Calloway? How could my dour, negative Uncle Nikolai be the Church in Exile's representative, authorized to rule over us?

Or was this some fault in me? Did everyone else think he was the right person?

I remembered a Calloway that worked together, a community that chose the Synod after open and lively discussion. How could the Synod then end up picking a man the people didn't want?

Elder Tuominen stood with us. He was one of the Synod. A man elected to the post. He clearly had no doubts about Uncle Nikolai.

The people?

My problem was that I couldn't talk to the people. I couldn't find out what they thought. I was Excluded and anyway, the majority of the population was too focused on keeping the crops and livestock and people alive. With so many stuck on the Great Farms, and no electronic communications, it was possible that almost no one on the planet, outside of the town, knew Bjorn and I had come back. I hadn't even been able to get out to the Great Farm where my family lived. They wouldn't know I was here.

Judge Nikolai was talking about getting Captain Kumara to take the ships and find a new planet for the Yorkham colonists to set up on. It was out of the question to allow them to stay here, he said firmly. Calloway was a planet belonging to the Church in Exile, he went on, settled under the terms of the Accords on the Settlement of Systems. It had been continuously occupied, and most importantly, legally, formally and correctly registered back on Earth. To land here without permission would be an act of piracy. To remain in the system without permission would be an act of piracy. His will, as the representative of the Church on the planet, was that they leave the system as soon as possible.

Of course, there was a literal huge distance between the documentation stored on Earth and the implementation or enforcement of the Accords in the depths of the Frontier. And pirates were real threats out here.

I was half listening to him and half thinking about how to wake up the people of Calloway to the death spiral they were in. How to present the information?

Facts and figures? The Church controlled all the numbers.

The shocking view of farms dying that you could see from the shuttle? That was technology and forbidden.

"Yes, Judge," I muttered in response to his request that I tell them of his decision.

That would go down well with Kumara.

The Yorkham people had unpacked the containers brought in the *Dark Star*. Most of them were in the process of creating a minimally viable space station in orbit, and the rest were assembling the shipments for the shuttle to bring down and bootstrap a planetside first base.

Repacking all that? After all the hopes raised, being told they had to find somewhere else?

It wasn't as if finding suitable planets was easy. It involved blind jumping to unmapped systems, a gamble where each spin of the wheel had a thousand more chances of death or failure than success.

And yet, the alternative was to seize Calloway by force. For the good of the people.

Not a solution that would sit well in the long term. Colonies with that sort of history never prospered.

"You seem distracted, daughter."

I snapped back to focus on the here and now. I'd lost track of what he'd been saying.

"I'm..." I cast around desperately. "I'm worried."

"Worried?"

"Yes... the Ceremony of Shriving." The first acceptable thing to say popped out of my mouth.

"Ahh." He nodded sagely. "It isn't as fearsome as it appears. Everyone there, is there to help you."

Everyone...

"Have you been thinking of your path back into the fold of the Church, Janice?"

The Ceremony of Shriving was open to everyone...

"I've thought of little else, Judge, since we returned to the system."

The bigger the sin, the more people, so that each of them might take a little of the burden into their own soul.

"How have you done this?"

My mind was in overdrive, but my mouth knew the right responses.

"As we were taught, in quiet contemplation and the self-knowledge rituals of the Mirror of the Soul," I said.

"What precisely is worrying you?"

"So many sins," I said. Not bad for making it up on the spot.

I needed a congregation. The bigger the better. I needed Judge Nikolai to give it to me.

He was frowning, but it was Elder Tuominen who saved me.

"Of course, it's normally not possible to reach out to all of the Lord's Farms without a lot of unnecessary diversion of resource," he said. "But tomorrow is Harvest Home. There will be some people from every Farm here, and the priest will be holding a thanksgiving."

The Judge was still frowning.

Elder Tuominen surprised me by standing his ground. It became clear that Judge Nikolai had decided that festivals like Harvest Home were a distraction from the more important business of feeding the people. It was actually a good argument, given everyone was starving, but I got the sense Nikolai had come at it from his hatred of seeing people enjoying themselves.

Not all Farms had managed the same success in the harvest, Elder Tuominen pointed out, and the meeting was necessary to ensure all families on all Farms had the same levels of sustenance. It would be a disaster, he said, to lose another Great Farm, like Fettle Bay.

They'd 'lost' Fettle Bay? It was the outermost of the Eastern Reach of the Lord's Farms, the furthest from the town and the other side of the landing field.

"Besides, it's too late to tell people not to come, Judge," Tuominen concluded.

Judge Nikolai conceded gracelessly. "Very well. I will have to speak again at the service. People must realize that they have to master their hungers, for only then they will be open to the Lord's grace."

Tuominen bowed deeply. "I'll inform the priest that there will be a ceremony as well," he said, and left us.

"Speaking of the hungers of the body," Nikolai said, his eyes watching me shrewdly, "you are of an age that your marriage should not be needlessly delayed."

"First I'd need to be taken back into the Church, Judge."

"Yes. Naturally. And you would need to perform your penance. But afterwards. It falls to me to select a husband for you."

"Yes, Judge." There was no other response possible.

"I gave it deep thought last night. I prayed to the Lord, and I believe He has revealed to me one with the purity of soul and the clarity of vision who would be a calmness for your excitability and a safeguard against the darkness. I think you and Zakai Stenstrand will be happy and fruitful."

I ground my teeth. Yes, fruitful all right. I remembered Zakai. That grasping little runt would want me producing babies every year to prove how manly he was.

"You're angry," he said.

Nova! He was a miserable bastard, but Uncle Nikolai was slyly clever and observant. And I still needed his agreement for my Shriving. I couldn't let him put it off. The way things were going there might never be another festival, or a congregation of sufficient size.

There was no point denying my anger.

"I was warned by Judge Yevenst," I said, speaking low. "I was warned that I would feel anger on my return. That it was to be expected that the darkness would struggle at the approach of the light."

He looked at me and I looked at the ground, unable to bring my eyes up.

He had to let me speak to everyone tomorrow. I had to do or say anything to get him to agree.

"I submit to your judgement, and I thank you for your efforts on my behalf," I said meekly.

"You say you submit, but do you accept my choice for you?"

I couldn't say no. "If the Church readmits me, then my choice is made for me, Judge. I will accept the Church in all matters, including your choices for me."

He put a hand under my chin and pushed my face up until I had to look in his eyes.

I thought of suns exploding in the cold silence of deep space. I thought of the terrors of war.

I would not flinch.

I thought of Hal, and Solveig, and Enoch, and their families. I thought of my family. I thought of Bjorn. I would do this thing for them. For all of them.

"I accept your choice," I said.

There was an unending moment of silence before he spoke again. "Good. You are worrying too much about the Shriving. Naturally you will need to perform penances. You will need private instruction by me afterwards, but such things should not be so fearsome as your imagination makes them."

"I understand, Judge. Thank you. There's so much to do before tomorrow," I said. "I must go."

"Yes."

He held his hand out. I'd gotten away with it last time because I'd been in a sealed suit.

No way out this time.

I knelt and kissed the Judge's ring.

He spoke a simple blessing over my head and turned away.

My lips burned as I hurried from the square.

My imagination.

They told stories of it. A liar's lips will burn with hell fire from kissing the ring.

The ring allows the Judge to see into the hearts of the people.

But they'd also said I'd turn out bad if I read all those forbidden books.

I hadn't, had I?

That pain in my lips was anger. Formless anger. It wasn't against the Church, or the people, so much as against how it had gone wrong.

It made me break into a run.

Good. I needed something to work the anger out, and exercise would help.

But I also needed to get back to the shuttle quickly. I needed to query the ship's legal databases, and if that went well, I was going to need to persuade Kumara. I needed every moment I could.

Because for the first time since the *Acid Penguin* had dropped out of Chang space into the Calloway system, I had a plan.

E4. Chapter 7

It was gloomy in the empty Great Church early in the morning.

It had been the first building they'd constructed after landing. They'd gathered all the rocks when they'd cleared the ground for the town. Some of them had been turned into high-density magma and then cooled to create the seamless frame for the building. Smaller rocks created the basis of the walls, held in place by a plasmetal web and sealed with synth-c. They'd torn apart steel shipping containers for the doors. All of the tech to achieve that had been part of the deal with the company that had transported us here. That technology had left with them.

I wondered if the new regime would decree the Great Church had to be rebuilt. How exactly would they go about destroying the existing one? Pick-axes?

Maybe that was the darkness in my soul speaking. A darkness that would stay with me, Shriving or no Shriving.

I was kneeling where I remembered kneeling on my last visit to this church, just before the five of us had left to go to the landing field. The memory was bright and vivid in my mind. Flowers. Sunlight blazing through the windows. A stream of words that I barely heard, but that had lifted us all up. Songs. Blessings. Tears. It had cleansed my soul.

That had all gone.

Try as I might, I could not recapture that feeling from where I was now.

There was just me, and the realization of the enormity of the task. And the certainty that I was going to do this, the knowledge that my mother didn't raise children who did things by halves.

Words came to me. Not prayers. Words from my time in the 1st Frontier.

There being no other course of action open to me...

Gunny had stood beside me, hissing the words into my ear until I had memorized them perfectly.

That had been my second time in a disciplinary? Or was it the third?

She'd gotten me through the hearing and back on duty. Punishment duty, admittedly, but that beat the alternative: full court martial. Possible execution.

She'd been good, had Gunny. I missed her. I really missed her.

There being no other course of action open to me...

I still remembered the speech she'd prepared for me to recite before the disciplinary board. My lips were moving to the words.

"It gladdens my heart to see prayer, daughter, but you have been Excluded."

I hadn't heard the priest come in. I stood hurriedly, guiltily.

"Even the Excluded have their right," I replied. That was straight from the texts. He couldn't deny me.

"Indeed. You are here to summon a Ceremony of Shriving?"

"I am."

He nodded.

It wasn't the same priest from six years ago. With the effect of the famine, I couldn't guess his age, but his shoulders were bent down as if by weight.

"I don't know how many will come," he said. "These are hard times."

"I understand. I need a lot of them."

He peered up at me. "I had heard that you're troubled by the number of sins you feel you bear, my child. There will be enough of a congregation. The Lord provides."

There had to be enough.

"Some of the Elders thought you would leave with the outsiders, the Unknowing. That your place was among them now. Others question that you have spent enough time in contemplation of your sins. I must ask: are you sure? This is your one, last chance to return to the light."

"This is my right, and none may hinder it." Again, straight from the texts.

"Then I give you my blessing, daughter."

He placed his frail hands on my head and prayed.

Strictly according to the texts, he should not have. I was still Excluded.

That gesture on his part certainly didn't reduce the guilt I felt.

When he finished, I escaped to the back where the bell rope hung.

It was part of the ritual of the ceremony, for the supplicant to ring the bell and summon the people to a Shriving. When I'd left, Shriving had been done on allocated days, with everyone alerted in advance by radio messages. People came in from the remote Farms, or attended by video conference.

By today's way of reckoning, that was sinful, and it had all gone.

It occurred to me at that moment: it was that particular decision—that electronic communication with each other was sinful—which had broken the sense of community and cohesion of Calloway.

The bell remained as the only way to summon people to a Ceremony of Shriving. The bell needed to be rung continuously. It was supposed to be a minute for every sin.

I looked up at the rope disappearing into the darkness of the bell tower and shook my head. It seemed fitting I was probably the only person left on the planet with the strength to ring that bell for as long as it took to count my sins out. Apart from Bjorn, who might disagree with what I was about to do.

There being no other course of action open to me...

I took hold of the rope and began.

An hour later my arms ached and my ears hurt.

"Enough, my child." The priest came to me and spoke, his words sounding like whispers. "Beyond a few minutes, the ringing is symbolic anyway. The whole town and all the folk attending Harvest Home from the Great Farms have come in response to your ringing. Everyone. They're waiting. Your Ceremony of Shriving may begin."

I followed him back into the main body of the Church and waited until he sat.

Row upon row of faces. Puzzled. Curious.

My mother and father.

My heart leaped to see them and then plunged. I wanted to go to them, but the rules for the Ceremony were precise and exact.

While I stood at the front and recited sins, no one was allowed to interrupt me.

Not even the Judge.

E4. Chapter 8

I told them what had happened to the five of us as a narrative, step by step.

The little steps—the unbecoming immodesty of communally bathing and sleeping in mixed company, the swearing, drinking to excess, gambling, listening to the Unknowing.

The creeping of darkness into our souls.

All the way to the big steps like killing people.

I listed my sins, and I could see tears of compassion in people's eyes, because they knew I did it for them.

This was still the Calloway I remembered.

It became easier as I went on. The memory of how to talk about religion was returning to me. But it struck me that it was easier to talk because I was describing the person I really was, not the earnest young woman who'd volunteered six years ago. The woman who didn't yet know herself.

Then I changed tack.

"All of these sins and burdens we knew about and anticipated. We accepted that there was no other way to get the payment for the bio-processors which we'd been told were what we needed to avoid the catastrophe that's happening to us right now."

"The Lord will provide," someone called out, and was hushed with the traditional call: "Hear her."

"Yes," I replied. "The Lord will provide. But the texts also say that you may not anticipate the agency of the Lord, lest your pride betray you into folly. Who has known His mind? Who has searched His judgements? Who will question His ways?"

There was stirring at that. Not least from where the Synod sat.

Good.

"But what I was talking about is the sin I did not anticipate. My own sin. My betrayal."

Silence in the Church. My mother covered her mouth and bowed her head.

"The Elders chose five of us. It was more than we could afford, but it was the smallest number the Elders felt could give support to each other. In Judge Yevenst's words: *That in the midst of sin, you will remain pure.*"

I held up my hands, fingers interlocked tightly to demonstrate the way we had been supposed to seal our true selves from outsider influence.

"But I was the flaw, I was the weakness that admitted the darkness. If anyone is to blame, it's me. I *alone* am to blame. Hal and Solveig and Enoch will not return, rest their souls, but Bjorn has. He should be held blameless, separate from me, and re-admitted without concern into the community."

It felt like a cold rock sitting in my chest, but if Bjorn chose to return to Calloway, I couldn't allow what I was doing today to cause him a problem.

I could see Nikolai stirring. If he hadn't been surrounded by the Synod, I knew he'd have broken the rules of the ceremony and called an end to it. He was probably clever enough to suspect where I was heading *wasn't* going to be where he'd thought it was yesterday.

"The Shriving will not work for me as it would for another."

Gasps in the gloomy recesses.

"The texts say the thought is as the deed, and to Shrive me, you will need to forgive sins I have committed since returning and those that I will commit because I have put actions in progress that will be regarded as sins, despite knowing that."

There was worry in the Synod now, and Nikolai needed the restraints of others to stop him from getting up.

That wasn't going to last much longer.

"I don't mean wearing a combat suit, synthetic clothes, eating hydroponic food or using electronic comms, because those aren't sins—"

More gasps.

"I mean that I have put into place actions which will save this community from certain death resulting from the actions of your own Church leaders."

Bedlam.

Nikolai fighting free of the restraints of the Synod and screaming I was darkness incarnate and should be burned to remove the taint I'd brought into the Church.

The Judge, whose word was law, called for me to be executed in a way that the Church in Exile condoned, but which had never been used to our knowledge.

"No!"

My parents leaped to their feet.

They were sitting among the representatives of the neighboring Great Farms. Some of those people stood. They frowned and shook their heads to show they didn't agree with the Judge, but they didn't join my parents in shouting.

Bjorn's mother, Mrs. Thorsson, did.

"No!" she yelled from the back. She began to push her way out of the pews, pulling someone with her.

Heads turned and people stood to see what was going on, even though Nikolai shouted for everyone to be seated. They spilled into the aisles, and my parents had to push through to reach me.

"No." It was a murmur more than a shout. A stirring in the body of the church.

My mother burst free and came to me, arms outstretched.

I could barely see for the tears as she hugged me. My father joined us.

After too brief a moment of hugging, he let go and turned back to the nave. He always had the clearest, strongest voice and he called out in the words of the Ceremony so that everyone could hear: "I share her sin."

Mrs. Thorsson reached me, touched my arm and turned. "I share her sin."

The woman behind her was Mrs. Osmundsen.

"Excluded," Nikolai shouted, but the people were gathered too thickly around us for the Elders to get through, and Mrs. Osmundsen called out over the heads: "I share her sin."

"Hear her!" came from the nave. It was a part of the ceremony and yet it meant much more today.

The community wanted to hear what I had to say, and the true heart of the Church was the people, not the Judge.

So I told them—all the things they didn't know.

I told them the first of the bio-processors were waiting in orbit, and then, I described the fraudulent claims about those bio-processors that had started the whole chain of events. I explained to them that the community *could* be fed, but biomes were required. I told them I hadn't gotten enough bio-processors yet, and I needed to continue with my plans to buy more.

I ignored the shouts that biomes were sinful and so was the food from them, because it wasn't coming from the people in front of me. It was coming from a few in the Synod—Nikolai's supporters.

"But we have no biomes, and no way we can build them," an Elder said.

"We do have a way," I replied, and told them about the Yorkham colony ship, a colony with everything needed to set up on a new world, but no world to go to when their ship's Chang generators had failed.

Which lead to having to tell them about Shami, Bjorn and me taking over the *Karakun* and *Tünjorgo*, my plan to use the renamed *Dark Star* to move the Yorkham people here and use the *Acid Penguin* to work my way back nearer to Earth so I could convert our Terran credits into usable money that would buy the bio-processors that *would* do the job *if* we had the use of the biomes that were part of the Yorkham's colony equipment.

It was a free-for-all. I had to answer questions thrown at me by people, while ignoring the Synod's attempts to wrestle back control. We had to stop several times when people fainted. Some kind soul brought in barrels of water and passed us all cups.

"But we won't have enough for both colonies," someone complained eventually.

I pointed out that the Yorkham had survived for years on the produce of their hydroponics, and that people on Calloway were still surviving, if barely, and besides, I had made plans with Thandi to profit from our trip and so I'd get more bio-processors and biomes.

I could feel the belief growing, so I tried what I knew would be an emotive subject.

"I'm proposing that the first of the Yorkham colonists come down and reopen the Great Farm at Fettle Bay—"

"No!" Nikolai shouted, and the rest of them had become quiet enough that everyone heard.

He climbed the pulpit and held up his chain of office for all to see and acknowledge. "I am the Judge. I have been elected to that position by the rules that were agreed between the Church in Exile and all of Calloway. As the Judge, I have the final say on these matters. Calloway belongs to the Church in Exile, and as their representative, I do not give my permission for these outworlders, these Unknowing, to pollute our lives on Calloway. If in our moment of weakness we allow these outsiders to descend on us, the people of Calloway will gain their meaningless, temporary bodily desires at the expense of their immortal souls." He was shouting now. I half expected him to faint, but I guessed his food rations weren't quite as bad as some. Anyway, I needed to confront this, so I let him go on.

"It is my duty to oppose this," he said. "I forbid it, in the name of the Church in Exile. I demand that these outsiders leave this system that belongs to the Church."

No one spoke out against that. This was his position of strength, and the people might question his absurd definitions of sin, but they wouldn't question his right to speak for the Church in Exile, *their* Church, on the matter of the ownership of the Calloway planet and system.

Every eye turned to me.

Good.

"It turns out, that's not the case," I said quietly. "And you, personally, were the one to throw away the authority to make those decisions."

I thought he *was* going to faint then, his face went so pale.

There weren't police as such on Calloway, but he was about to order the Elders to silence me somehow.

"You see," I went on quickly, "the ownership of a system is granted in the Accords on the Settlement of Systems, held back on Earth. The Accords are legal documents, and they are very clear and precise on the ownership of systems. There is no doubt that the Church in Exile completed the documentation faithfully, and that when the colony arrived on Calloway, as far as any human justice system was concerned, the Church owned this planet and system. There's also no doubt that they charged those people elected as Judges to maintain that ownership correctly."

Again, silence in the Great Church.

"The Accords are also clear and precise on the maintaining of ownership of a recognized colony." I took a printout from my pocket and held it up above my head. "As it says here: At all times, it is the duty of a colony wishing to preserve their ownership of a system to always maintain a functioning navigational beacon, that visitors may approach in safety and be duly informed of the existing ownership."

Nikolai staggered, grasping at the rails of the pulpit to prevent a fall.

"When you switched off that beacon, Judge Nikolai, you failed in your commission to the Church in Exile, and you surrendered ownership of this system."

"No... no. That's not right."

"I'd say look it up on an InfoPad, but you've banned those."

"Lies," he said, licking his lips. "It's all lies, and the texts warn us that nothing good ever comes from lies and liars."

But they weren't listening to him. They crowded around me to find out how this was going to work.

E4. Chapter 9

"We gotta go," I said to Shami in the shuttle. "Things to do, places to be."

I always hated long goodbyes, and I couldn't bear to look at the small crowd who'd gathered to see me off.

"Not going anywhere until I've completed my checks. Talk to Captain Kumara while you wait."

I hadn't had time to do anything other than transmit a brief message via Shami saying the temporary committee on Calloway had agreed to the proposals I'd hammered out with Kumara.

The *Dark Shark* shuttle would be bringing the first Yorkham colonists down today. Of course, they weren't calling themselves that now; they were calling themselves the second wave of Calloway colonists. The system belonged to Calloway, but its control no longer resided in the person of the Judge.

It was going to be a difficult few months while they worked out the details. Details on how the two communities would interact. How the new Calloway town committee was going to reconcile itself with the former administration, who were trying to Exclude everyone.

While that went on, the former Yorkham colonists would reopen the Great Farm at Fettle Bay, and install the biomes and bio-processors as quickly as I could deliver them. As more colonists arrived, they would start a new town called Yorkham on the far side of Fettle Bay.

Those Calloway people who did not wish to mingle with the Unknowing would never need to. The Great Farms neighboring Fettle Bay would handle distribution of food and essentials.

What would happen at the end of the atmospheric cycle? I didn't know. There were a million details to be agreed on, but it was already starting to work.

Kumara came in on the comms and Shami routed it through to me.

His opening question was: "Did you get as far as discussing the threat of pirates with them?"

"Yes," I replied. "But they don't understand. They hear the words like 'drop a rock', and they understand that a large meteorite forced out of stellar orbit and impacting the planet would kill everybody, but they can't grasp that there are people who would do that, so it's not a real situation for them. Even when I told them about rebuilding your station in orbit here to protect them and open trading possibilities, it's about as real to them as if I were describing the plot of a holovid."

"At least they didn't blame you for the pirates," Kumara said. "And in future, the kids will understand."

"Yes, the next generation."

This generation was going to be too frantic with work to be able to worry. Kumara's people were building a defense system based on the parts of their space station they'd brought with them and the *Dark Star*'s shuttles. The *Dark Star* itself would be racing back and forth between Calloway and Yorkham, bringing more bits and colonists.

Everyone hoped that by the time any pirates arrived in the system, they'd be ready.

"Your ship and your crew..." Kumara said, and hesitated.

"Yes?" I knew there were going to be problems.

"Most of the crew have elected to stay with the *Dark Star*."

I'd scared people. My fault. The tricks I'd pulled trying to kill Maykn were the sort of risks that I took for granted after six years of fighting Earth's wars. Not the same for the temporary civilian crew I'd picked up. The *Dark Star* would be safer. It was a bigger, more powerful ship, and more importantly, *I* wasn't in command.

"Talking to them," Kumara said, "it seems that it's common for merchanters to pick up crew from stations they visit."

"Nice to know. Who have I still got?"

He cleared his throat.

"Thandi and her husbands. They're reasonably skilled in cargo handling and medical. They have basic training in life support systems and hydroponics. Of course, they'll be handling most of the actual trading in stations that you do."

"Okay. And?"

He cleared his throat a second time. "And Prasad."

My cargo boss.

"And me," Shami said with a grin.

"That's it? So no engineer?" That was a *bad* loss. Not that Guillaume had been an actual engineer, but it had felt comforting to have *someone* down in the engine room. "You can't loan us one?"

"No, I'm sorry," Kumara said. "With taking a space station apart in one star system, building it in another star system, creating a defense, constructing biomes on the ground, installing and maintaining the bio-processors... I haven't got enough as it is. I did divert a team while we were waiting. They installed some better weapon systems on the *Acid Penguin*, and they checked your Chang generators and engines."

He paused and my heart sank.

"More bad news?" I said.

"Not as such... but it would be better to limit your jumps. The two you did from Ensylas to here were too far. You'll need three or more on the way back. And you'll need to find an engineer as soon as you can."

"Okay." Frustrating, and it would slow us down, but I could live with that. I tried to remember which star systems were closer that I could use to head back to Ensylas. Preferably one which had signed the Piracy Accords, so we could get rid of the ones we'd captured and get paid for it.

I'd have to access the navigation computer as soon as I was back onboard my ship.

My ship.

Fully, legally registered by Calloway, and licensed to act both as a mechanter and as the official Calloway Navy Anti-Piracy Unit, commanded by Lieutenant Commander Skelling.

I laughed. Part sheer joy of my own ship, part sheer ridiculousness.

"What?" Shami said.

"A navy comprising one Lieutenant Commander and one beat-up old ship."

"And a couple of lieutenants. We could make Prasad a bosun, too. Think we're out of luck recruiting Thandi's harem though."

"A couple of lieutenants?" I asked. "Who's the other? Thandi?"

The hatch banged open. A great oaf with sweat streaking down his shaved head and his combat suit flashing warning lights showing almost no power remaining crashed into the seat next to me.

"Damn, but I'm out of condition," he said. "Lieutenant Bjorn Thorrson reporting for duty, ma'am."

My mouth moved for a couple of seconds before I managed: "I thought you were staying."

"Yeah. Then I remembered I promised Gunny I'd look after you. She'd give me hell if she found out I'd let you escape."

"Asshole." I punched him on the arm, hurting my knuckles on his armor. "But your family? The Great Farm? Not enough people to work?"

"Funny that. There's been an outbreak of common sense, following some idiot shooting her fool mouth off in the Great Church. They've done what I always said they ought to do: close down the neighboring Farm and bring all those families to our place, which has plenty of room and much better soil. They don't need me anymore."

He wiped his face and sniffed dramatically. "I was all upset, but I'm over it."

"Strap in, children, takeoff in thirty seconds," Shami said.

"That's ma'am to you, Lieutenant," I said. "Or Captain."

"Aye, aye, Captain Ma'am."

We were all laughing as we took off. I wasn't sure why. The way home hadn't gotten any shorter.

E4. Chapter 10

Aside from personal reasons, as it turned out, I was *very* happy to have Bjorn with me at our first stop out of Calloway.

I'd opted to keep away from dead star systems, and the nearest inhabited system on our path back to Ensylas was a small colony called Endellion. There was nothing in the ship's database about them.

Our engines and Chang generators were fine, as far as we could tell, and we'd have transited straight through, but the navigation beacon held a message that intrigued me.

It was a standard arrangement at many systems. The beacon transmitted the system's registration, all the navigational data, updates on star charts and so on, but there was a secondary channel. Usually the second channel was full of marketing for the system, explaining why their fruit or mechanized goods were the best in this sector of space. This one had a single message on it.

Require passage to Ranier system, with cargo less than 30 cubic meters, query Trader Jessop on secure channel for highly advantageous rate.

I'm the curious type; I queried. Trader Jessop came back with a rate to be paid in Terran dollars that would cover half the cost of a new bio-processor. On top of that, he offered five percent of profits on his cargo, without being willing to discuss what it was. He made a point of saying it was not a 'live' cargo and had no support requirements. Which made me even more curious.

Ranier *was* in the general direction of Earth from Ensylas.

It *was* a lot of money, and we *were* trying to be merchanters.

We could do with a top up on fuel.

So despite feeling uneasy, a week later, we docked at a space station even smaller than Orion's Wheel in Ensylas.

Once the engines powered down, our comms system was finally allowed to connect to their general feed, rather than the dedicated Space Traffic Control.

Data flooded in.

The video feed from the concourse was like looking at a human zoo.

Every different style or mode I'd seen while being transported around human space by the army was present. But flicking through the video feeds of ships' berths that were active showed every single one of them locked tight and guarded.

There were no offices visible. Business seemed to be carried out on the concourse or in rough bars. Some of the 'bars' were no more than a canopy that stretched out into the concourse.

No police in sight.

"Hey! My kinda place," Bjorn said.

Despite his words, the sense of unease was growing.

"Just leave?" Shami asked.

I bit my lip and shook my head. "That business is too tempting."

"Got to wonder why no one here is willing to take it, though."

"Let's find out. I am officially scrapping task 2."

"Which was?"

"Find an engineer. I'm not trusting anyone from here. Including our potential client."

"What about supplies?" Thandi asked. We'd left our food on Calloway. We'd been eating the tasteless produce of a minimal hydroponics setup that the Yorkham crew had installed.

"Maybe. Bjorn and I will go out to contact Trader Jessop. If we think there may be something worth buying, we'll come back and fetch you."

∞ ∞ ∞ ∞ ∞

It was clear that crew went dockside on this station with weapons, so I felt much better that Bjorn and I had our military TAWs in holsters strapped to our legs. Anyone looking at us would have no doubt about the power of the weapons we were carrying. We were also wearing impact vests underneath big jackets, and we'd both opted for the style of having a black bar sprayed across the eyeline. We looked like trouble.

We fitted right in.

Halfway across the concourse and Bjorn's confident stride faltered. He was wearing a comms link earbud, and he touched his ear.

The threat of a frown appeared on his brow.

"What?" I asked, when he finished listening.

"Shami update. Seems Endellion isn't a signatory to the Piracy Accords." His eyes started to scan the concourse in military mode.

"It's very small. Maybe…"

He shook his head. "Dock gate one down from us. People in cages," he replied.

I gestured back at the *Acid Penguin's* berth as if we were having an argument about something inconsequential, and took the opportunity to look back.

I saw them.

I'd seen small trains of cargo pallets being moved dockside on the station's video feed, but the cameras were fixed high above the surface. The tops of the rolling stock were blanked off. But down at this level, I could see Born was right. They were cages and there were people in them.

"Station prisoners?"

But I could see there was no uniform, no signs that these were official prisoner transports. They were just cargo, ready for loading on a ship.

Trader Jessop's comment came back to me—not *live* cargo. He meant not slaves.

I looked around. There were more of them, some not even in cages, just chained together.

My heart was suddenly in my mouth. Breathing came hard and I could feel my pulse pounding in my head.

"You okay?" Bjorn asked.

"See that bar straight ahead? The Dark Horse?" I said.

"Yeah. Why? What's up?"

"Keep your eyes on it until I say. Do not look around."

Bjorn's forehead was creased in his famous frown. The one that usually ended with him going full berserker.

"What's up?" he repeated.

I counted to three.

"We're about to have a public argument, and return to the ship. This is very important, Bjorn. We are going to walk back to the ship. Everyone will see we have a minor problem. Not their business. We are *not* going to call attention to ourselves, and we are *not* going to do anything else. Whatever we want to do. Agreed?"

"Back to the ship. Acting out. Nothing else. Got it. Can I turn around? What the nova have you seen?"

"Yes. Turn and look at me."

He obeyed.

I got hold of his arms, acting as if I was trying to restrain him from doing something.

I was.

"What the nova, Jan?"

He *was* angry now, getting more angry by the second.

"Keep looking at me. You are going to *pretend* to be angry, but you are going to be *calm*, whatever the provocation."

"Got it."

I gripped tighter.

"When I tell you, one quick glance and straight back to me." I waited until he nodded. "Over my left shoulder. There's a line of slaves in chains. Third from the end."

His face went blank and then his eyes bulged.

"Eyes! Eyes here," I said, my fingers digging frantically into the muscles of his arms. "Now!"

He did it. He looked back at me. He was furious; trembling with the urge to do something.

"It's..."

I nodded. "Gunny. Her ship back home must have been taken."

Something changed then. I'd seen him roaring mad, berserker. I'd seen him charging and shouting and throwing people around. I couldn't hold him when he got like that. Not a chance.

But now he began to go pale with anger, deathly pale, and I hadn't seen him like that before.

"We need a plan," he said, forcing the words out.

Episode 5
Break the Chain

E5. Chapter 1

"Stop!"

Back in the *Acid Penguin,* and Bjorn was ready to suit up in combat armor and go assault the ship where Gunny was being held as a slave.

"We can't get this wrong," I said, keeping a grip on his arm. "It's too important. You know the first task of an operation is always *recon.*"

"You mean to go back out there like that?" Thandi said.

We'd just seen Gunny in a line of chained slaves, being herded towards one of the ships, and no one on the concourse had blinked. They hadn't even turned to look. It had looked like business as usual on this orbital station in the Endellion system.

"We're playing it cool," I said. "Not attracting attention. We came in for a meeting with Trader Jessop. Got a call as we left the ship, had to come back. Fixed the problem. Now, we go back to what we were doing. Pretend everything is normal while we gather intel."

"Eh! And what if they're part of the same pirate fleet as Maykn?" Thandi said. "What if they're just waiting for the opportunity to jump us? We should leave immediately, while they're busy."

"No. Not leaving Gunny," I said. "Those ship names..."

"One of the ships was the *Korçë,* and the other the *Yli Bezan.* Neither of them appears on any list we have," Shami said. "Doesn't mean we know every name of every ship that runs with Maykn."

"No, but even if they *are* his friends, it's unlikely he's been able to tell them. Bjorn hit the *Sambuk* a couple of times with the pulsar. Maykn's gone somewhere to repair. It's vanishingly small odds that these ships have just come from wherever he went."

A small risk, but not zero, as Gunny herself used to say.

Bjorn still wanted to gear up and go in with weapons blazing. I pointed out that we didn't have enough ammunition for more than a few minutes' fight, and we didn't have any idea what those ships were like, or how well armed the pirates were. Combat suits were being sold in the market on

Ensylas. There was nothing to say that wasn't the same all the way around the Frontier.

He grumbled that learning to use the suits was another matter, and I had to admit he had that point.

I set Shami and Thandi to finding out whatever they could about the *Korçë* and *Yli Bezan*.

Then we were back out on the concourse, striding toward a bar that Trader Jessop had suggested for a meeting, with my stomach rebelling at the thought of Gunny and others in chains. There were no more slaves in view this time, but I forced myself not to look to either side.

Both Bjorn and I had earbud comms in place now, and in addition to the two ships, Shami was updating us with anything she could find about this pirates' nest we'd stumbled into.

"Not good news," Shami said. "The spoke where they've taken the slaves has been cleared of any other traffic. There's only the *Korçë* docked. It's so big they couldn't fit anything more than a small in-system ship anyway." She hummed. "Good news, maybe; they have no scheduled departure on the boards. We should have time."

I could hear Thandi in the background calling her attention to something.

Shami spoke again. "More bad news. I'm looking at the concourse video feeds. The entrance to the *Korçë*'s spoke has been sealed and they have guards posted outside. I'm looking at schematics for the station. I'm sure you can get past the guards on the gate easily enough, but then there's just the elevator and the stairwell to get to the dockside level. And even then, if it's like our dockside, it's all blast-sealed between the stairwell and the dock. There's no way in without a huge fight."

"There's always a way in," I muttered.

"We're getting eyeballs from some of these people," Bjorn said.

"They're sizing us up," I replied. "No law enforcement around. Just don't look like easy pickings."

Bjorn ostentatiously resettled his TAW in its thigh holster. Whether or not the people looking us over could tell what the weapons were, they looked impressively bulky.

"Like you say, we're going to need more ammunition," Bjorn said. "I can't say this is my favorite place, but I'll bet we can buy some here."

"Good point, I guess. Like you, I don't much like the idea of spending money here, but the bigger problem is I don't see any stores open."

On any other space station I'd visited, the concourse was lined with stores and bars which used the purpose-made spaces in the structure of the station itself. In this station, what we were seeing was that those spaces were sealed off from the concourse by heavy emergency shutters.

There were 'bars' and 'restaurants' touting for custom, but some of them were little more than trolleys wheeled out onto the concourse with some plastic chairs and tables. They didn't look inviting.

The place Trader Jessop had said he'd meet us was called the Bar With No Name. It was the real thing, built into the structure of the station. Its sign was as tall as the concourse sidewall, about thirty meters high. It was a dark silhouette of a man wearing a long coat and a hat with a wide brim, the sort people wore on planets where the sun was a problem. He was smoking a cigar. His coat had been pulled back on one side to display an antique handgun in what looked like an animal-hide holster hanging from the man's belt.

I was about to wonder aloud how this bar got to be open, when I saw the answer.

There was a guard standing at the door.

"We're here to see Trader Jessop," I said to him.

"Say your ship name and personal names," the man said, holding up an InfoPad toward me.

"*Acid Penguin*," I replied, checking the voice transcriber got the name right. "Jan and Bjorn. What's that for?"

"Ship's name for credit check. And your names so we know how to label the body bags if there's trouble."

He jerked his head back, indicating another guard standing inside the bar. The man was carrying a Renshaw scatter gun, held across his chest. We didn't use them in the 1st Frontier, but we knew about them. They were horrendously inaccurate, and the rounds had little genuine penetrative power, but if you wanted to make a mess inside a building and didn't care who died, they were the go-to weapon.

"Understood," I said. "We're not here to start anything."

The guard sucked his teeth noisily. "Don't much care who starts it. We finish it."

His pad had logged our data. It beeped to show confirmation we had entered a credit with the station. The guard stood to one side as the outer airlock door opened.

"Nice place," Bjorn muttered. "One by the door, two in the galleries that I can see."

He was spotting guards with Renshaws.

"Can't have many more of them," I said. "It's not economical."

He grunted. "Depends on what they charge for their beer."

The door cycled slowly and eventually let us in.

It wasn't as dark inside as it had looked, but quite busy and I couldn't see anyone waving at us, so I stopped one of the staff.

"Do you know a Trader Jessop?"

"Sure," she said. "Middle of the gallery level, front of the building." She indicated upward with her spare hand.

We climbed the stairs and a man waved us over to a booth.

"*Acid Penguin*'s crew?" he asked, in a polite, careful baritone.

"Jan and Bjorn," I said, not ready to give anything else away. "I guess you're Jessop?"

"Oliam Jessop, at your service." He bowed. "Welcome to Endellion's orbital station. Please, join me."

He waved for one of the serving staff.

"A drink? Something to eat?"

"Mr. Jessop, the sooner we're gone from here, the happier we'll be."

"Ah. The visitors on spokes 2 and 4. Understandable. Give me a minute to explain." The waiter approached. "The salt beef special for everyone, and a bottle of the Tallina red, please."

Bjorn and I traded glances.

It wasn't that we couldn't finish a bottle of wine quickly, it was just that we tended not to be invited back to places where we did that. But if we wanted Trader Jessop's money, I guessed we had to start by having a meal with him, and drink wine from a glass. More important, he might be able to provide us with the information we were going to need to get Gunny freed.

I sat back, and Bjorn nodded agreement. We'd stay and behave for the moment. The trader had to know things about the pirates that wouldn't appear on the data banks.

Another waiter laid our places, with table mats and cutlery and balloon-shaped glasses. I couldn't remember when I'd had that kind of service before. This was not the sort of place I normally ate in, and surprising for such a small, out-of-the-way station.

The waiter clearly knew Jessop and they exchanged good-natured comments about the wine he'd ordered for us.

When we were alone again, Jessop's attention returned to us. His fingers tapped a brief nervous drumbeat on the table, quickly stilled. I kept silent, taking the opportunity to look closely at him.

He looked about forty years old, in good shape. Steady gray eyes. Short sandy hair combed straight back. Neatly trimmed goatee and mustache. Tense body. His clothes were formal and businesslike. More like some kind of planetside professional, like a lawyer or a doctor, than an orbital station trader. But his jacket didn't hang so straight under his left arm. I guessed he had a weapon there. His hands looked out of place, too; they were hard-working hands. They were scrubbed clean now, but I'd lay odds there was work grime under those nails more often than not.

"What you're seeing out there isn't the real Endellion," he said. He nodded with his head to indicate the concourse. "This is a tiny station in a backwater system. They don't have the means to stop unwelcome visitors."

"Cut the crap and call them pirate slavers," Bjorn said.

Jessop's eyes twitched left and right, but he didn't disagree.

"You're saying those two come in here and do what they want?" I said. "Everyone gets out of their way?"

He nodded again. "They call once they emerge in the system, so the station has a few days' notice. The police and administration disappear into shielded rooms. Most of the operating traders drop the emergency barriers over their shop fronts. No one challenges them. Most exhibit a sort of blindness: don't look, can't see. The brave or desperate try their luck trading on the concourse." He waved his hand to indicate the bar. "And places like the Clint hire extra guards."

"I thought this was called the Bar With No Name?"

"Officially. Everyone calls it the Clint, though the reason for that seems to be lost in time."

"So those pirates come here to buy supplies?"

"Partly that, and partly this is more convenient than meeting in space. They need a place to transfer what they've stolen in their attacks, including the slaves. You see, these pirates, they have to operate as pairs—"

"We're familiar with pairs of pirate ships," I said. "The reaver to ambush merchanters and sell slaves in systems that allow it, the pirate merchanter to sell the stolen goods in systems that abide by the accords on human trafficking."

Jessop looked startled and then his face went carefully blank.

"We're not slavers," Bjorn said. "In fact, we have a problem with them, and they—"

I interrupted before he could spill the information that we had to be especially careful around slavers. "Are you going to be able to get your cargo to the dock with them around?"

"Can I expect assistance from your crew?" he countered.

"Handling and security once the cargo is delivered to shipside in the spoke," I said. "We're not coming out to fight a battle on the concourse."

Jessop's eyes narrowed, but he nodded. "They don't mess with the cargo delivery system. I'll keep everything off the concourse, so it'll come from the sub-level monorail straight up the spoke."

From his words, I guessed this station had the same bulk cargo delivery mechanisms as Orion's Wheel. Good. The amount he was talking about would be difficult to handle on trolleys in the concourse. A nova-cursed nightmare if there were pirates who could act with impunity. Why bother to take it in space if you can steal it on the station?

The image of that started me thinking.

What if...

Jessop had paused to let a couple of waiters serve us our meals. When they left, he spoke as he poured out the wine.

"As I say, the pirates don't mess with the monorail, but they do watch the trading boards. They might come sniffing around your dock if they see that shipment being loaded."

"They won't cause a problem at *our* dockside," Bjorn said grimly. "But what's appearing on the manifest that's going to draw their attention?"

"The manifest will not give details of my shipment, but the size itself will attract attention."

I sat back, chewing on the tastiest piece of salt beef I'd ever had.

"Well, that's good news," I said, chasing it down with a swallow of wine, "because that'll work neatly with my plan."

Bjorn choked on his salt beef, and I had to thump the poor boy's back.

E5. Chapter 2

It was a very productive meal with Trader Oliam Jessop.

At the end of it, we had a deal agreed for shipping him and his cargo to Ranier, but even better, we had a mine of information on the pirates. So much that I wondered how a station trader knew it.

He confirmed what we already knew: the *Korçë* was the reaver. Again, we already knew it was bigger than the *Dark Shark*, but from Jessop's description, it was faster and more powerful as well. It was a genuine fighting ship. The *Acid Penguin* would have no chance in a space battle.

It wasn't much less formidable while docked.

From the supplies he knew they'd ordered, Jessop suspected they had a large crew of around eighty. They operated under discipline. The crew were only allowed out onto the concourse in groups of a dozen, and only for a limited time. They drank in concourse bars, ate at the restaurants and paid. They didn't wear uniforms, but they were easy to spot, armed and quick to threaten violence if they were approached in the wrong way. The gate to the spoke they were docked on was always guarded, and the guards changed shifts every couple of hours.

Sounded like it had to be a military unit gone rogue.

From the number of slaves moved across from the merchanter to the *Korçë*, and the stolen cargo moved in the opposite direction, it was a reasonable guess they were about to split up. The *Korçë* would visit a system where they could sell the slaves.

The other ship was the merchanter and they would be heading to somewhere like Ensylas to trade the stolen goods. The *Yli Bezan* was a much smaller ship, about the size of the *Acid Penguin*. It had a crew of a dozen or so, and they were currently engaged around the clock in loading up all the cargo that had come out of the *Korçë*.

Jessop told us that the pair of them used Endellion as a regular stop, taking up to a week to exchange cargos and resupply. Whenever they visited, not only did the shops close down, but even ship and station maintenance stopped. The pirates designated which spokes they wanted, and any other visiting ships were moved to other spokes. Traders stayed behind their barriers, although they did sell supplies to the pirates. Deliveries arrived in trolleys on the concourse or through the monorail system, but everything was handled by the pirates from then on. No one from the station was allowed in either spoke where they were docked.

The pirates had no contact with any of the officials on the station beyond issuing curt orders to Space Traffic Control, but they limited their violence against the station. They even paid docking fees. Jessop's opinion was that they valued this place for its convenience, and wanted to keep using it.

The trader must have known he was being pumped for information, but apart from his narrowed eyes, he gave no sign of it.

"So, Oliam," I said when we'd reached the end of his information, "all this money you're offering for transporting your produce to Ranier... would you like to make some of it back?"

The eyes narrowed even more. "I'm listening."

"We don't want our crew to come out and trade on this station, but we do want supplies. We'll need them in the same time it takes to load your cargo, and we want that to happen quickly. Very quickly. I think you're the sort of person who can make that happen."

He grimaced, but didn't complain when I set up a connection between his InfoPad and Thandi, back on the ship.

As they haggled, Bjorn and I made our own list. When Thandi declared herself satisfied and logged off, I sent our list through to Jessop's pad.

His lips pursed as he read it through, as if he was trying not to smile.

"I see you're intent on starting a small war," he said. "I trust that will be *after* you've delivered me to Ranier."

I finished my wine.

"I'm not going to make any promises like that."

"Why should I risk my life then?"

"Because you're in a nova-cursed hurry, otherwise you wouldn't be hanging out an advertisement on the navigation beacon. Because whoever you *were* going to ship with hasn't come through or has backed out. Because common sense would tell you to keep your business secret until the pirates have gone, but for some reason, you can't. Because there's no one else who's going to come along soon who will take you to Ranier, and if there were, they'd have exactly the same problem keeping the pirates away while you load your mysterious, valuable, urgent cargo on board right in front of them." I leaned forward and stared him in the eyes. "And finally, because if you fill that shopping list we gave you, what we *do* promise is that the pirates *won't* be a problem."

He sat back and looked coolly at us.

"You're ex-mil, aren't you?" he said.

Bjorn nodded slowly.

Jessop picked up his wine glass by the stem and twisted it thoughtfully in his fingers. "Now I may have heard that there are some military personnel in that last shipment of slaves. Something about the army using civilian freighters to transport demobilized Frontier soldiers back to their home systems. Easy pickings." He finished his wine and went on. "Military personnel are prizes."

Bjorn's frown was back.

I laid a hand on his arm. It wasn't one strange trader with a mysterious cargo we needed to be concentrating on. It was Gunny.

"Prizes?" I asked. "How's that?"

"Some of them end up joining the pirates. They bring useful skills to such enterprises." He shrugged. "If they don't join, they fetch good prices as strong, healthy slaves."

Bjorn's hands clenched under the table, but he was still in control.

"What you may have heard, may be correct," I said.

Jessop was watching Bjorn, and I thought I knew why.

He was an odd man, this smart, well-spoken trader out on the wild Frontier. A man accustomed to evaluating risks. I reckoned he was assessing whether Bjorn was going to go berserk at the wrong time and get us all killed.

Bjorn understood. He consciously relaxed and leaned back in his seat.

Good man.

Jessop probably thought we had a ship full of soldiers or mercenaries, and we were the only reasonable option to get him to Ranier for whatever urgent business he had there. That message he'd put on the navigation beacon was desperation. The pirates were evil, not stupid. They'd be wondering what he had that needed to be in Ranier so quickly.

If we moved it while they were in dock, they'd come looking.

I was depending on it.

"I get that these supplies will take a while to purchase and deliver," I said. "How long?"

"On the contrary, your munitions, the evac chute and maneuvering packs will be at your dockside in a couple of hours. Your food supplies and my main cargo will be ready to load immediately after that." He gave me a lingering stare. "If you can handle it."

"We can. Payment for the munitions will transfer to your account the moment we have them. I will then send you a message. I have some precise requirements about how the remaining deliveries need to be arranged and presented. For instance, the food supplies will arrive by sealed trolley on the concourse. They will be guarded by some gentlemen with Renshaws, like the guards here in the Clint, who you will have hired to look like guards. Meantime, you will arrive with your cargo, on the monorail. You will obey instructions and you will not interfere with my crew's loading process." I matched his stare. "If you can handle it."

A trace of a smile slipped across his face as he stood.

"I'd better be about my business."

E5. Chapter 3

It was over two hours later, T-10, ten minutes from the formal start of my plan, and the sweat was running down my body as the combat suit struggled to cool me.

Bjorn had no problems with my plan, but everyone else did, Jessop included. So many critics.

Luckily, once events start to roll, they got a momentum and it would have taken much more to stop things from happening than it had to start them.

It was scary stuff.

I knew the plan wouldn't survive contact with the enemy, like damn near every military operation Bjorn and I had ever been involved in, but there was nothing we could do about *that* in the planning stage. When that countdown clock hit zero the plan would be set in motion, and we had no way back. Only forward.

If we were going to get Gunny back, there was no other option I could see. There was no way the *Acid Penguin* stood a chance of fighting the *Korçë* once it had undocked. We wouldn't even be able to catch up with it. Not that I thought they were going to undock. There was someone over there on spoke 4 who was watching us, just as we watched them. They wanted to know what Trader Jessop was shipping and they knew we were displayed on the trading boards as the designated shippers.

T-8.

Gunny's voice seemed to whisper in my ear: *There being no other course of action open to me...*

Despite that meaning we had to go up against a pirate reaver with a crew of unknown size, with unknown weapons, on a ship whose internal layout we didn't know and on station with innocent bystanders...

Yes. No other course of action open.

We'd done what we could. Our spoke, number 3, was now cleared of stationers. We looked and acted like pirates, so that had been the easy part.

Now, everyone was in position and ready, which for Bjorn and me meant we were in combat suits, crouched like fleas on the back of the whale that was the pirates' reaver ship.

T-6.

Jessop's first delivery had come right on time. Bjorn and I were as well armed as when we'd been in the 1st Frontier. The maintenance crew maneuvering packs had jetted us across from the *Acid Penguin* to the *Korçë* with none of the drama from our last space flight, which had been powered by failing fire extinguishers. We'd positioned the explosives Jessop provided based on reasonable guesswork about how the *Korçë*'s propulsion systems worked. We had the largest capacity emergency evacuation chute in its packed state, but ready and waiting for its part in the plan.

Of course, just setting off explosions to disable the *Korçë*'s engines would leave us with a large, pissed-off crew of pirates, with us on the outside and them on the inside of what looked to be the battle armor of a former military ship.

I had a plan for that too.

T-4.

"I have movement on the concourse." Shami's voice came through the comms system. "The emergency doors on a store half an arc away are rising."

"That's got their attention." The other voice was Thandi's, and I could hear the stress in it. She was not cut out for fighting. "I can see the guards on spoke 4 getting agitated. One of them is speaking into a comm."

"Good," I said.

"Nova!" Shami swore. "Got a connection from Jessop coming in. Wants you. Patching it through on channel 5."

I could hear the click and hiss of a relay as I switched channels.

"What, Jessop? We're busy."

"Understood. Minor amendment. Get all your crew involved in loading the monorail cargo. I understand you're trying to lure the *Korçë*'s crew out. Leave that to my people. You get my cargo loaded quicker."

"Your *people* are supposed to be only for show," I said. "We have two minutes."

"I assure you they're not for show. Go with it, Skelling. Your crew has to do miracles with loading as it is."

I cut back to channel 1. "Shami? You heard that? What do Jessop's guards on those trolleys look like?"

"Like they mean business," Shami replied. "They have a concourse truck to pull the trolleys just emerging, and I can already see four guys in impact vests with Renshaws."

Back to channel 5. No other options now; I had to trust him.

"Don't mess it up, Jessop. Get all those containers inside our spoke. Make a barrier with them inside the entrance. Send just two containers up to the dockside level on the elevator and then jam the elevator open with them."

"Just as I thought. Got it."

"And then follow orders." I cut him off and switched back. "Thandi, everyone onto cargo loading. Leave the fighting to Jessop." I could hear her relief as she ordered her husbands back to the hold to help Prasad with loading. It did make sense if Jessop's people could do their bit.

If they could.

"Shami, update."

"The trolleys are moving across the concourse at speed. I've put the Jessop monorail shipment up on the boards, and the train is moving, so *Korçë* will be aware. ETA 5 minutes. Nothing from the *Korçë* yet, but their spoke gate is now open." She paused. "Wait one."

A wash of static. The station spun on, still unaware of what was about to happen.

Shami was back, speaking in a rush: "We have two squads from the *Korçë*, armed and wearing impact vests. About twenty of them. They're running down the concourse now. Jessop's trolleys are entering our spoke. Station knows something is up. People are getting off the concourse in a hurry."

Good.

T-0. We'd arrived at the point at which I had planned for Thandi's husbands to twist the *Korçë*'s tail by firing weapons at them.

Now it was down to Jessop's people to do that. I needed the *Korçë* crew to be so angry that everyone from their ship came down the concourse to teach the upstart *Acid Penguin* a lesson.

Shami's rapid updates drew the picture for me.

Jessop clearly understood what was necessary: as the last of the trolleys tried to enter the crowded spoke entrance, a half-dozen of his men came back out and started to fire their Renshaws into the squads from the *Korçë*.

Those squads' impact vests saved their lives, but they didn't prevent injuries.

Under the barrage, half the twenty people from the *Korçë* were on the floor with wounds in less time than it took for the first half-dozen of Jessop's men to change over with the second half-dozen. The second set of Renshaws completed the job.

The pirates were so surprised that someone was willing to fight back, it broke them. They fled, most of them limping or crawling. Only one or two had even fired their weapons.

"Step one completed successfully," Shami reported.

"The monorail delivery has arrived at the base of the spoke," Thandi said. "It'll be alongside our hold in seconds."

"Hand all that over to Prasad. Same method we used to speed-load in Ensylas. He has to make sure they're secured in the hold as well."

They knew that was very important. We were in serious trouble if the *Acid Penguin* couldn't be maneuvered.

I cut back to Jessop. "Get your men up to the dock, and they will obey *every* order."

"To be sure you understand, the spoke entrance is open," he said. "There are too many trolleys. We can't close the doors."

"I know. Deliberate. Leave it and get up to the dock level. Everything depends on getting your cargo, and now your men as well, safe inside the *Acid Penguin*, before the rest of the *Korçë* crew arrive."

"What? You can't load —"

"Shut up and do as I say."

I cut him off again. If he didn't obey, he was going to die, and I really didn't want that, but freeing Gunny and the others was our main objective.

There were stages in my plan where it worked or it didn't. The pirates died, or we did. We'd just arrived at the major one. How did the *Korçë* respond to our loading valuable cargo and shooting at the crew they'd sent to investigate?

E5. Chapter 4

They responded the way I'd hoped. It took the *Korçë* crew fifteen minutes to organize a new attack, equip them and return to the concourse.

Which sort-of matched my plan.

They were forty strong this time. That wasn't the problem.

They were five minutes quicker than I had anticipated. *That* was a problem.

Shami sent a video feed to my InfoPad. I couldn't use the pad from inside the combat suit, but it was good enough to show me the attackers.

The majority of them were in the sort of protective armor that police use. Better than the simple impact vests of the first wave, but not very good. There were five in some sort of combat suit. I couldn't see details, but that could be a problem too.

"What's the status with loading?" I overrode the common channel.

"We need another ten," Prasad said.

I switched back to Shami. "Gotta delay them," I said.

Jessop broke in.

"I'm on that," he said.

"How the hell did you—" I stopped. How he was patching into our comms wasn't relevant at the moment. Something to discuss later. "We need that ten minutes, and then we need *everyone* inside the ship."

"I understand what's needed." He switched off, just as the picture on my pad showed the crush of *Korçë* attackers at the entrance to our spoke.

They were forced to slow down. Immediately inside the spoke was a hallway with the elevator and stairs at the other side from the entrance. The trolleys with the food supplies that had come across the concourse filled that hallway so there was no room. So full, that the last one had jammed the spoke entrance open.

The elevator was up at the dockside level where Jessop had jammed it open. The only way for the attackers to get to the ship was to climb on top of the containers in the hallway and crawl across to the stairwell. Then they had to come up the stairwell, with no cover.

I had hoped not to be fighting in the stairwell, but there was that rule about plans and contact with the enemy. If Jessop could hold the stairwell for eight minutes and then run back to the ship, that should delay them enough. Anyone who'd been fired at in the stairwell would be hesitant about running up them just because the shooting paused.

"Nova!" Shami yelled. "Explosives in the stairwell."

That made everyone stop and think.

The shaft that comprised the elevator and stairwell was as solid as the rest of the station, but two of those walls were external. Blow a hole through them and the stairwell would vent to space.

"Low penetration fragmentation," Jessop's voice cut in. "No danger to the integrity."

He knew a worrying amount about weapons.

I switched back to the common channel. "Prasad?"

"Nearly. Four minutes, Skipper."

Back to channel 1. "Jessop?"

"Here."

"Fall back, get onto the dockside and be ready to sprint for the ship."

"Understood."

Jessop didn't sound military, but he sounded trained, and when I had time later, I was going to have to ask him some hard questions.

Unfortunately, the *Korçë* crew weren't stupid. The five in combat suits were crawling over the containers in front of the rest. They'd seen that the explosives hadn't damaged the stairwell and so more of the same wasn't going to get through their armor. And combat suits would climb those stairs in less time than Prasad needed to close the hold.

I had to divert their attention.

Which was the exact moment the plan really took off and gave me the opportunity for that diversion.

Standing on the back of the *Korçë*, we'd had about as much knowledge about what had been going on inside the ship as if it'd been on the other side of the sun. That stopped when they began to spool up their in-system engines and maneuvering jets. We could feel the ship tremble.

"Time to rock and roll," Bjorn yelled, and braced against the cables we'd strung into position.

I closed the contact in my hand. The signal shorted an electrical charge in a sealed unit at the other end of the ship, which ignited a primary charge. Which ignited the base charge. Which blew holes into the engine room.

An armored ship is really tough, unless you can get your explosive *underneath* the shielding. Then the shielding actually directs the explosion to where it does the most damage.

We'd found *good* places to pack the explosives.

We felt the shock of it through the ship. We saw the flash, then the random tumble of debris and unsecured items vented into space.

Lots of things happen when there's a disaster in a spaceship, and a breach of the engine room is high on the list of disasters. Emergency doors seal shut. Sirens go off. Everyone panics. It doesn't matter if the ship happens to be docked at the time. But when it *is* docked at a space station, the station's emergency systems also activate.

That's a nova-class distraction in anyone's book.

Although we couldn't see it from where we were, emergency doors between arcs would be coming down. Emergency shielding was already in position for most of the stores on the concourse, but even the Clint would be disappearing behind one as well.

Dockside doors sealed.

And every spoke entrance was sealed with a blast door that could only be opened once the whole system was reset.

The *Korçë* crew was divided into groups. Forty were trapped in the stairwell leading to the *Acid Penguin* dock. Twenty from the first squads were probably in their sick bay getting treatment for minor injuries and wondering what the nova was happening. There would be some on the dock alongside the *Korçë*. Anyone in the main engine room was dead. That left, according to our estimates, maybe a dozen or so distributed around the ship. The important ones would be on the bridge, which would have been sealed off from the remainder of the ship as soon as the explosives went off.

Which is why I had another plan for the bridge.

I flipped my visor to dark.

"See if you can hit the target, big guy," I shouted at Bjorn.

"See if you can shut up for a moment," came back.

He was carrying the plasma cannon from the *Acid Penguin*.

The same forces that provided pseudo-gravity on the concourse acted here, on the back of the *Korçë* and halfway along the spoke. The cannon had been a monster to move around, but luckily, it didn't need moving anymore. We'd pointed it at the junction of the ship where the main body joined with the forward section, and the armor was thinnest.

The forward section contained the bridge and living quarters. Bjorn angled the cannon slightly toward where we judged the bridge was.

"Knock, knock," Bjorn said and pressed the activator.

Even with my visor on dark, it maxed out as the plasma bolt contacted the skin of the spaceship.

The *Korçë* was armored and, at the distances ships shot at each other in space, our popgun would have done little damage, unless we got really, really lucky. At twenty meters, we didn't need luck. It blew a hole the size of my helmet through the ship.

Incandescent pieces of liquid metal exploded outwards, followed by a blast of superheated atmosphere carrying bits of fixtures torn off their mountings. Inside my combat suit, I was shaken like a leaf in a storm and battered by debris.

My suit's warning lights lit up like the Milky Way, but if the Earth's military industry did one thing well, it was building combat suits.

"Suit status?" I said to Bjorn.

"Couple of minor breaches. Self-rep taking care of it. You?"

"Good to go."

We'd only been able to bring one of the bulky charge capacitors, so the plasma cannon was finished as a weapon today.

Time for a more standard approach.

I reached inside the glowing hole opened by the plasma bolt and placed two more explosive charges on the underside of the ship's skin. I could feel the heat from the plasma bolt's damage even through my suit.

Bjorn hauled me back as the charges blew, deforming the spaceship skin and enlarging the hole.

The pair of us tore at the damage, suit servos whining, until the hole was big enough to climb in.

Lots to do, but everything was going to plan.

And then, as we were about to climb in, Shami came through on the comm.

"Skipper, sorry. Jessop and his men didn't make it to the ship. Something happened in the stairwell. It's vented to space. Apart from the attackers in the combat suits, they're all dead in there."

"Shit. Shit. Shit." I punched the *Korçë* as if it were the ship's fault, my suit-enhanced strength distorting the damaged skin under my blows.

Jessop had been a man full of secrets, with an agenda of his own, and he'd volunteered to fight the *Korçë*'s crew, but he'd been part of my company today, and I'd failed him.

"His decision, Jan," Bjorn said. "Not your fault."

I bit my lip and tried to get my head back in the right place.

"We still have a job to do," Shami said. "And we're on a timer now."

"Yeah. You're right. The plan remains the same, Shami. As soon as Prasad confirms the hold is secured, you blow the docking clamps and move. Even if you're not completely ready and the *Yli Bezan* moves—"

"I blow the clamps and disengage from the station quicker than them. Yes, Skipper."

Bjorn climbed into the *Korçë* and I followed him.

He'd broken into the main passageway which ran the length of the ship, interrupted by hatches at key points. Unlike the *Penguin*, this was a military style ship. Under normal operating conditions, with the acceleration compensators providing artificial gravity, it was a passageway you would walk along.

Since the *Korçë* was docked alongside the spoke, with the bridge at the front of the ship pointing toward the hub of the station, the passageway was a vertical shaft: bridge at the 'top' and the engine room at the 'bottom'. No engine power, no acceleration compensators.

The ship was long enough that the pseudo gravity provided by the rotation of the station was minimal at the bridge and would grow larger the further 'down' we went.

"The bridge area is still sealed." Bjorn lit up his helmet lights and pointed them upwards. I could see the hatch above us. The plasma bolt had angled in, missing the hatch itself and the bridge it protected.

"Then we have to fix that now."

With only two of us against an unknown number of them with unknown weapons, we had no chance for subtle options. If there was someone in that bridge thinking clearly, they were getting evacuation suits on. They could be arming themselves.

If it were my ship, and I had a combat suit, under these circumstances, I'd be getting into that. The *Korçë* probably had former military personnel on board.

I didn't like it, but we had no other options: we fired penetrating rounds from our TAWs into the bulkhead above us.

Atmosphere burst out.

We stood, our TAWs pointed up at the bridge, but once the air had gone there was no movement.

"Climb," I said to Bjorn. "I'll cover you."

"*Yli Bezan* has blown its docking clamps!" Shami's voice came on the comm. "Prasad! We're moving."

Prasad's voice in panic: "Last container to secure! Last one!"

"Go, go, go!" We couldn't risk the *Acid Penguin* being attacked by *Yli Bezan* while it was helpless in dock.

"Clamps blown," Shami said. "Dockside vented. Maneuvering clear of station, minimal acceleration."

We stood there, hearts thudding in our chests. An unsecured container weighing several tons would quickly become uncontrollable in the hold when the *Acid Penguin* moved abruptly. It would smear Prasad and Thandi's husbands against the sides like overripe fruit. Even if they escaped into the rest of the ship, the container would damage the middle of the ship under heavy maneuvering.

"All secure!" Prasad's voice broke. "Goddess be praised. Containers are stowed and we're in harness."

"Go get them, Shami," I said.

"Skipper."

Bjorn and I had the plasma cannon from the *Acid Penguin*, but the *Yli Bezan* didn't know that. They were in a blind panic. Their big bad reaver buddy had just been disabled and was under attack by an unknown force. A ship of unknown capabilities was chasing them.

If it came to a fight, Shami had one more weapon that the Yorktown engineers had installed. Not the greatest, but it might do the trick, and I'd back Shami over some pirate pilot any day.

Shami had one final message for us through the comm. "The station has vented all docks on all spokes. If there were *Korçë* crew on the dockside, they're either suited up or dead."

Which was one problem down, and another one up.

"Got it," I replied. "Good hunting."

Time to put her out of my mind and concentrate on our tasks.

First was to make sure the *Korçë*'s bridge was dead.

We couldn't delay. With the engines down and holes blown in the top and bottom sections of the ship, the middle section, the cargo area, would be on emergency life support.

We had between thirty to forty minutes to defeat any pockets of resistance, find the prisoners and get them out of this dead carcass of a ship before the air started to run out.

E5. Chapter 5

There were bodies on the bridge. One of them had been getting into a combat suit when we'd depressurized it.

Not the sort of standard combat suit we'd seen the *Korçë*'s attackers wearing in the attack on our spoke. This suit looked more like the sort of high-specification gear we'd seen the marines demonstrating on their recruitment drive back on Earth. He even had a Mark 4 Tactical Assault Weapon. One model shy of the latest equipment.

And Terran Marine tattoos on his arms.

Bjorn and I exchanged looks, but there was nothing we could do about it now.

Bjorn took the TAW 4. He checked the ammunition and safety while I broke into systems looking for information on the layout of the body of the ship. Most importantly, where the prisoners were kept.

I couldn't make sense of the schematics. All I could find was the emergency warning system that told me we had an average of twenty-seven minutes of air left in those parts of the ship that were still airtight. After that, it depended on how many people there were in each sealed area.

The power for life support was being provided by backup batteries, and it had reacted to the amount of damage we'd done breaking in by cutting back everything but the essentials. There was no functioning comm system with the rest of the ship, so I couldn't even threaten someone for information.

We began to work our way back down the main passageway.

Immediately behind the bridge, there were empty cabins.

Beyond the damaged area where we'd broken in was the medical section. It had functioning seals, a clear panel to look through the hatch and a voice-only intercom that appeared to be partially functioning.

I pressed buttons and banged on the panel until someone came to the other side, looking terrified.

"This is Lieutenant Commander Skelling of the Calloway Navy Anti-Piracy Unit," I said into the intercom. "The *Korçë* is now under my control. Assuming there is no resistance, we will attempt to evacuate everyone in the time that you have life support remaining. If there is resistance, then all bets are off. If you can communicate with any other sections of the ship, I suggest you warn them of that and point out that any resistance will be met with deadly force."

All the man on the other side of the door could see was a figure in a military combat suit, and I left it to his imagination to fill in a platoon of similarly equipped people stalking the passageways of the disabled ship.

He nodded jerkily. He tried to speak on the intercom, but there was nothing but noise coming through. He showed me a handheld comms device and began to use it.

He had no suits in there, so we left him and his injured charges in their sealed unit.

We climbed down further. It took us five minutes to break through the airlock hatch sealing the cargo area from the forward section. They still had atmosphere inside the cargo hold. The storage area had been reduced in size to accommodate an extra-large crew, so the first section we came to was divided into small dormitories. They were all empty.

The next section was living area. Eating, exercise, storage. Also empty.

It still took us another five minutes to sweep though it and make sure there wasn't anyone waiting to leap out and ambush us.

Which left about fifteen minutes of fresh atmosphere in the hold generally. If we could get the prisoners to the dormitory or living area, they could breathe there for a while longer.

"Lots of hatches and bulkheads," Bjorn commented.

He was right. This kind of modification wasn't something you saw on merchanters, but it was exactly the same work we'd seen on freighters converted for military use when we'd fought in the Dimitras Incursion.

"You reckon they did all this work, or they captured it like this?" I said.

Bjorn grimaced. "Pirates paid for a modification to make in-space docking feasible between the *Karakun* and the *Tünjorgo*. The same thinking would apply to this. If there's that much money to be made in piracy..."

We climbed down. We found the hatch to the next section had a red light flashing above it and a stenciled set of rules on the bulkhead mentioning that entry required the code of the day.

We'd found the prisoners' section.

I wasn't interested in trying to open a code-locked hatch. We were down to our last couple of charges, but one of them proved more than sufficient to get us through.

There were guards who hadn't got the message from the sick bay to give up. As the smoke from the explosion cleared, they fired small handguns at us.

Plain dumb.

Combat suits are designed to shrug off that kind of attack. The guards had no such protection. It was over in seconds and we were inside the prison section. The passageway was split into three stacked walkways with cellblocks off either side. Each cellblock was behind a hatch, and each hatch had stenciled rules beside it. Because the rotation of the station was providing pseudo gravity along the axis of the ship, those walkways were actually more like ladders at the moment.

The orientation wasn't a problem.

No way we had enough explosives to open all those doors.

No way there was enough time to get more, or even to find out what the codes were to open the doors.

"We have to get life support connection from the station—" Bjorn started.

"No time. They're in lockdown and the dock itself is depressurized. It'll take hours to reset their systems." I checked my suit timer. "We have less than ten minutes, and then whatever air there is in the cellblocks."

We were helmet to helmet, looking at each other, desperately hoping one of us would see something the other hadn't. I saw Bjorn's eyes squeeze shut. When they opened again, his face had gone hard.

"We find Gunny," he said.

He leaped to the topmost of the passageways.

Feeling sick, I raced to the lowest level and started looking through the view panel in each hatch. Each block formed a unit that reoriented itself when under a station's rotational pseudo-gravity. The units were all the same: an area separated from the rest of the block by bars, with space so that one person at a time could come forward and offer their hands to be cuffed together. Behind that area, an open space with bunks and primitive sanitation features. Each cellblock had people in it, crushed against the bars, panicking, shouting questions I couldn't hear.

They didn't know who I was or what I was doing there. All they knew was that they'd felt explosions through the structure of the ship and the fact that the lighting had gone from standard to low-intensity backup.

They were spacers. They knew what was happening.

There was far worse. On catching sight of me, some cringed and backed away, thinking I was a member of the pirate crew.

I hated the pirates more with every view panel I looked through. I hated myself for not being able to do anything for these people. I hated myself for not being able to communicate with them. To explain. I hated myself for rushing away, leaving them screaming soundlessly, hopelessly behind me.

I found Gunny on the middle level just before Bjorn joined me. Almost the last cellblock I looked in. We had less than five minutes left.

There was no screaming in Gunny's cellblock. Everyone was standing still, looking scared, looking at Gunny, who stood right in front so I could see her easily.

"Gunny!" I shouted uselessly, my voice cracked.

"Tell her to stand back. We'll blow the door." Bjorn had the last charge in his hand.

"Wait."

Gunny had become animated. She was signaling at me.

"Wait," I said again. "She's trying to say something."

She held a hand up next to her head, one finger extended toward me and jabbing in a pattern.

"Code! She knows the code!" I shouted. "Of course, she knows the nova-damned code."

"Okay, okay," Bjorn said, but he couldn't hide the flood of relief in his voice.

Gunny laid four fingers on her upper arm, like she was doing charades.

"Four digits." I was still yelling.

"First digit. Nine." I traced nine on the view panel, she nodded, and we hurried through the remaining digits. 9573.

I had to hold myself back from stabbing my combat-suited finger right through the code panel buttons.

The light went green on the panel. Bjorn pulled the latch and the seal opened with a hiss.

"Took your own sweet time, Skelling," Gunny yelled at me. She blinked, swaying and looking around. "How many of you are there?"

"Just Bjorn and me. Backup power's down to three minutes."

"Nova," she whispered.

Now that I could see her fully, Gunny wasn't looking too well. Her face had partly-healed scarring and fresh bruises. She was holding onto me, and her eyes didn't seem too well focused.

"Just you and Thorsson? Got to get others out. Same code."

I pulled Gunny to one side and yelled at the others in her cellblock. "We need all of you to help. Open the hatches. Code 9573. Go, go, go."

Gunny had them well organized. Given half a chance, I could imagine her leading this group on an attack against the pirates with nothing more than their fists. Those that could, ran up or down the walkway/ladders to do their tasks. Those that couldn't run, hobbled. There weren't too many hobbling. Injured slaves didn't fetch as good a price. Bruises were another matter.

I hated the pirates with a feeling like a fire eating my belly.

"Priority," Gunny said, still holding onto me. "Top walkway. Cellblock 3."

I didn't ask questions. I picked her up and jumped across the gap to the top walkway. Cellblock 3 was the end one and the prisoners flooded out when I opened the hatch, their lungs already heaving. Emergency air supply was failing all through this section.

As the freed prisoners came out, I directed them along the walkway to open other hatches on this level. Gunny's cellmates had already opened the middle walkway cells.

But there was something else going on here. Gunny slipped off my arm and began snatching people and throwing them to the side. She forced her way inside through those remaining.

I followed her.

The last one couldn't make it out himself. There was something about the way he was lying on the bunk that told me he couldn't walk.

"This is Werner. Pick him up and follow me," Gunny said.

Six years in the 1st Frontier. I did what she said without question.

We climbed back up towards the bridge.

"Sit-rep on the ship," Gunny gasped.

"Bridge dead. Both the bridge and main passageway in that section are open to space. Only known survivors up there are in the sick bay. General engine section unknown. Engine room itself holed. Remainder of cargo hold unknown."

"Good enough. We can redirect life support from the engine section."

"And the bridge," Werner said. "That won't affect the sick bay. The routing junction will be in the last fore section of the cargo hold."

Gunny nodded and kept climbing. We went back into the crew areas, all the way to the airlock between the cargo hold and foremost section.

"There!"

A panel with stencil markings indicating a utilities control junction.

"I can't get in without keys," Werner said.

I put him down carefully, stabbed my fingers through the cover and ripped it open.

He used his elbows to drag himself closer, then reached into the complex array of valves and switches. He started muttering under his breath.

Three minutes later, he finished and relaxed, lying back down.

"We have an hour before the life support runs out in the hold now," he said. "Given the volume of the crew quarters, I'd say another hour after that before air becomes a problem. About the same for the sick bay."

Gunny slumped against the bulkhead.

"That'll be more than enough," she said. "Even if we have to break hatches open, we can get through the hold to the dockside and walk out in, what, half an hour?"

I cleared my throat.

"Ah. Slight problem there. The dock has been vented."

E5. Chapter 6

We had too many people to get to somewhere safe, and too little time.

My original plan had anticipated forty or fifty slaves. We'd have loaded them into the evacuation chute, sealed it and used the maintenance maneuvering rigs to drag them across to a station access hatch. The towing itself would have taken ten minutes maximum. Another five minutes at the start and end to connect the chute to hatches. Another five minutes at each end to cycle though the airlocks. Thirty minutes in all.

Simple. Frightening for the people in the evacuation chute, but quick and simple.

We didn't have fifty. We had two hundred and fifty.

Bjorn and Gunny were arguing about doing it in shifts, fifty at a time, five trips. Two hours thirty minutes if *nothing* went wrong. *If* there was enough propellant in the maneuvering packs. *If* there was enough air. *If* we got going immediately.

On the other hand, even I had to admit evacuation chutes weren't designed for multiple use. Merely 'frightening' became 'terrifying'.

Werner tapped my arm.

"The station won't help us?"

"They're locked down, and they'll have their own problems," I said. "Three spokes have been vented. Emergency shutters will be down and locked between arcs and so on. Reset procedures are going to take them hours to go through."

"So we are going to die," he said, nodding thoughtfully.

"There is the chute," I pointed out.

His eyes defocused as he thought about it and then he waggled his head. "That would possibly save half of us, at best. Mechanical analyses of typical chute construction have proved that the entire tube body must be recycled after one use. On the basis of standard safety margins, I estimate two uses would have a thirty percent chance of failure, rising to one hundred percent by the fourth reuse."

"Engineer, huh?"

"Yes. Of course."

"Purely hypothetically, suppose there were a shuttle that might have sustained some hopefully minor damage—"

He frowned. "You can't fit even a dozen people in a shuttle."

"Not in the cabin, no. But shuttles have cargo grabs for up to two containers."

His frown deepened.

I prompted him. "A standard container is three meters square and six deep..."

"54 cubic meters," he said. "1,000 liters of air per cubic meter, so 54,000 cubic meters of air. 5 liters per person per minute—"

"They'll be scared. Let's give them 6 liters a minute—"

He waved his hand. "We tell them to sit still and be calm. 300 liters an hour. 100 people in a container. 30,000 liters. You would have more than two hours to move 100 people onto an open dock if you can get the air in the container."

"A return flight to the hub dock would take twenty minutes. We'd need two trips to get all two hundred and fifty people to safety, including those in the sick bay. Now, if we can get to the shuttle, it has compressed air tanks inside as a standard safety measure. Not enough for long, but maybe enough to make the plan viable. Better than the evac chute."

Gunny had been listening. "Then why are you still here?" she said.

"Because we fired a plasma cannon into the forward section. There may be some damage to the shuttle, the bay doors, the clamps. There's no power down there. And I'm not an engineer."

Which was why, thirty frustrating minutes later, I was dragging Werner in an emergency space suit through the guts of the damaged forward docking bay.

Bjorn was behind, struggling with the plasma gun capacitor and a random collection of connectors and tools we'd found in a scavenger hunt. The capacitor didn't have enough charge to fire the cannon, but it might be what we needed to operate docking releases and things like that.

Murphy's Law was operating, and our plasma bolt had gone straight through the shuttle cabin.

Werner laughed. "You missed," he said. "You almost completely disabled this shuttle."

He swam around on the floor, dragging his legs, re-routing cabling for 'safety', and laughing every time he said that.

He directed Bjorn to connect the capacitor to a power junction which fed the mechanisms for the bay doors and the clamps that kept the shuttle locked down.

Apart from electric arc flashes that drained more of the capacitor, that went acceptably, despite swearing from Werner.

Bjorn then had to disappear back into the main body of the *Korçë*, carrying the emergency oxygen tanks from the shuttle with him.

I carried Werner in and out, while he made a cradle of connections between the shuttle and the docking bay mechanics.

Finally, he attached test meters and started checking readings.

"Ready!" he said. "Leave me here and get to the pilot's seat. The bay doors will close again after the capacitor is exhausted. You must take off immediately I say."

"Yeah. About that..."

I got distracted reading the board as I hit the standard buttons to bring the shuttle systems on line.

Green. Green. Green. Amber. Low pressure on hydraulics.

Nova! It would have to do. The *Korçë* pilots probably flew it like this all the time.

No reds. Focus on that.

I looked up.

"The bay doors are opening," I said, as Werner couldn't see from his position. I could feel the docking clamps lift through the structure of the shuttle.

"Of course the doors are opening and you must fly out. You didn't finish. You said 'about that'. What about that?" Werner replied.

"Oh, *that*. Just I've never flown a shuttle before. This is going to be fun."

There were several moments of silence on the comm as I started the maneuvering jets and we jerked forward in ungainly hops.

People who aren't used to suits sometimes speak aloud things they don't mean to communicate. Werner did as the shuttle banged off the sides of the docking bay and slithered toward the open doors and the looming station hub that seemed far too close.

He muttered: "At least the end will be very quick this way."

"You of little faith! Eat your words!"

"We are not landed until we come to a halt," Werner shouted.

All the shouting put me off. The descent down to the hub had been so good up to then, it had almost made up for the tricky bit of actually snaring the cargo containers, which I didn't do well.

I decided the landing was Werner's fault. His, and the guys who were supposed to be helping me. One on comms screaming unintelligible instructions and another on the landing pad waving lightsticks. It dented my confidence when lightstick guy jetted himself away. Flying was all about confidence.

The shuttle's nose slewed around.

The landing pad started to slide away underneath.

Stick up, stick down, rotate the cluster, hold your attitude, level, descend.

I ignored the noise on the comms, turned off what I thought of as the 'up' jets, and blipped the power on the 'down' jets.

We landed on the edge of the pad.

Hard.

Red lights on the board flared, like a cascade rippling down.

No!

This was our first trip. I had to be able to make a second flight.

"They'll have a pilot," I said as I started turning things off. "They'll have someone who can fix this and get the next containers."

"I think you may have broken the release mechanism," Werner said. In null-G, he'd floated over to a board. "I will re-route power to disengage. This may take a while."

No!

Bjorn had reported the remainder of the people all loaded into the next two containers. Their air was getting low already.

The comm crackled.

"Any landing you survive is a good landing, Skipper."

"Shami! Nova! Where are you?"

"We're back. The *Yli Bezan* is disabled and I have her crew in our holding containers. I'll use the *Penguin*'s shuttle and I'll have those two other containers in the hub, probably about the same time you clear that junk off it."

E5. Chapter 7

The station master's desk in his office was a beautiful thing.

It was about three meters long, slightly curved. It was made of what was probably hugely expensive wood from the planet of Endellion, and it had been polished until the surface looked like it was water.

There was nothing on the expanse of the desk apart from a comms console. And a couple of huge indentations where I'd planted my combat suited fists into it.

I'd come straight from the hub. Werner had waved me on my way immediately after Shami finished speaking. "Null-G is pleasant for me," he'd said. "I've had my excitement for today. Thank you. Goodbye."

Between the hub and this executive office in the rim, there was a trail of stunned guards and broken doors. Civilians should not get in the way of a combat suit. At least they'd been smart enough not to escalate to firing weapons at me, so I'd restricted my responses to match.

On my arrival through the shattered door to his office, the station master had tried a stuttering tirade about the costs of damage to the station and imminent confiscation of the *Acid Penguin*.

That was when my fists had come down into his desk.

He was being quieter now, trying to argue his way out.

"Piracy, Station Master," I said. "Provable conspiracy in piracy on multiple occasions. All those in positions of authority, starting with you."

Even in the chill of his office, with life support reduced to emergency levels, he was sweating.

"We're not signatories to the Piracy Accords," he said.

"Neither are pirates," I replied, "but the accords still apply to them. I still get a bounty for handing them over to stand trial in any system which is a signatory."

"The trials are a mockery!"

He had a point. Further into human space, in the Inner Worlds, pirates might get a formal and even-handed hearing. Extenuating circumstances might be taken into account. Appeals. Prisons that were maintained to a standard.

Out in the Frontier, resources were short, so trials were too. Expectations were low.

Tough.

"Then I recommend you make every effort to ensure you don't end up on the wrong side of those trials."

I leaned over the desk and made two more impressions in his furniture.

"I see I'm just in time."

I spun around, the TAW up and pointed at the doorway.

"Jessop! You're dead."

"You exaggerate, if only slightly."

He had his hands raised and spread, and waited until the TAW's muzzle dropped a bit before he came in.

The station master knew him. "Jessop! I should have known you'd be behind this."

"Actually, very little to do with me, sir. I was only looking for a charter and, well," his face screwed up mock-apologetically, "I got swept up in the excitement. From what I gather, you have fallen foul of the new Calloway Navy Anti-Piracy Unit."

"Calloway doesn't have a navy," the station master blustered, but his eyes latched onto my military combat suit.

"They do now. Not sure if introductions have been made, but the lady in front of you is Lieutenant Commander Skelling, the captain of that naval ship on spoke 3. And piracy *is* a problem out here in the Parvi arc, don't you agree?"

The station master visibly wilted.

I let Jessop do the talking. He had a real grasp of what needed to be done. On the other hand, my list of questions for him got longer and longer.

He got half a point for calling me a lady.

I nearly snorted, but that wouldn't have been ladylike.

The two pirate ships were going to be stripped of weapons systems by Bjorn and Werner in whatever time we had before setting out to Ranier.

The hulks were then to be made available, with basic assistance provided by the station, to the freed slaves. The aim was to rebuild one functioning ship from the two. There were enough ex-prisoners for five or six entire crews, and enough space on the *Korçë* for all of them, if they wanted.

The stolen cargo on the *Yli Bezan* would be impossible to return to its owners, some of whom were among the slaves anyway, so it was agreed that they could use it to barter for supplies and building assistance.

All the pirates, dead or alive, were transferred to the *Acid Penguin*. The living would find themselves in cells with the survivors of the *Karakun* and the *Tünjorgo*. The dead in the deep freeze. All of them would be handed over for the bounty at some, as yet undecided, Inner Worlds destination that honored its Piracy Accords obligations.

The Endellion system agreed to never again become the resupply base for pirates, even unwillingly. Steps would be taken to provide a police force capable of enforcing that, and some basic defense systems for the station.

We reckoned it would take somewhere between two hundred and three hundred days to make the *Korçë* serviceable. Plenty of time for Endellion to keep its promises as well, so I pointed out we'd be heading back to Calloway in that sort of time and would make a point of stopping here to check on progress.

All of which concluded my business with Endellion station.

Leaving me the unfinished business with Trader Jessop.

E5. Chapter 8

"Sorry for the inconvenience. We took some minor damage. Nothing to worry about, but we've closed the main passageway to the bridge area, just to be safe. You need to come through this temporary passage. Follow me."

As anyone would expect, the corridor was crammed with maintenance tools and parts, forcing all of us to move through in single file, into a similarly narrow corridor.

The temporary corridor was not much more substantial than an evacuation chute. It had clear panels on one side so they could see they were on the outside of the ship.

I didn't expect them to be nervous about it, and Trader Jessop's team weren't. For a supposedly random group of people collected off the dockside, they'd behaved as if they knew their way around everything from guns to spaceships.

Oh, it was long past time to ask Trader Jessop some hard questions.

The temporary corridor had a safety system preventing use of the exit hatch while the entrance hatch was open. They all dutifully crowded in and closed the entrance behind them, pushing the locking bar down until the safety light showed green.

It was all standard practice. The sort of safety feature you expected to see when a ship was being repaired. There was a single person airlock arrangement to exit to the bridge.

I went through.

Jessop followed.

His team now found that the exit airlock didn't work. And neither did the entrance. They were trapped in the corridor on the outside of the ship with very little between them and hard vacuum.

Jessop knew what was going on as soon as he came out of the airlock, probably because I was pointing a Renshaw at him.

He went very tense, very still.

"My apologies, but I need to ask you some questions, Trader Jessop, and six armed men on my bridge makes me plain nervous. Keeping your hands in sight, walk into the briefing room, please."

He nodded his head, his face unreadable, but he obeyed instructions.

I gave him a hand-held comms unit linked to one in the corridor. "Sit down and talk to your men. They're in no immediate danger, but they should be aware that corridor can be vented to space in a millisecond."

We had Thandi's husband, Meson, standing like a statue in the briefing room. He was dressed up in a naval uniform with my TAW held across his chest. He'd never fired anything like it before, and had no idea how it was used, but he played the part perfectly.

Shami ran a detector over Jessop and removed a handgun in a shoulder holster and an interesting knife from his boot.

"Piracy or Anti-Piracy?" Jessop asked quietly when she'd finished.

"Anti. You, your men and your mysterious cargo are safe, and you will be delivered to the Ranier system orbital station in the time stated in our contract, or less. We *are* the Anti-Piracy Unit of the Calloway Navy, and although we didn't intend it initially, our actions on this station have been entirely within our remit."

Sounded grand. Gunny would have been proud of me.

"So, you *are* a disguised naval ship and there *is* a genuine Calloway Navy? I wasn't feeding the station a line?"

"The Calloway Navy is two ships. A former reaver and merchanter pair originally from Zilkum, a small Frontier system at the other end of the Parvi Arc."

"It would have been easier if you'd had your reaver partner here," Jessop said. "Where is she?"

"On naval business, not your concern. Now, it's my turn for questions."

He was keeping his face blank, but he knew he wasn't in a position to argue.

"A trader puts out a message on a navigational beacon that can only be described as an invitation to pirates, when he happens to be on an orbital station that is being terrorized by pirates. The sensible traders on that station all hide behind emergency blast shields and sell to the pirates when asked to."

"Being foolish is not against the law, Lieutenant Commander."

"On the contrary, it's a capital offense in the unwritten law of the Frontier, Trader. The Dark takes fools."

He shrugged, but didn't argue.

"The same Trader," I went on, "when faced with a difficult demand for military-level weapons and ammunition, not only supplies them, but manages to do so in less time than it should have taken to locate them, let alone negotiate a deal."

Jessop's eyes narrowed.

"Impossible," I said. "Unless that Trader happened to have them ready and waiting. What exactly does your cargo comprise, Jessop?"

"We discussed this. It's confidential. It's a point-to-point contract and any liability—"

"I'm not interested in the legal situation. You can't stop us opening those containers, so why don't you just tell me."

His fingers drummed the table for a moment, and stopped.

"Weapons," he admitted.

"Military weapons."

His nod was short and sharp.

"Enough, as you put it in the Clint, to start a small war on Ranier."

He made an expansive gesture and smiled. It didn't reach his eyes. "What can I say? The lure of large profits."

"Mmm. Just in it for the profits? So this Trader, only interested in profits, reinterprets the plans to lure the *Korçë* crew into a position in our stairwell where they could be neutralized. He hires 'some men' to assist him in this far more dangerous plan. These random recruits lay down fire like a military team, wound the first group and successfully trap the second group in the stairwell. As neat as if they'd practiced it."

"We lured them, but trapping them was *your* plan, and it was *your* actions in attacking the *Korçë* itself that caused the blast doors to come down."

"At which point you and your recruits managed to take out five attackers in combat suits and then retreat to a couple of the same containers you'd just moved across the concourse, which had been carrying not food supplies, but oxygen and evacuation suits, so when the docks vented and killed the rest of them, you were all okay."

"A bit of forethought, but mainly lucky, I guess. Close thing."

I snorted. He didn't for one moment believe that I believed him.

"I bet it was. We always pray for luck," I said, "but we depend on training and planning."

"We?"

"People in the business of military operations, Mr. Jessop."

He didn't answer and we watched each other like a pair of Calloway's dueling river snakes.

He was a spy, or an insurgent. The station master knew him as a troublemaker. He had military-style training. He was probably the product of some rogue government department from somewhere in the Inner Worlds. Or maybe a group of Frontier merchanters had pooled money to sponsor someone to hit back against the pirates.

I'd get answers from him if I put him under enough pressure, but whether those answers should be believed was another matter entirely. I had problems with that.

We'd fought on the same side in Endellion, but that was no guarantee we'd be on the same side in Ranier. He'd invited himself to my bridge with armed men, which gave me no good feelings at all.

And yet, he'd put himself in danger in the fight against the pirates. We'd benefited.

Endellion had been about freeing slaves. Maybe. What if Ranier *wasn't* about slaves? What if he was a mercenary hired to overthrow a legitimate government there?

He seemed to sense where my thoughts were heading.

"Ranier is far, far worse than Endellion," he said. "Ranier is the local center of the slavery business out on this part of the Parvi arc, and it isn't a station master cooperating under threat, it's a station master who's a senior man in the pirate gangs. You broke a chain here, but Ranier's where the chains meet."

"It doesn't sound like you're starting a small war on Ranier, Jessop. It sounds like it's a big one. So, I hope that's *after* we've left. The *Acid Penguin* isn't a reaver with a full complement of military troops. We got lucky here in Endellion."

"You don't believe in luck, Lieutenant Commander. As to before or after... that depends when we get there," he replied.

"I've no wish to emerge into a full-scale battle," I said. "Fortunately, we have a reasonable chance of getting there much earlier than we agreed."

"Oh?" Jessop raised his eyebrows. "Not going to burn out your Chang generators, I hope?"

"Not exactly. At least, not according to our new engineer, who will either get us there in a couple of jumps, or end up feeding us to the Dark."

Episode 6
Absolutely, Positively

E6. Chapter 1

"We're agreed? Absolutely, positively *not* getting involved in any uprising on Ranier, regardless of whether it's a good cause or not."

Bjorn and I had decided we needed to be very clear on this before we emerged from Chang space in the Ranier system, which was why we'd gathered everyone in the rec room for a beer and a talk.

Even Shami was 'there': physically on the bridge, but connected through the comms onto a display screen. We were developing a set of ship's rules, and one of them she'd insisted on was that there would never be a time when there wasn't someone from the command team on the bridge.

Jessop and his team *weren't* in the room. As much as I liked him and acknowledged his assistance on Endellion, I'd be a fool to trust him, and the Dark takes fools.

I knew he'd try to get us to help. He'd use words like *justice*, *obligation* and *honor*, in the same way he'd use any tool at hand to achieve what he wanted. However noble the aim of his enterprise, he refused to discuss important background details like *who* was backing him and *why*, so I wasn't listening to him about this.

Shami and Bjorn nodded agreement with me. We had our own obligation to our home planet, which was now Shami's as well. That obligation was to get far enough into the Inner Worlds that the credits which we'd been paid for our service to Earth in the 1st Frontier Brigade and the 5th Frontier Wing could be converted to usable currency. With that money we'd buy the bio-processors which would save the lives of everyone on Calloway.

Whether they wanted it or not.

To get that far into the Inner Worlds, we were going to have to trade to pay our way, and that was enough of a complication in itself. We couldn't afford to be diverted into side escapades, however righteous the cause, however much we wanted to.

Absolutely, positively not.

Thandi nodded as well. "Thank you for including me and my husbands. Eh, we're not permanent members of the crew. As you all know, we have an entire satellite communication system in the hold. We have to sell it to get our investment back, and the sooner we travel into the Inner Worlds, the better chance we will have. We are simple traders. We can't help with real fighting, and the slightest damage from a stray shot might mean our ruin."

Only her most senior husband, Meson, was with her. He took her hand and squeezed.

I knew Thandi hadn't made plans beyond the sale of the satellite system, and I knew we'd really miss her trading skills on the way back. Not to mention she and her husbands were managing our canteen.

"We stocked well at Endellion. We don't need supplies from Ranier," Thandi said. "I say we undock as soon as Trader Jessop and his cargo clear the ship."

Meson wasn't going to disagree with his wife. Sensible fellow.

Which left three more to voice their opinions.

"Not agreed," Gunny said.

That wasn't a surprise. After we'd rescued her, Gunny hadn't spoken much about being held as a slave, but Bjorn and I could see the anger in her, the darkness in her eyes.

Trader Jessop had made an argument about the Ranier system being the center for the slave trade in the whole Parvi arc. *That* was all the motivation Gunny needed.

Which put us in a quandary.

When we'd brought Gunny on board, Bjorn and I had discussed what role she should have. After all, we'd spent six years with her as our immediate commander in the 1st Brigade, and she'd been a damn good one. Should she take over the command of the ship?

She hadn't been in a state to talk about who should run the *Penguin* before. But now...

She stirred in her seat. "I'll go along with your decision. Personally, my reason for being here is to wipe out the slave trade wherever we come across it, but I don't feel much like starting a mutiny today," she said.

She turned to Prasad, who was sitting next to her. "What about you, Pras? What's your reason for being on the *Penguin*?"

Prasad laughed. "My reason for being here? I must not go home." He shook his head and became more serious. "I was also a slave, rescued by the valiant Calloway Navy. I hate thinking there are more people in the situation I was in, but I owe my freedom to Jan and Bjorn. I'll support them."

I was about to turn to Werner when Gunny raised a hand.

"Yes, Gunny?"

"I take back what I said." She stirred uneasily again, and I felt my heart skip beats.

Was she about to take over?

That interpreted itself directly into my gut as *take over my ship*. It was ridiculous for me to feel I had a better claim to the *Penguin* than Bjorn, for instance. On the other hand, it would probably be a good idea for someone with more sense than I had to run the ship.

None of which made it feel good at all. Quite the opposite.

But that didn't seem to be what Gunny wanted.

"I apologize," Gunny said. "Not just about what I said, but the way I said it, and not just about the decision for Ranier, but the whole situation."

Everyone frowned, and Gunny let the silence deepen before she went on. "This ship is part of the Calloway Navy, and we're all behaving as if that's just another fake identity, like the one we're set up to broadcast when we arrive in the Ranier system. It *isn't*. This *is* a navy ship, with an important mission, and with a chain of command. Some of you aren't in the navy. You're here as advisors. That's fine, but we're all in the same relative position. Lieutenant Commander Skelling is the captain of this ship. We provide our specialist advice. She decides what we're going to do. We salute, or agree, or we request to leave the ship at the next dock."

No one spoke. It was one of those glaringly obvious things that hadn't been obvious to me until Gunny had pointed it out. This was a difficult mission and it would end in disaster if we ran it by committee.

"I'm offering my services," Gunny said. "I guess my rank equivalent would be Bosun. If you'll accept me."

Then she stood and saluted me.

Military reactions made me rise to my feet, and I returned the salute.

"Of course," I said. "Welcome aboard."

"I think Gunny will sound better than Bosun Gunny," Bjorn said.

They laughed and the mood lightened.

Which left Werner as the last to say his piece.

The engineer had converted the engine room to a zero-gravity environment, so his spinal injury would not restrict him, but up here in the gravity of the rec room, he was sitting in a cargo trolley that he'd adapted as a wheelchair.

"I guess this would make me Engineering Officer," he said and shrugged. "Awaiting your orders, skipper."

"Okay." I smiled. I could tell he had something to say. "I'm seeking opinions."

"Well, we all have to die sometime, but I would prefer it not to be because the engines in my care blow up. Whatever happens, I would strongly suggest we dock on the Ranier orbital station, and buy some replacement parts."

"You've damaged the Chang generators?" Shami's tone of voice from the bridge spoke volumes, even over the comms.

"The most stressful operations for the Chang generators are entering and leaving Chang space, and since I've *reduced* the number of times we've done that on this trip, you can take it that I have done the exact reverse. I'm talking about the in-system engines, which have been run in the red and operated to give the appearance of misfiring. That's not good for them."

"How expensive are the spares?" I asked, dreading the answer.

Werner shrugged. "That depends on the local market."

Thandi pursed her mouth. "Staying at dock will also cost us."

Great.

I'd liked her idea we would get off the station as soon as Jessop and his cargo cleared the doors. Now it looked as if we were going to have to stay a while.

But absolutely, positively not get involved in any takeover or revolution.

E6. Chapter 2

"Ranier Orbital Docking Control, this is merchanter *Spiral Song*, ESS512, inbound to you, ETA fifteen minutes to matching orbit, requesting trading berth."

"*Spiral Song*. We have your details from Traffic. Proceed to twenty-meter stand-off on berth S5-01 where you will surrender maneuvering to dockside control on channel 16."

"Roger that. Stand-off twenty on Spoke 5, Berth 1. Dockside on 16."

Shami handled the maneuvering and chat with the station as we approached. It was eerie to watch her sit motionless while the *Acid Penguin* moved in response to her commands through the interface in her head.

We'd come in as the *Spiral Song* because it was always going to be possible to backtrack to which ship had brought Jessop and his cargo in. If things went well for him, no one would care. If they went badly, then the ship would get labeled a gunrunner. I didn't want that description attached to the *Acid Penguin*. We had enough to do without that.

Ranier's space station, named only as Ranier Orbital, was *big*, much bigger than Orion's Wheel in the Ensylas system. And not only bigger, but busier. There were two other ships in the process of docking, and a mega-hauler standing off, waiting for tugs to load it up with cargo modules bound for the Inner Worlds.

While Shami was handling docking, I was reading station information and news feeds. My most important task was trying to assess how close the station and system was to the open revolt that Jessop claimed to be involved in.

There was nothing to indicate that. After Orion's Wheel and Endellion, Ranier Orbital seemed downright boring. Half the information in their feeds was about trade. The station's trading arc seemed to be stuffed with the offices of small financial institutions, or contact agents for Inner World corporations.

Bjorn came up and read over my shoulder as the docking proceeded.

"Nothing suggesting dissent," he said. "Maybe there's censorship?"

"Don't know. There are pieces here that are rude about station management and politicians down on the planet. Very rude."

He grunted. "Concourse video show anything?"

I switched one display to a video feed of the station arc closest to our docking spoke.

"What does a station about to break out in a revolt look like?" Bjorn asked.

I snorted. "Not like that."

On Endellion's station, people had been hiding behind the blast doors designed to isolate them from whatever was happening down in the concourse. Not here.

"Okay, different question. What should the 'slave trade center' of the Parvi Arc look like?"

That was the description Trader Jessop had given us of Ranier.

"Again, not like that," I said. "There's nothing going on out there that tells me there are slaves here. I mean, half the ships docked are from the Inner Worlds and Margin. They're not going to come trade at a place that deals in slaves."

Bjorn went quiet. Our opinions about how law-abiding those worlds were didn't quite match, but there was one clear fact in my favor: *all* Inner Worlds were signatory to the Anti-Piracy Accords. An Inner Worlds ship docking at a Frontier slave trading station? They'd be making themselves liable to prosecution when they got home.

I could feel through my seat when we came under dockside control, and the *Penguin* began inching down to the dock in careful steps.

"Did Jessop lie to us?" Bjorn asked.

"Gut reaction? No. But I guess the situation here is complex. Not our concern though. We get Werner's replacement parts and we're gone. All I'm interested in is being sure that no fighting breaks out until after we leave."

Bjorn straightened and stretched. "Fair enough. Who's going with Werner to get the spares?"

"Prasad to take charge of loading. Me and you."

Shami rolled her eyes, knowing that would mean she had to stay on the bridge, at least until we returned.

Bjorn wrinkled his nose. "Why not take Gunny and Thandi instead of me? Werner knows what he wants, but it's Thandi who does the negotiating."

"Fair enough. Why Gunny rather than you?"

"Whether the situation is volatile or not, I'm recommending one person in armor. I'm kinda noticeable suited up. And Gunny needs something to do."

I chewed that over.

Yes, we had scavenged enough bits and pieces at Endellion that we could suit Gunny up as long as she didn't have to spend a lot of time in it. And she was a whole head shorter than Bjorn. Taking him dockside in armor would look aggressive. With Gunny along, I might get away with just looking cautious.

It was a mistake to look too careless in the same way it was a mistake to look too aggressive.

Gunny *did* need something to do. And with her experience of being traded as a slave, she might spot signs about Ranier's station that I hadn't from the video feeds.

Bjorn wasn't finished. "And include three-way comms. Gunny, the bridge and Jessop. We don't want to get caught if their rebellion kicks off suddenly."

"Done."

I sent messages through the comms.

Ranier was efficient. The sounds of Jessop's containers being unloaded into the monorail system were already ringing around the docks as I walked off from the forward bay, pushing Werner's trolley-wheelchair.

Thandi and Prasad walked alongside me. Thandi was in one of her splendid robes that shimmered and glowed as she moved. Prasad was in his working coveralls.

Gunny came up behind us in a junkyard mix of armor that made her look like a pirate. It worried the guards at the dock gates, but we passed some test of acceptable average lethality and they let us through.

I could hear the servos whining in her suit and Werner winced at the noise.

Werner's trolley's right front wheel squealed. On top of that, every five steps or so, it spun around and made the trolley swerve.

What was it with me and trolleys? I *always* got the bad one.

"Tell you what, Werner," I said. "We have some work to do on Gunny's suit, but you need to fix this trolley."

"I'm a spaceship engineer," he said. "Not the same thing as a trolley engineer."

"Beneath your dignity," Prasad said, suppressing a smile.

Werner twisted around. "What did you mean back on the ship, Pras, when you said you *must* not go home? Are you a criminal?"

Prasad laughed. "No, nothing like that. It's just... I will be home no more than ten minutes before Grandmother will announce a very remarkable young lady of a splendidly good family happens to be coming to visit, quite unexpectedly. This will continue at hourly intervals until I surrender or escape again."

Everyone laughed.

"Marriage is not the worst thing that could happen to a person," Thandi said.

"You should know, but I am allowed only one," Prasad countered, and they both laughed again.

Thandi's home system considered her domestic arrangements a matter for her and her husbands to agree on, and would only intervene if there were children at risk or a nuisance was caused.

By the time we'd finished teasing each other about the social differences in our home systems, we'd reached the trade section, in the arcs to either side of Spoke 1.

Ranier was *so* much bigger than Orion's Wheel, or Endellion. The rim was five levels high above the concourse, with living accommodations in the two upper levels, and businesses and shops below them. Each level had a gallery that overlooked the main concourse, and plants trailed down attractively from each level's balcony.

It was busy without being crowded. There was a hum of chatter around us and teenagers skated past, cutting swooping curves around the pedestrians and the plant boxes that broke up the walkways.

"Not exactly what I was expecting," I said to Thandi.

She shrugged and frowned. "Eh. A lot of evil can hide under a pleasant face."

I felt a familiar itch that usually meant someone was watching me, but there was no hint of danger in the crowds in the trade area.

We had a short list of three traders, based on what Werner had found in their advertisements on the boards. At the first, Thandi took over Werner's trolley and pushed him inside while the rest of us waited outside. I looked up and down the row of businesses.

"I'm just going to check out the exchange rate in the bank across the way," I said, but the squeal of Werner's trolley came from behind me.

The engineer's face was pale and rigid.

"Reconditioned," Thandi explained.

I shivered, and the bright concourse suddenly seemed a little darker all around.

Naturally, there were ships that undertook repairs or upgraded their systems. The repaired or superseded parts would find their way into the market. But Werner had pointed out that the largest potential return pirates got from capturing ships was the value of the actual ships themselves. The cost of buying a new spaceship was so high it had created a thriving market for secondhand ships. And if the ships were damaged or too easily identified, pirates would strip them for parts. It was extremely likely that at least some of the 'reconditioned' parts being sold by this trader came from a ship that had been a victim of a pirate.

I cleared my throat hesitantly. "What if that's all anyone has?" I asked.

Werner's face twisted and then he shrugged. "The *Penguin* has a basic fabricator for the mechanical parts, and it would only take me suitable raw material and a few days for those. The electronics and photonics? No way we can manufacture those. Look, it's not only that these parts might have blood on them, it's that you can't be sure whether they'll work in a system. If they came in the legitimate way from a maintenance facility, why was the ship getting rid of them? Either they were faulty, or someone decided they weren't good enough. In either case, you're depending on reconditioning with no way to test it." He thought for a minute. "If there was absolutely no other way, I guess we could buy, let's see... three reconditioned units for each part that needs replacing, and my bet would be I could salvage one set of decent photonics and an emergency backup from them."

It didn't let my face show my dismay. "Okay. It's a plan," I said.

More costs.

"And don't forget," I said to Werner, "in this port, the ship's name isn't the *Penguin*, it's the *Spiral Song*."

He nodded and I guided his trolley down the concourse.

The second trader looked more promising; on its advertising signs outside, it was claiming a connection with Inner Worlds spaceship manufacturers. Thandi and Werner went in.

I saw a bank three doors down and headed for it, leaving Gunny and Prasad to wait.

The financial institutions that advertised on the boards had all shown they exchanged currencies and provided letters of credit, but they'd all been cagey about their rates. That gave me hope that there was competition on the station and I *might* get a good enough deal on Terran credits that I could cut the trip short and go buy the remaining bio-processors at Ensylas.

Of course, I *might* see a purple unicorn flying through space too.

The bank was set up with the standard airlock-style isolation from the concourse, and they had thoughtfully put a general enquiry terminal in the middle section, so I didn't need to go all the way in.

It didn't look like my kind of place anyway—more like some kind of club, with subdued lighting and a receptionist that looked as if he'd just finished modeling fashions at a show. The deal on exchange wasn't my kind of deal either. Much, *much* better than Ensylas, but not even enough to clear the bio-processors they were holding for us.

I tapped the screen to clear it, and the display blanked for a second. While it did, it provided me with a mirror to look over my shoulder and out onto the concourse.

Not a good mirror, but good enough to reveal the face of Captain Maykn of the pirate-merchanter *Sambuk* as he ran past.

E6. Chapter 3

"Gunny! Urgent. Thandi has to stay inside that shop." My pad comms were set up with a direct line right into her suit helmet.

"On it."

There was a moment's silence before she came back.

"Okay, Pras went inside with instructions. What's up?"

"There's a guy on the concourse running past. Wearing one of those heavy brown coats."

"Got him."

"That's Maykn. The *Sambuk* must be docked here under a different name for repairs."

She'd heard all about our experience at Orion's Wheel and the battle after, so she knew exactly who I was talking about.

"Shit! Did he see you?"

"I don't know. He only passed the bank while I was inside, I think. Last time we met, my hair was all colors of the rainbow and I had a black horizontal strip painted across my eyes. I'm not sure he'd recognize me."

"Might depend on whether he's looking," Gunny said.

"Hold the line." I stabbed the party connect icon and got through to the ship.

"Shami. I've just seen Maykn on the concourse. Lock the access and prep the ship."

She swore.

"Jessop is clear of the ship," she said. "I'm closing the doors, but what about Werner and his parts? What about you?"

"I'm just three doors down from the rest of them. I'll join them as soon as Maykn gets out of sight. I'm not sure if he saw me. The only other person he'd recognize is Thandi and she's inside a shop, out of sight."

"I should have thought of Maykn coming here." Bjorn's voice in the background. "When he confronted us in the bar on Orion's Wheel, he mentioned the Ensylas-Ranier trade run."

"If you should have thought of it, so should I," I replied. "But it would have been a pretty remote probability anyway."

"Hold on, I'm checking ships having repairs done..."

"This doesn't look like his sort of place," I said, half to myself. "He was alone, without his mutant security team."

"They'd stick out here," Gunny pointed out. "He wouldn't want that, if this is where he pretends he's legitimate."

She had a point. The gene-tricked mutants *were* illegal, even if places like Orion's Wheel turned a blind eye.

"Got it!" Bjorn's voice broke through. "The *Sambuk*'s claiming to be the *Sun Weaver*. Docked on... S2-05. Spoke 2. Three spokes away from us. Repairs finished today according to the boards. No flight time or destination filed."

I thought furiously. Three spokes from the *Penguin*'s dock, but right next door to the trade section.

"We need those parts, so I'm going to take the chance he didn't see me—"

Gunny interrupted. "Werner says he got what he needed. The big stuff is being delivered on the monorail in fifteen minutes. The small stuff he's got on the trolley. We're ready to head back."

"Keep them inside the shop for the moment," I said. "Is Maykn out of sight?"

"He is," Gunny replied.

"Okay, I'm coming back, but Thandi should still wait inside." I jogged out of the bank, still talking. "She's going to need a cloak or something—that dress catches the eye."

Using her pad, Thandi found a store which sold robes.

It was half an arc around the rim in the same direction Maykn had gone. I trotted there, cautiously checking ahead that I wasn't catching up to Maykn. At the shop, I bought a robe for Thandi and an odd cap with a long peak in front for me. I probably didn't need it, and caution never was my middle name, but I had a ship to get back to.

I scurried back, peaked cap pulled down to hide my face.

Ten minutes after I'd seen Maykn, we set off, heading the long way around, so we wouldn't go past the dock spoke where the *Sambuk* was moored. We were traveling as fast as Werner's squeaky, wobbly-wheel trolley would allow.

I was still talking to Bjorn.

"What was Maykn doing?" I asked. "Can you access video feed from the concourse in the market arc?"

"Shami's on it," he replied. "There's rim-round surveillance, but it's not for public viewing except for the docks."

What he meant was, she was hacking the station's security systems. I winced.

"A bank?" Shami was muttering to herself in the background. "He went to one of those banks?"

She was interrupted as Bjorn swore furiously.

"What's up?"

"The station just closed the concourse around Spoke 6. Sealed for 'minor repairs'."

My gut froze. I didn't believe in coincidences. "If Maykn can do that," I said, "we have a whole station to fight our way through to get back to the ship."

"Not sure," Shami said. "They had maintenance scheduled for Spoke 6. There were alerts posted on the boards for days before we arrived."

"Yeah, but why right now? When they posted, did they say the time the work would be done?"

"No."

"It stinks," I said. "Bjorn..."

I couldn't find the words, but I had to speak. The silence on the comms seemed to grow.

When the mind falters and the voice must speak, fill your mouth with the words of the Scriptures.

"Blessed is the gathering," I said, "but the light must not die in darkness."

I could hear Bjorn's sharp intake of breath.

"Bjorn. Shami," I said. "Our mission is more important than any one of us. File a departure with Docking Control before Maykn can pull another trick. You've got to be able to get away, whatever happens to me. If we make it, we make it. If not, it was just our day to die."

I felt tears threaten and shook them away.

I could hear Shami talking on another channel to Docking, but Bjorn was still on our channel.

"I'm not leaving you, Jan," he said. "We *will* gather and prosper. You and I. We'll do it together."

But a new voice joined the circuit.

"It's not Maykn shutting down the spokes." The voice wasn't crew, and for a second I thought our signals had been hacked. But they hadn't.

"Jessop!" I said. "You're kicking off your revolution!"

"It won't be a revolution. Probably. It's very quiet, very limited. I can't explain now, but there's going to be a minimum of fighting—"

"Good to hear," muttered Gunny. She had a point. Fighting on a space station could end with everyone dead.

"An absolute minimum," Jessop went on. "But I need you to get the hell out of the market sector. We're closing that next."

"What the hell is so strategic in the market?"

"Banks. Money. Secret accounts. No time to explain. Now go! Maykn knows you're here, but he's too busy getting underway to ambush you. He knows about us as well. That's why he was in the bank; he was closing his accounts. He knows his pirate fleet won't be able to use Ranier as a safe port for their legitimate face. He won't be coming back, so *don't* get trapped in dock when he clears."

Because if he wasn't coming back here, he might think about taking a shot at us as he departed.

We were already heading back at a trot. We tried sprinting, but the swerves at speed caused by the nova-damned wheel in Werner's trolley threatened to overturn it and spill the cargo all over the concourse.

Up ahead of us, where the upward curve of the concourse hid the isolation junction between arcs, we could see the reflection of amber warning lights flashing. Loud station announcements began, telling everyone in the businesses and accommodations to seal their doors, and to clear the concourse for temporary emergency depressurization.

People began running, and for a moment, we didn't stand out so much. But the people on the concourse were doing what station training taught them to do: dive into a shop. In seconds the concourse was almost empty.

People at the shops' entrances screamed and waved at us to get inside.

The warning lights went red just as the junction came into view.

Gunny grabbed the trolley and lifted it so the front wheels were in the air and the back didn't touch the floor. That meant she had to run doubled over, but the suit helped.

A maintenance crew at the junction was waving frantically at us to get into one of the shops.

We kept going.

I could see the huge junction doors begin to slide closed.

We weren't going to make it.

E6. Chapter 4

As it turned out, it wasn't our day to die of suffocation in the evacuated arc of a space station.

Bjorn came through the door like a missile. He was wearing his combat suit, running at full power, and *no one* was going to get in his way.

He grabbed me around the waist like a child's toy and picked up the back of the trolley.

Gunny was able to straighten up and she picked up Thandi with her spare arm. Prasad leaped on and clung to the trolley, helping Werner keep all the purchases from falling off.

Two people in battered combat suits, four helpless passengers and a defective trolley shot back through the closing doors with an inch to spare.

People scattered and fell in their hurry to get away. Bjorn and Gunny had to slow way down. We needed to get out of this arc and back to the ship, but injuring bystanders wasn't part of that.

A group of teenagers on skates, who I'd seen weaving in and out of pedestrians earlier, came swooping in and one of them made a fancy spin and took up a position moving backwards a meter from me. He wore lurid, skin-tight overalls with padded joint protection and his hair, either dyed or gene-tricked, was amethyst-purple and gelled to stand up like he'd been zapped with a huge static charge. At a guess, he was all of fifteen.

"Was razz, t'way you come through t'doors like that," he said, looking at Born's armor. "Got you nova-speed in t'suits. You 'kay?"

His Ranier slang took a second to process, before I realized Bjorn was still holding me captive. Our skating friend was worried I'd been abducted.

"We're all good, sort of," I said, grinning. "Just trying to get back to our ship on Spoke 5 in a hurry."

He spun around expertly on his skates a couple of times, taking in the numbers of people.

"We can do," he said. "Want to see how fast you go in t'suits."

He whistled a strange sequence of notes. It was clearly some kind of code the kids used, because they formed an arrow in front of us and started charging down the middle of the concourse. People ran to get out of their way.

"Crazy kids!"

It was too late to stop them, so Gunny and Bjorn powered up and began to sprint after the hooligans. We might be losing friends on station, but the thought of what Maykn might do if we didn't clear the docks was justification in my mind.

If any of Maykn's crew was on the concourse, they didn't attempt to stop us. It wouldn't have been a clever move against Gunny and Bjorn, but my gut told me it was more likely that Maykn and his crew were too busy finalizing their departure to bother with us.

We passed out of Sector 2. There was no stopping. Bjorn and Gunny sprinted after the skaters the whole way back to our dock, ignoring everybody else.

"Shit, he's going to crash!" Bjorn yelled.

The kids had been going faster and faster once we'd gotten away from the crowds in Sector 2. Now their purple-haired leader was skating backwards again, so he could see how quickly we were moving after them.

All fine, but the bare expanse of the concourse was broken up at intervals with plant boxes and he was heading straight at one.

My heart was in my mouth. We were too far away to do anything.

Purple-hair shot straight up the smoothly-ramped side of the plant box, converting all his energy into a vertical take-off, then tucked up and spun half a dozen times before returning to the surface of the concourse with an air of studied nonchalance, standing tall and crossing his arms as soon as he'd landed.

The kids hooted and whistled in their code as they bled off all their high velocity energy in less exhibitionist ways.

"Razz! Razz!" I shouted and tried whistling, as we raced in through the open doors to the dock.

"I hope that means what you think it means," Gunny grunted as she and Bjorn took the stairs four at a time, still holding on to everything.

There was no thought of waiting for the elevator. Armored suits would beat any elevator, even carrying a trolley.

Shami had prepared for our return, and thanks to the kids, we'd gotten back quickly enough that they were probably still pumping air out of the market arc when the forward loading bay of the *Penguin* was closing behind us.

"Pras," I grunted as Bjorn put me down. "Secure the trolley and get Werner back to the engine room. Bjorn—"

"On the plasma cannon. Got it."

I was already running for the bridge.

"Shami?"

"Still on channel," she said over the comms. "Docking control is arguing with me. The *Sambuk* is also lifting. They don't want two undocking at the same time. Also, there are reports of shots fired in the market arc, and Sector 6."

"Patch me in," I said.

"Docking Control," Shami said, "I'm putting Captain Skelling through to you."

"It doesn't make any difference, *Spiral Song*," a brusque voice replied. "We're not lifting two ships at the same time. Regulations—"

"This is Captain Skelling," I cut him off. "This station is experiencing anti-piracy action in Sectors 1 and 6. The ship you call *Sun Weaver* is in fact a known pirate called *Sambuk*, and they're running."

I half expected Maykn to say something, but he didn't. The controller did: "Remain docked. I won't breach safety rules because of some wild allegations—"

"I'm not asking you for permission to undock. I'm telling you that if the docking clamps aren't open in..." I made the bridge and stared at Shami's screens, "...fifteen seconds, then we will blow them. *Spiral Song* out."

I strapped into my seat.

"Dockside is sealed," Shami said, flicking through the station comms. "All spokes are being sealed and all sectors in the entire station. Taking it seriously."

The *Penguin* was coming alive around us.

I patted my armrest to apologize for calling her the *Spiral Song*.

I broadcast on the ship comm: "All hands, sit and strap. We don't know how this is going to go."

I felt thumps through the ship.

"Clamps disengaged. Someone made the right choice," Shami said. "Can lift now."

"Go."

E6. Chapter 5

"*Spiral Song*! *Sun Weaver*! This is Station Director Portiac."

This was a different voice on the Traffic Control channel. Urgent and panicked.

"We have you both lifting. We take no sides in any dispute between you. Please clear the vicinity."

He meant *don't start shooting*, because space battles got messy. If one of us had our containment vessels breached, the resulting explosion would take the whole station with us. Even if that didn't happen, bits of spacecraft crashing into the station was a nightmare scenario. Each arc of the station was closing and being sealed, but damage one sector enough and the whole station would tear apart. And if that happened, seals would break and whole sectors would vent.

Maykn wouldn't care. If Jessop succeeded and Ranier became a no-go system for pirates, he wouldn't ever come back. It certainly looked as if Maykn thought that was the likely outcome, with his visit to his bank and hurried departure.

I cared, whether or not I ever came back.

What options did I have?

Maykn knew of our claim to be Calloway navy from our last fight. He also knew the *Dark Shark* was out there, somewhere, and even if he thought he could beat us in a fight, he was justifiably scared of the bigger ship. What he didn't know was the *Dark Shark* was busy shuttling between Calloway and Yorkham.

I couldn't magic a signal from the *Dark Shark* to send him running.

From our last fight, Maykn knew that the *Sambuk* was a more powerful ship than the *Acid Penguin*.

But we'd both had work done.

Time to bluff.

"Bjorn, okay to open the forward bay?"

"Yes," came back.

"Point us at them, Shami," I said.

The *Penguin* began to swivel. I could see the *Sambuk* doing the same.

On the Traffic Control channel, Portiac's voice became ever more agitated. I switched him off.

"Spool the Chang generators and light him up, Shami."

"We've got nothing to back it up..." she complained, but she did what I asked.

The engineering team from the Yorkham had upgraded our sensors and support systems. We had military-grade sensors that would look like navy targeting systems. And Inner World navy ships had experimental shields using Chang space projectors.

But all we had to fire with was one small, lousy plasma cannon in the forward bay that we aimed by syncing Bjorn's combat suit with the sensors, and a rail gun that fired out the back, which we could only aim by moving the whole ship. We had no shields.

If we'd been in free flight, Shami's skill would make a difference, but we weren't. We were effectively at a standstill and right next to the station. Far too close for any maneuvering.

"He calls our bluff..." Shami said, "and the best we can hope for is we kill each other without blowing up the station."

"Got that," I said.

The *Sambuk*'s sensors came on line.

"Almost as good as ours," Shami said. Her hands were relaxed by the controls, but I could feel the *Penguin* tense, almost straining at the leash, as she controlled it through the interface in her head. Her face held no expression other than concentration, but beads of sweat stood out on her forehead.

Seconds ticked by.

Both ships were drifting away from the station.

My comms board was pulsing. Station Director Portiac, no doubt still begging us to move away. Thandi wanting to talk. Werner wanting to know why we had the Chang generators online. Icons for dockside channels flashed to show incoming calls stacking up. Part of the comms display was switched to station public channels, and emergency notices crawled over the screen.

I ignored them all.

I was watching Bjorn's suit feed, which showed the plasma cannon locked steady on the weakest point on the *Sambuk*. He couldn't miss and neither would they.

Then the image drifted. The aspect changed. Bjorn's suit moved the cannon, locked on another weak point.

And again.

The *Sambuk* was moving. Turning away.

Maykn didn't want to die today.

"Stay where we are, or get between him and the station?" Shami asked.

"While his weapons sensors are locked on us, we stay here," I replied. The station's orbit was carrying it away from us slowly.

Another agonizing minute passed. The *Sambuk* was only using maneuvering jets.

"Can we tell if he switches his targeting from us to the station?"

"Yes," Shami replied. "I've set it up as flag 235 on the tracking signal."

"Bjorn? Flag 235. Key that in so the plasma cannon fires immediately if he does that."

"Done."

"His in-system engines are powering up," Shami whispered. Then: "Narrow beam transmission for you."

She passed it to my console and I opened the channel.

"This isn't over, Skelling." Maykn's voice.

"No, it isn't. We'll find you, Maykn. Then, it'll be over."

The channel clicked off and the display showed the *Sambuk* picking up speed.

"I have a clear shot at the engines," Bjorn said.

"Stand down," I replied. "We haven't got enough firepower to be sure we can take him, and I wouldn't put it past him to hit the station out of spite."

Shami nodded curt approval. She kept the targeting systems active and tracked the *Sambuk*. It looked like Maykn was aiming for a close pass on the planet of Ranier to pick up speed in a slingshot maneuver.

The *Sambuk*'s in-system engines came up to full power and suddenly the ship was racing away from us, accelerating hard.

The flashing icons on the comms board gradually reduced.

I sat there shivering and sweating. Every muscle had been tensed, as if that would have made a difference in a confrontation that was all about spaceships and physics and plasma cannons.

Now those muscles relaxed and the aftershocks took over.

I can't do this!

I hadn't even registered she'd come onto the bridge, but Gunny appeared at my shoulder, still in her junkyard combat suit minus the helmet. She bent down until her mouth was right beside my ear.

"You did well, skipper." Even in the hush of the bridge I could barely hear her words.

I shook my head sharply.

"Every single person on that station," I whispered. "Everyone on the ship. They'd all be dead if he'd called my bluff."

"But he didn't. You're more inside his head than he is in yours. If we'd stayed in dock, he'd probably have fired on us anyway, and the station would have blown up when he did. We had to launch. The standoff was a *good* call. It was the *right* call, *skipper*."

I shook my head again.

"Don't call me that. I'm no ship's captain. I'm not trained for command. I'm not even trained for the navy. I can't take responsibility for the lives of thousands of people like this."

"You already have," she said. "You're the person responsible for thousands of lives back on Calloway. You're the person who saw what needed to be done and made the plan. That means you're the one who has to see it through."

That brought a snort from me. "Me? I'm a mess. I'm shaking so hard I couldn't even stand up at the moment."

"Then sit a while. Let Shami and Bjorn handle the ship, and I'll stall the station. I'll say you're busy until we're sure the *Sambuk*'s not coming back. Which is true."

She had that kind of voice, at least when she wasn't yelling at some poor grunt; the kind of voice that could convince people what she said was right.

"You know, not *every* junior officer that passed through my unit had this kind of reaction to command responsibility early on in their career," she said. "Only the best ones did."

E6. Chapter 6

It took less than half an hour for the *Sambuk* to reappear from behind the planet, and the ship was on a hard-burn, minimum-time course to escape from the Mez, the Mass Effect Zone.

There were no more transmissions from Maykn.

After another hour Shami said that the time it'd take him to slow down and reverse course toward the station made it unlikely he was returning, and would give us lots of time to prepare if he did.

Most of her attention was on running through simulations of maneuvers that would give us an advantage against a ship like the *Sambuk*. She looked thoughtful, lost in her own world of physics and firepower.

Which left me with one pissed-off Station Director Portiac to deal with.

I had used the wait to make an extract of our sensor recordings from our last encounter with the *Sambuk*, and I sent it to him a good fifteen minutes before I was ready to talk to him.

It didn't help.

I had broken some regulations, apparently!

Well, scuttle my bucket. Who'd have thought it?

Luckily, *this* kind of thing was well inside my comfort zone. Bjorn was listening, and as he pointed out on our internal comms, I had *lots* of experience with breaking regulations. I had to mute the mics when he got me laughing about one instance that he exaggerated horribly.

Not that Portiac was making any effort to listen to anything I said.

And then the station director found out he was in trouble of his own; the emergency notices on the public channels changed from repeating emergency lockdown broadcasts to public information about the cause. I was half-expecting Jessop to appear, but he was a behind-the-scenes man. Instead, someone I'd never heard of or seen started talking about the dozen banking and trading establishments that had been knowingly involved in piracy. Owners were in custody. Funds, assets and data already seized in one swoop. Air was being pumped back in and the seals between sectors were opening.

Portiac had left his mic open. I could hear him start shouting at people, putting out demands for the station police to close down the broadcasts.

From the talking head in the broadcast office came an announcement that the administration, while probably not directly engaged in criminal activities, had been negligent in allowing traders and banks to behave as they had.

Video feeds of the concourse came back up, showing police were there in little groups of two or three. They mostly looked a little anxious, but were making efforts to walk slowly in a relaxed fashion, look calm and smile as people approached them. Clearly the police were onside with what Jessop had been doing.

The revolution was over, bar the shouting, most of which was coming from Station Director Portiac, even as he ran out of the Space Traffic Control offices.

Another voice came on the channel to replace Portiac.

"Spiral Song, this is Ranier Orbital Docking Control. Request you return to berth S5-01, and stand off twenty meters to await maneuvering from dockside control on channel 16. Mr. Jessop will meet you on the dock."

Shami looked at me.

"We don't actually need to re-dock," I said, breaking in on the channel. "We have all the goods and supplies we need for the next stage—"

"Special request by Mr. Jessop," the new controller said. "He says it'll be worth your while. He's waiving docking fees and all the fines Station Director Portiac was compiling in error."

I'd forgotten that wrinkle about docking. Normally, dock twice, pay twice. And although Portiac was a stuffed shirt trying to fine the *Penguin* for breaking regulations while saving the whole station, it would be sweet if those fines were officially erased. *If* Jessop had that authority.

I sort-of trusted Jessop, enough to waste some time confirming we owed nothing, and checking out what he might think was additionally worth our while.

I nodded at Shami.

"Roger that, Ranier Orbital," she said. "Stand-off twenty, Spoke 5, Berth 1, dockside on channel 16, ETA 12 minutes."

Shami turned the Penguin and we slipped back to where we'd come from.

As he had promised, Jessop was waiting for us on the dock.

He was wearing his everyday business clothes again, but a couple of his team were with him, still in military gear, carrying Renshaws and with their eyes on a constant sweep of the docks. Whatever Jessop really was, his team were elite military and my gut said they were current, not mercenaries.

Jessop had some government somewhere that was backing him. The questions were still *who* and *why*.

In any event, even if I sort-of trusted Jessop, this station had just undergone a change in circumstances, so walking behind me were Bjorn and Gunny in their full combat suits, carrying assault weapons. I'd also brought Thandi out with me because Jessop was nominally a trader, and 'worth our while' made me suspect there was some bargaining to do. Thandi and I had impact vests on, and I could see that amused Jessop when he glanced over at us.

He was surrounded by a group of stationers, all talking at him in the way of those people who think what they say is really important.

He stopped them and excused himself to come talk to us. The important people were furious, but one of Jessop's team carefully positioned himself so they'd have to walk around him to follow Jessop. They decided against trying that.

"That looked like fun," I said to him. "Sorry to break it up, but you wanted to talk to us."

His mouth twitched.

"I swear however much fun the rest of it is, this part sucks," he said. "But I want to get you on your way quickly."

He pulled out his pad and waggled it. I drew mine warily.

Beep.

Confirmation that docking fees were waived for *both* times we'd docked. Original fees returned to us.

Beep.

Confirmation from the Assistant Station Director that there was no unnecessary breaking of regulations in our maneuvering in the vicinity of the station, no fines, and we had the thanks of the government of Ranier for our assistance in clearing suspected pirates from the station.

Beep.

"Pursuant to the terms of the Piracy Accords, Ranier Station officially accepts from the *Acid Penguin* (currently IDed as *Spiral Song* for Calloway Navy operational reasons) the submission of prisoners suspected of involvement in piracy, including those no longer alive..."

The document went on for pages. Jessop had known we had pirates and their dead colleagues locked up on the *Penguin*, but he'd gone further and managed to access the records we'd been compiling on them. There was the full list of names, their ships and their systems of origin.

And at the bottom, the bounty as stipulated in the Piracy Accords.

A number that made my eyes go round. I'd never seen it added up till now.

"Hold it, Jessop," Thandi said. "First off, Ranier isn't a signatory, and—"

"Ranier signed..." Jessop glanced at the clock above the dock gate, "ten minutes ago."

"Okay, okay," Thandi went on. "You held a gun to Portiac's head. But you're only going to pay us half."

I bit my tongue and said nothing about looking gift horses in the mouth.

Jessop nodded. "Half paid in Ranier franks on your agreement, half held in credit. Ranier franks are honored through the Parvi arc, and Ranier is good for the credit, but with accounts being frozen at the moment..." He shrugged.

I tried to nudge Thandi in the ribs unobtrusively. *Take it! Money!*

"What about interest on that credit?" she said, ignoring me.

He glared at her, but opened the document and added a paragraph.

While he was doing that, I got Gunny's whisper in my earbud.

"What does he want them for? What's he doing with them?"

Good point.

I cleared my throat and asked the questions.

Beep. The amended document came back.

"They're to be interrogated. As much as we've done, we're still in the dark about the way these pirate fleets operate. Who sets them up? How? Why? Where does the money go?"

He ran a hand through his hair. "If we take these pirates out of circulation without understanding what's causing them, we could find we have to do the whole job again. And again."

It was a fair point.

"This interrogation..." I said.

"Ranier is now signatory to the Accords, and any interrogations will be done under those rules."

"You just said 'we take these pirates'," I pointed out, "but any time you talk about Ranier it's 'Ranier', not 'we'. Who are you working for, by the way?"

"You're right, not Ranier." He frowned. "More than that is not for public knowledge."

My gut told me we'd quickly reached a point where he wasn't going to say any more, and I didn't have any objections to offloading the pirates. I glanced at the others and got subtle nods.

Beep.

The document went back signed.

"Police will attend the dockside in half an hour for the exchange," Jessop said.

E6. Chapter 7

Managing the secure transfer of prisoners from their sealed containment in our holds would have been a nightmare, but Jessop's team turned up and I was happy to leave it all to Prasad to arrange.

I went down to check when they were close to finishing. It was all going well, and I got to give dejected, former-captain Satybal a smile as he was led off *my* ship.

I didn't expect Jessop would be there, but he turned up at the end.

"Can I talk to you privately?" he asked.

I let him lead me to one side. We were still in full view, and Gunny wasn't more than fifteen meters away.

"Is this where you tell me what your favors are going to cost me?"

"So cynical in one so young," he muttered. "But you might look at it like that."

I snorted.

"Shoot."

With his back to everyone else and hidden from the dockside cameras, he handed me a data card.

"Hide that, please."

I slipped it in a pocket.

"What is it and what am I supposed to be doing with it?"

"It's the full analysis of our knowledge so far. Pirate fleets, where they operate from, what they use for currency and where their money seems to go, when it leaves the Frontier. I might update you by encrypted message before you exit the system, if we get some lucky breaks with interrogating your pirates."

"Not my pirates any longer. Yours now," I said. "Okay, what do I do with it?"

"First, read it. I know you're heading into the Margin and the Inner Worlds, and I'm guessing you think you'll be leaving the pirates behind in the Frontier. You won't. They're just better hidden and they run banks and corporations."

I swallowed. He was absolutely right. Shami and I had looked at the next system we were visiting. It was a Frontier system on the border where we should be able to exchange our Frontier currencies for Margin currencies. The system after that would be in the Margin, and I'd had almost exactly the thought Jessop had suggested.

"Okay, I'll read it. What comes second in your list?"

He was silent for a moment. "I want it broadcast. That's not something I want you to do directly, because it would make you too easy a target, but I reckon if you pass it secretly to every Xian ship you come across, they'll have safety in numbers."

I frowned.

Xian was an oddity. The best way I'd heard them described was as a multi-system trade organization. They spanned all sections of human space, from the Inner Worlds, through the Margin and out into the Frontier. No system claimed to be the leader, but Xian set the whole thing up and what Xian said tended to be taken as official. Xian was about a third of the way around the approximate sphere of human space from where we were now, in the Margin, and the other systems which formed part of the organization were mainly clustered around that.

A long way away, but I could see why Jessop picked them. The Xian fleets dominated trading for the Inner Worlds and the Margin. They visited everywhere, even the depths of the Frontier. There would be no better way to spread information than to give it to them.

I didn't have Thandi to negotiate, but I knew she would be disappointed if I just said yes.

"What does the *Penguin* get for being your messenger?"

He laughed. "You'll be trying to sell me Thandi's satellite comms system next."

"Funny you should mention it, but what a great idea for a rich system like this! The sort of comms that would engage every part of the planet equally and might even have averted the problems—"

"Nice try. No money at the moment. Ranier has had some unexpected expenses."

I grinned.

"No actual money, but here's a favor you may need as you make your way inwards."

He checked again that no one could see what he was doing, and then passed me something slim and light which I thought was another data card. It joined the first one in my pocket.

"What's that?"

"It's a special communicator for last resort situations. It sends out an encrypted signal. If there's one of the right ships in the area, they'll know you're owed a favor."

"Which ships?"

"Can't say."

"Nova! Back on Calloway, we'd say that's like selling a hog in a forest."

He laughed again. "One that's not yours to sell and which there's no way for the buyer to be sure to collect?"

"Pretty much."

"Fair enough, but not completely accurate. It is mine to 'sell', but there's no way I can be sure you'd be able to collect, and I can't tell you more, other than it's more likely to work the deeper you go into the Inner Worlds."

"Because there's more traffic! Of course it's more likely I'd come across your mysterious ships there."

He nodded, and his name was called from the dock gate.

One of his team was pointing up at the clock above the gate. Time for him to go.

He started to back away slowly.

"One last thing..." he said.

"What's this going to cost me?"

"Nothing. Just for interest. I know your regiment was called the Acid Penguins, and I guess that's why you called the ship that."

"Uh huh."

"Where the nova did you get a name like that?"

"You know they recruited us from every hick planet in the Frontier?"

He nodded.

"Can you imagine what the first drill instruction session was like? Started off just clumsy, but we have a bad sense of humor out here. People started turning left instead of right, that sort of thing."

Jessop's mouth twisted in half a smile.

"Gunny looked like her head was going to explode, and at the end, she signed off with what she thought was a great put-down; she told us we were about as good as penguins on acid."

He wore a definite smile now.

"We were from the Frontier: no planet we came from had flightless birds that waddled, and once we'd looked up the birds on the InfoPads, the phrase 'on acid' for us suggested penguins panicking as they had to walk across corrosive chemicals, picking their feet up and going double-time. We loved the image, and the Acid Penguins were born."

"You know you're crazy," he said, laughing and shaking his head. "But the sort of crazy I like. Safe travels."

I watched him as he walked off.

The way he talked showed he wasn't from Ranier. He'd admitted that. My gut said he wasn't from the Frontier either. Which left Earth, the Inner Worlds and the Margin. Earth didn't care enough what was going on out here, as long as it didn't stop people from emigrating. He knew the meaning of 'on acid', which was an old Earth phrase to do with psychedelic drugs, so my guess was he was from one of the Inner Worlds, where it might still be used.

Fascinating.

Not that I wanted to get so badly into trouble I had to use his mysterious communicator as a last resort, but wouldn't it be interesting to see who turned up?

Prasad and Gunny were waving at me and the amber departure warning lights started flashing. I trotted to my ship.

E6. Chapter 8

A week later at the end of our jump in Chang space, I decided to sit in on the bridge.

We were due for a recalibration pass through a dead system, one of those so marginal it didn't have a name or a navigation beacon. The star was a late cycle white dwarf, too small to go supernova, and on its leisurely way to depleting all its hydrogen and helium fuel.

It was designated GC 10799-63844. Not a name you conjured with.

On the other hand, it was the sort of place that pirates might use and it was an easy Chang jump from Ranier.

Shami, as always, had organized her shift so she was on duty for entry and exit of Chang space. She was running system checks from the main pilot console and nodded to me as I entered the bridge.

I sat in the captain's chair, and slaved my consoles to hers.

Bjorn was suited and down in the forward docking bay. Not that we would need our plasma cannon. Just to be sure.

The bridge was quiet and calm as a library.

I checked Shami's navigational computer output. With the speed we'd picked up from the relative motion of the system we'd come from and the system we were arriving at, we'd pass through this one at a good fraction of lightspeed. Given this system had no navigational beacon, and we were only in transit, she'd routed us to pass through the zenith of the system, 'above' the star and the orbiting planets, at 4AU.

At that distance, the star would be small, and the planets invisible, but the computers had created a visual for us, based on a guess from the latest navigational information and the distorted view of masses that the sensors got in Chang space. The innermost planets were small, bare lumps of rock. The outermost were large balls of gas. They were displayed in their approximate locations with a volume around them to indicate the level of inaccuracy. All of them were spinning and circling well below where we'd pass through. Nothing unusual for a failed star system.

Of course, out here in the deep Dark, it was foolish to think there was anything 'normal' about a transit through *any* star system, and the Dark took fools.

"Thirty seconds to emergence," Shami broadcast shipwide.

As this was a routine passage, she didn't warn anyone to strap in or take any precautions.

However, Shami's navy training took over, and she went through what I was beginning to recognize as her routine.

Buckle in.

Pick out standard channels to monitor on emergence: nav beacons, Space Traffic Control, ID broadcasts.

Main display set to cover the immediate path in front of us.

"Ten seconds to emergence."

The lights started to dim. Power was being diverted to the Chang generators as they spooled up for the burst to take us back out of Chang space.

I patted my armrests. "You go, little *Penguin*," I whispered.

"Emergence."

No more than a shiver passed through the ship.

The *Acid Penguin* was so much smoother than she had been before we got Werner down in the engine room.

The main display blinked and started replacing the guesses the computers had made about planetary positions with real-time data, spreading out in a sphere from our point of emergence.

Nothing in front of us, or in any proximity.

The visual model of the system soon showed the star and its planets where it had been predicting they would be. Everything normal. Calm.

"Goddess!" Shami gasped.

"What?"

I looked around wildly. I could see nothing out of place.

Except on the comms channels, where there *should* have been nothing.

The system had no nav beacon, but the comms were trying to make sense of a signal on that channel.

"Navigation info?" I asked.

Shami shook her head, staring at the display with its 'Unresolved Signal' banner. She changed the display parameters so we got a separate visual of the signal. It was groups of pulses, coming and going. A second image showed the computers at work, overlaying the timelines where the signal was strong, then matching patterns. Reconstructing them until the second image gave way to a clear view of the signal that was too short and simple to be navigational information. A signal that was being repeated over and over.

"Old tech," Shami said eventually. "Real old."

"How old are we talking?"

"Hundreds of years," she said. "Before we adopted conventions like separate channels for Space Traffic. Back then, there was one primary channel—the one that later got chosen for navigational beacons when they divided them up by function."

A shudder ran through me.

That far back, there were no maps of the systems you visited, no list of hazards with formulas that navigational computers could plot to achieve a safe route into a system. Every exit from Chang space was a leap into the unknown. Hundreds of ships had simply disappeared. To counter the risk of emerging only to collide with a random rock, ships had emerged from Chang space *much* further out. So much further that the ability to choose the exit point accurately was compromised. A situation that had been jokingly called being between a rock and a deep space.

We might be looking at a ship that had emerged so far out, its resources were exhausted before it made it to the system.

"At least it's not alien," Shami said.

We looked wordlessly at the hypnotic, unintelligible pulse of the signal on the comms display for a full minute.

"Probably."

AFTERWORD

Thank you for reading *The Dark Takes Fools*,
book 1 in *The Long Way Home*.

I hope you've enjoyed reading it as much as I enjoyed
writing it.

Reviews!
Reviews are writers' fuel, every bit as much as coffee.
Please follow this link to Amazon
http://mybook.to/TLWH1-TDTF
and leave a review.
Short or long.
Reviews make books. Seriously.

Book 2, Out of the Dark, is on Amazon here:
https://mybook.to/TLWH2-OOTD

Books in *The Long Way Home* series so far

The Dark Takes Fools
Out of the Dark
Born in Fire

Meanwhile...

Read on for details of more Science Fiction
written by me and set in the same universe
(but much later)

AMONG THE STARS
1: A Name Among the Stars
2: A Threat Among the Stars

An heiress fleeing for her life. A forbidden and terrifying Artificial Intelligence let loose. A telepathic alien race secretly living hidden alongside humanity. A deadly conspiracy spreading through human space. The untold shame and sorrow of a whole planet revealed for all to see.
Vows that must be broken. Loves that must not be.
Duty and *honor*.

A huge and developing story set in the distant future with a sweep that encompasses the whole of humanity, told mainly from the perspective of Zara Aguirre, daughter, and last of the great Founding Family Aguirre, who abandons her home world and the burden of her Name to save her life, only to find she must take it up again and fight on, to save humanity.

A review of Among the Stars by
Charles de Lint
The Magazine of Fantasy & Science Fiction
"It's a delicious mix of the Brontë sisters, murder mystery, sf drama,
space opera, and just general romance and derring-do...
I could sense the joy of storytelling on every page.
This one hit the mark on every point."

http://mybook.to/Among_the_Stars

Keep going for other books by me in a different genre...

BEST SELLING URBAN FANTASY THRILLERS

BITE BACK

Prequel: Raw Deal
1: Sleight of Hand
2: Hidden Trump
3: Wild Card
4: Cool Hand
5: Angel Stakes
6: Inside Straight
7: Queen of Diamonds

Charles de Lint
in the Magazine of Fantasy & Science Fiction:
"They represent some of the best the field has to offer."

http://mybook.to/Bite_Back_Series

More books? Yes, keep going...

Also from the BITE BACK universe

Characters from these books appear in the main series

BIAN'S TALE
1: The Harvest of Lies

Anticipated series of 6 books following Bian from her early life in 1890 Vietnam to the point she becomes Daikon of House Altau, prior to the start of BITE BACK

BITE BACK: OUTSIDERS
1: The Biting Cold
2: Winter's Kiss

A short novella series with a PNR flavor introducing the background of House Lloyd
This miniseries fits between books 5 and 6 of the main BITE BACK series

LONG ISLAND ATHANATE
Change of Regime

Stand-alone novella set between books 5 and 6 of the main BITE BACK series providing some insight into House Altau in New York

You can also keep in touch on my Facebook pages:

https://www.facebook.com/TheBiteBackSeries

https://www.facebook.com/groups/1203689013307118

I welcome feedback!